MW00531746

I'll Be Home for Mischief

Also available by Jacqueline Frost

The Christmas Tree Farm Mysteries

Stalking Around the Christmas Tree

Slashing Through the Snow

'Twas the Kinfe Before Christmas

Twelve Slays of Christmas

The Kitty Couture Mysteries (writing as Julie Chase)

Cat Got Your Crown

Cat Got Your Secrets

Cat Got Your Cash

Cat Got Your Diamonds

I'll Be Home for Mischief

A CHRISTMAS TREE FARM MYSTERY

Jacqueline Frost

NEW YORK

This is a work of fiction. All of the names, characters, organizations, places and events portrayed in this novel are either products of the author's imagination or are used fictitiously. Any resemblance to real or actual events, locales, or persons, living or dead, is entirely coincidental.

Published in the United States by Crooked Lane Books, an imprint of The Quick Brown Fox & Company LLC.

Crooked Lane Books and its logo are trademarks of The Quick Brown Fox & Company LLC.

Library of Congress Catalog-in-Publication data available upon request.

ISBN (hardcover): 978-1-63910-906-7
ISBN (ebook): 978-1-63910-907-4

Cover design by Rich Grote

Printed in the United States.

www.crookedlanebooks.com

Crooked Lane Books
34 West 27th St., 10th Floor
New York, NY 10001

First Edition: November 2024

10 9 8 7 6 5 4 3 2 1

This book is dedicated
to Jerry Weible

Chapter One

Downtown Mistletoe, Maine, was a merry and bustling place any day of the year, but just ten days before Christmas, my hometown really put on a show. Twinkle lights trimmed shop roofs and outlined windows. Flickering, faux-gas streetlamps were wrapped in pine greens and topped with big red velvet bows. Banners announcing our town's 150th Anniversary Celebration bobbed on strings of bistro bulbs high above the tourist-filled streets. And everyone in sight seemed to be celebrating.

"Can you believe all this, Holly?" my best friend, Caroline West, asked from beside me on the heavily salted sidewalk. "I don't think I've ever seen so many people on the square." Her cheeks were pink from the biting winter wind, her blue eyes curious and delighted.

"I don't think so, and I love it," I said.

This amount of business was great for everyone in town, most of whom relied on holiday commerce to keep their families financially afloat the rest of the year. My family was included in that bunch. The Whites had owned and operated the Reindeer Games tree farm for five generations, and it was still going strong today.

Caroline pushed thick blond waves away from unfairly porcelain skin as we slowed behind a crowd of shoppers on the corner. "I love knowing that we're strolling along the same paths, outside the same buildings, that others walked and visited a century back," she said thoughtfully. "It makes me feel like part of something bigger. Less insignificant, somehow. Connected. You know?"

Nothing about Caroline was now or had ever been insignificant, but I knew exactly what she meant. "Totally."

Caroline and I were complete opposites from an outsider's perspective. The daughter of our mayor, she was average height, perpetually poised and camera-ready. At five foot eight, I only felt small when standing next to my lumberjack father, and my propensity for jeans and sweatpants usually turned cameras away.

On the inside, however, Caroline and I were exactly alike in all the ways that mattered. And those things made us the best of friends.

My gaze dragged over the picturesque row of shops and cafés while we waited to cross the street. Each storefront and window display was dressed in its holiday finest and fully embracing this year's Victorian Christmas theme.

"It's a little like falling back in time," she said, looping an arm through mine.

She wasn't wrong.

Wooden barricades had been erected on each side of the square, protecting the area from traffic and preserving the historic authenticity of our anniversary celebration. A private security team, working in conjunction with our sheriff's department, rerouted modern traffic to designated areas outside the perimeter. Cell phones and abundant electricity aside, everything else in sight was decidedly Victorian.

The passing horses and buggies cleared out of our way, and the horde of shoppers began to move. Caroline and I stepped into the street behind them, she with an armload of shopping bags, and I, towing my red canvas wagon.

"I wonder if it was really like this back then," I asked. "So adorable and inviting at Christmas."

"I like to think so."

A choir of carolers in Victorian garb passed on the opposite curb. They swayed jovially as they belted the lyrics to "God Rest Ye Merry Gentlemen," and I bobbed my head along in time. Children dressed as newsboys passed flyers into the hands of eager shoppers, and folks in vintage Santa costumes collected donations outside stores.

Caroline stopped to help me tug the wagon out of the crosswalk and onto the sidewalk. "We should do this theme every year," she said. "Everyone seems to love it, and tourism is up seventeen and a half percent."

We pulled on the wagon's handle, but the little craft didn't budge.

I didn't have to ask where she'd gotten such specific tourism numbers. Her father kept a close eye on Mistletoe's economics. Keeping a seasonal tourist town like ours in the black wasn't always easy, but he never ran out of ideas about how to make it happen. This year he'd encouraged a partnership between the Historical Society and the Chamber of Commerce. Together, they'd turned Mistletoe's one hundred and fiftieth anniversary into a financial wellspring.

Shop owners, employees, and most of the town, had agreed to dress the part. With a little luck, the collective efforts would charm every visitor into making a few more last-minute purchases. Maybe they'd even go home and tell all their friends about the trip, then come back next year to do it again.

"This kind of positive turnout is exactly what we need, given our town's more recent history," Caroline said.

I refocused on the wagon, not commenting on her reference to Mistletoe's unfortunate past.

There'd been a murder this time of year, seemingly like clockwork, for the past four Christmases, and I didn't want to think about death while the backside of my wagon was stuck in the road. The previous years' crimes had been unrelated, but it certainly felt as if the deaths were part of some twisted cosmic script.

I was glad I'd never meet that author.

"For the love of snickerdoodles," Caroline complained, giving the wagon one final heave onto the sidewalk. "This thing must weigh a hundred pounds."

"Probably," I agreed. "Mom is determined to prepare for every possible outcome before the big bake tomorrow."

I creaked upright and pressed my hands against my back to stretch. Then I wheeled the wagon close to a building and bent at the waist to catch my breath. "She asked me to buy extras of all the ingredients in bulk, in case she somehow lost or ran out of everything Dad already brought her."

Caroline nodded in understanding. "I did the same thing while planning for my cupcake shop. I overprepared, overspent, and overstressed. I'd needed a full body of spa treatments before I'd even opened. My hair and skin are still recovering, and it's been three years."

She dropped into a graceful squat on high-heeled boots and peeked at the wagon's contents. "Did you get everything you need?" she asked, turning tubs and boxes for a look at their labels.

I raised one mitten-clad hand and attempted to tick off on my covered fingers. "Twenty pounds each of flour and brown sugar, five jugs of molasses, plus cinnamon, vanilla, ginger, and baking soda in whatever quantities I could find."

My mom was an incredible baker and an enthusiast of all things Christmas. So it surprised no one when she announced her decision to bake the world's largest gingerbread man. Within a month she'd completed extensive research and contacted the *Guinness Book of World Records* to request judges be sent her way. She'd scheduled the big event for tomorrow, when Mistletoe was traditionally the busiest.

I was all in on anything I could do to help.

Caroline stood. "If she needs anything else, I just got a shipment. There are enough eggs and butter in my shop's walk-in freezer to help in a pinch."

"I'll let her know."

"Remind me how big this gingerbread man needs to be," she said. "I've added too many things to my short-term memory this week, and I'm losing details."

I considered her question a moment, struggling with my own mental capacity. "The largest gingerbread man on record weighed over one thousand four hundred pounds, so more than that." The record had been set in Norway, and it hadn't been broken in fifteen years. "I don't think it matters how tall he is."

Her eyes widened, and she turned to reevaluate my wagon. "Goodness. I'll text her to let her know I'm available to help measure the ingredients or navigate the recipe." She looked back at me. "Are you helping with the batter or baking?"

"Only if she asks," I said. My ability to burn water was well-known and rightly feared. If Mom turned to me, there were probably insurmountable obstacles afoot. "She's mixing the ingredients today, spreading the dough into the giant gingerbread man–shaped framework, then letting it set overnight."

Dad and his farm crew had tenaciously created a twenty-one-by-ten-foot cookie tray and a massive cookie cutter from enormous sheets of metal. They'd stored both in the old hay barn onsite. One of the cookie cutter's arms had to stick through an open window to make the rest of him fit. For a week it looked as if the barn was waving whenever I walked past.

"They rented a crane to lift the tray and dough-filled form onto the dump truck tomorrow," I added.

Caroline shook her head slightly as she processed. "I really hope your mom makes it into the record book. She deserves a Christmas win."

I sighed, easily hearing what she didn't say. My mom needed a holiday win because I'd become repeatedly entangled in the annual murder investigations these last few years. As a result, I was oftentimes threatened, and occasionally abducted, by the killer. All of which greatly distressed my mother.

Poking proverbial bears was one of many bad habits I'd been trying to break since New Year's Day. Unlike my vow to eat healthier and take more walks, I'd held strong to my stay-out-of-criminal-investigations resolution so far this year. Possibly because there hadn't been a murder in the last eleven or so months. I liked to think it was due to my incredible self-discipline, but the cookie crumbs on my coat and pile of unworn exercise gear in the closet suggested otherwise.

"When do the world record people get here?" Caroline asked.

We moved in the direction of my truck once more.

"Tonight." The team had reservations at the inn on my family's tree farm, where I was the innkeeper. "They're on a red eye, so I might not see them until morning. I emailed instructions for check-in if I fall asleep. The Snows, on the other hand, should be here soon." I paused to check the time on my phone.

"That's right," Caroline said, her pleasant smile drooping slightly. "I've been invited to dinner at my parents' house tonight so I can meet Mistletoe's founding family, or what's left of it. I hope they're nice."

"I do too," I said. Especially since the Snows were also staying at the inn, and it was my job to make certain they enjoyed their stay.

Caroline released a deep breath. "Dad's giving the son a key to the city, because he thinks local taxpayers will appreciate the nod to town history."

That made sense. It'd been the mayor's idea to invite the Snows into town to celebrate the anniversary. The son, Elijah, was in his early forties, and he'd never lived in Mistletoe. His mom, Violet, was a widow in her late sixties. She'd been a resident until her late teens, when her family pulled up one-hundred-plus years of roots and never looked back. I'd heard that she'd married but had chosen to keep her maiden name, an unusual choice so many years ago, but one I strongly supported.

There was definitely a story there, but I hadn't gotten wind of it, and not for a lack of trying. Everyone I asked claimed it was a mystery. The Snows had simply left, and that was that.

Maybe one of the Snows would be more loose-lipped.

"Dad's enjoying all the praise for this event," Caroline said, "But Mr. Lincoln at the Historical Society did all the heavy lifting, if you ask me. The folks at the Chamber of Commerce were great too, but it takes a history fanatic to get all these details right."

I cast my gaze around the square, taking in the scene once more. A pair of familiar men caught my eye, and I frowned. "Ugh."

The duo had dropped their coats onto the snow in favor of taking selfies in their ugly Christmas sweaters and pointy red hats.

Caroline followed my line of sight. "Do you know them?"

Unfortunately, yes. "They're the podcasters."

Tate the Great and Harvey from the Harvest were a set of obnoxious true crime podcasters with a show called *Dead and Berried*. They'd taken an obsessive interest in our town this year. Much like my friend Samantha, who owned the local wine shop and paired various vintages with food and desserts. This two-man team gained notoriety pairing recipes with reports on criminal activities, usually murders. They had a devoted following and frequently visited locations they felt would boost their popularity.

I'd looked into them last summer after they reached out in the hopes of having me on their show. They'd just returned from a trip to Charleston, South Carolina, where they paired a crawfish recipe with a tale of triple homicide. I had to block their numbers when they refused to take no for an answer.

"Oh dear." Caroline's prim expression collapsed briefly before popping back into place. "Well, pay them no attention. They're here to create a spectacle, that's all. And we won't give it to them. In fact, I'll bet no one in town will say a word about any of our tragic Christmases past. We've all got your back." She patted me as I picked up my pace toward the truck. "In fact," she said, brightly, "the exposure they're giving Mistletoe will only help the town's existence find a new audience and possibly increase tourism for next year."

I forced my head to nod in reluctant agreement, but I suspected the twosome wanted to exploit our happy little community. I could already hear their on-air voices posing questions like *"Does Mistletoe, Maine have a sinister underbelly?"* and *"What is this town hiding behind their unrealistic facade?"*

"I hope you're right," I said. "But all I want for Christmas is to avoid them until they leave."

"Speaking of gifts"—Caroline flashed me a mischievous look—"have you decided what to get Evan for your first wedding anniversary? I'm dying to know. I'll bet it's great."

My husband, Evan, was also known around town as Sheriff Gray. He had been a Boston homicide detective, transplanted to my hometown while I'd been living across the state, regretting a number of life choices—namely, agreeing to marry my cheating ex-fiancé. I'd developed a deep and abiding friendship with the sheriff. That relationship had slowly become rock-solid love, and we'd married in a heartbreakingly perfect ceremony last Christmas Eve. It was hard to begrudge my ex for his infidelity these days because his bad behavior had brought me home, and I couldn't imagine being anywhere else.

"Well?" Caroline nudged.

I glanced sheepishly in her direction while dodging a woman with a double stroller and two crying kids. Slush splashed onto our boots as she passed—one more reason I preferred function over fashion. My footwear would clean up with fresh water and a towel. Caroline's boots were probably ruined. "I have no idea," I admitted. "I can't think of a gift good enough for him. He's been a perfect husband, and I don't have the first clue what to buy. Nothing comes close to reflecting how I feel."

"How about a mug?" Caroline teased. "'World's Best Husband.'"

"Don't tempt me."

Evan had sent me a single red rose on our one-month anniversary in January. Two roses in February. Three in March. By June, the blooms started arriving interspersed with baby's breath and greens, swaddled in floral papers with holiday prints. I had no doubt I'd receive something indescribably fabulous on Christmas Eve. The flowers were merely to build anticipation. The pressure to equally impress him was smothering.

I'd thanked him with my words of joy and appreciation, but I'd never tried to reciprocate the gifts. Every time I brainstormed ways to surprise him, my ideas paled in comparison, and I'd shut the whole thing down. Now I was nine days away from our anniversary and still had nothing in mind.

"Maybe I *will* order a mug," I said.

Caroline rolled her eyes. "You'll figure it out. Let me know if you want help collecting ideas."

A familiar voice cut through the crowd, and we slowed outside the alley where I'd angled my pickup behind a dumpster and prayed local law enforcement would look the other way.

"Is that Cookie?" I asked, scanning the area for signs of my dear friend and Caroline's business partner.

"I think so," she said. "But I can't see her." Caroline rose onto her toes, attempting to peer over the cluster of shoppers headed in our direction.

I moved my wagon out of the way again, nearly losing a mammoth bottle of ground cinnamon in the process.

"Three," the voice said, growing clearer and nearer. "Theodore, Clementine, and me. No kids. A human and two goats."

That was definitely Cookie.

I smiled and waited for her cloud of white hair to appear.

Cookie had been in my life from the beginning. She'd been on earth an indeterminant amount of time, and no one dared guess.

Based on her stories of being a cigarette girl in Vegas and meeting Frank Sinatra, I had a general idea about her age that I'd never voice. Aside from being a lifelong friend of my family's, Cookie was a community staple, wealthy from a lottery win, and eccentric by nature. She lived with her pygmy goat, Theodore, and his wife, Clementine. Cookie named Theodore after her late husband, who, according to her, was also handsome and wore a salt-and-pepper beard. She'd officiated a ceremony this year that had bound him to his goat wife. Now she lived with the couple.

She popped into view a moment later, scowling, cell phone pressed to one ear.

I couldn't imagine what the call was about, but knowing Cookie, it could be anything.

"Oh!" She froze before us. "I have to call you back."

Cookie disconnected and tucked her phone into the pocket of her hot-pink vintage swing coat. "I was just on my way to Reindeer Games. Are you headed there too?"

Caroline shook her head. "I have to cover breaks at the cupcake shop, but I'll be there later if I can get away. Are you going to help Mrs. White with the gingerbread dough?"

"You betcha," Cookie answered. "What about you, Holly?" She eyed my wagon. "I'll bet those are for the big event. It's going to be a hoot knowing a world record holder. I've been trying to think of a way I can beat a record too. I figured I shouldn't waste an opportunity while the judges are in town. But I'm stumped."

"You're not alone," Caroline said. "Everyone's been wondering how to get into the record book."

I was lucky to get half the chores crossed off my to-do list on any given day. There wasn't any time left to think about setting a world record. As a matter of fact, I wasn't sure I'd finish any of today's tasks if I didn't get back to Reindeer Games soon. "I hate to rush off," I said, my gaze moving from one friend to the next, "but I'd better deliver these supplies and get the inn prepared for our guests."

Caroline's expression lit, and she clasped her mittened hands to her chest. "You have to tell me when Christopher's wife checks in and how soon I can meet her."

I grinned despite myself.

Caroline was convinced that the bearded man who'd built the inn in record time, collected toys for local children, and had a work crew that skewed toward the short side, was Santa Claus. His wife and her friend were slated to spend several days in Mistletoe before Christmas.

My dad had met Christopher at a fundraiser for the local children's hospital several years back. They'd hit it off and become instant friends. Christopher didn't live in Mistletoe, but he popped up quite a bit this time of year, a huge fan of our town. I loved him all the more for that. And like Caroline, I couldn't wait to get to know his wife.

"Maybe you can meet her at the wrapping party," I said. "My office is overflowing with donations for the toy drive. I'll need all the help I can get. Since her husband organized the event, she might want to hang out and help."

Caroline rocked onto her toes, eyes wide. "Text me the details."

"Will do." I smiled as I loaded my wagon and its contents into my truck, then climbed aboard.

The sun was warm on my cheeks and nose.

Mistletoe was bustling. Christmas was coming.

And something told me this would be the best Christmas ever.

Chapter Two

I parked my big red truck at Reindeer Games and climbed down from behind the wheel. Giant brown antlers wiggled above the window frames as I closed the door. A bulbous red nose hung merrily from the shiny silver grill. I loaded all of my newly acquired goods back into the wagon and set off for the Hearth, our tree farm's little gingerbread-themed café.

Cheery holiday music filled the icy air as I traveled, pumped from speakers hidden around the property and attached to lampposts. The place was hopping, partially thanks to news of Mom's world record attempt and partially because of Dad's brilliant addition to the festivities. He'd capitalized on the town's anniversary theme by designing and creating an authentic-looking Victorian marketplace on the property. He called the area Santa's Village and had invited artists and small businesses to rent a booth during the twelve days of Christmas. The response had been overwhelming. There was already a full wait list for next year.

The farm usually increased in traffic and sales about twelve days before Christmas, when our reindeer games began, but the addition of Santa's Village had already blown last year's profits out of the water. If things continued this way, we'd probably set a financial record to go with Mom's gingerbread man.

I towed my wagon past the strip of land where one of our most popular games was already in motion. Build a Big Frosty was a long-time favorite and exactly what it sounded like. Groups and individuals built snowmen to be judged on size and creativity. Winners got a picture of themselves and their creation in the annual newsletter and sometimes in the local paper. They also received a goodie package from the Hearth and bragging rights for the year. The snowmen had unofficial height limits of around twelve feet, since visitors were only so tall and few brought ladders larger than eight feet. But the winners weren't chosen by size alone. A recent winner had fashioned the snowman to look like two children, one stacked on the other's shoulders, wearing a trench coat. Another had been little more than a small cone shape with stones for eyes and twigs for arms. I simply couldn't resist the set of preschool-aged twins who'd worked long and hard on the project.

I waved, wishing my wagon were a sled as I trudged past busy contestants.

I dropped the ingredients off in the storeroom at the Hearth before hustling back into the day. A man I recognized as Henry Moore, the local mistletoe farmer, came into view, and I called out in greeting.

"Hello, Holly!" he said, eyes bright beneath bushy gray brows. His cheeks were rosy, and his shoulders hunched against the wind. The knit cap stretched over his round head was slowly winning its battle against gravity, creeping upward with each arch and wrinkle of his brow.

I tracked the hat's movement with my gaze, wondering what would happen when it reached the summit.

As if on cue, he tugged the material over his ears, and the cap began its ascent once more.

Mr. Moore was old enough to be my grandfather, and his farm was as old as the town. My dad had worked closely with him during the holidays when I was young, coordinating sales or helping the older man harvest his mistletoe. But Reindeer Games's popularity had grown by leaps and bounds since then, keeping Dad busy and on our grounds more and more every year. I'd often wondered what Mr. Moore had gotten up to since then.

"It's so nice to see you here," I said, meaning it to my core. I paused to shake his hand when I reached him. "Are you shopping? Or just stopping by for something sweet?" I winked. It was hard to leave Reindeer Games without at least one trip to the Hearth.

"No, no," he said, waving a gloved hand. "I'm participating in Santa's Village." He pointed to the collection of carefully crafted booths along the front of the farm. "Selling mistletoe wreaths, plants, ornaments, and decorative bundles to hang above the door. A few have little bells."

"Oh, that sounds lovely. I'll have to stop by and check it out."

"I hope you will," he said, patting the breast of his coat. A small collector's pin from the days when Mistletoe made the annual enamel accessory was stuck to the breast of his thick wool coat. My parents and grandparents had saved ones marking special years, like when they were married or when their children were born. Mr. Moore's pin featured the town name across a ball of mistletoe with holly berries. The perfect choice for this man.

He turned to keep pace with me when I began to move again. "If you buy anything from my booth, don't leave it where your cat can reach it," he said. A frown drew deep lines across his forehead. "Mistletoe is poisonous if you eat it raw or consume it in tea."

I slid my eyes in his direction. "Thank you. I'll keep it away from Cindy and try not to make it into tea."

He nodded. "Good. That's smart, but mistletoe isn't all bad, you know? Historians confirmed it's been used medicinally in the past, treating conditions like epilepsy, asthma, arthritis . . ."

I felt my eyes cross and go a little unfocused as he continued. Memories of why I'd gone to Moore's farm less and less often with Dad as I'd gotten older came back like a shot of mistletoe tea. I certainly appreciated his enthusiasm, but I could not relate, and I wasn't sure how to politely make my exit.

"It's parasitic too," he said. "Mistletoe stays green all year by leaching everything it needs off the trees it grows on."

"How romantic," I teased.

"Not really," he said. "The trees ultimately die. But it's interesting, isn't it? The plant's scientific name is *Phoradendron*, which is Greek for 'thief of the tree.' Appropriate." He chuckled, and the sound came with an intense nostalgia.

A smile tugged my lips. I'd been a dedicated *Beauty and the Beast* fan in my early years, admiring Belle's courageous, kind, and bookish ways. Mr. Moore had always reminded me of Belle's well-meaning but delightfully odd father in the cartoon movie.

"The Druids thought mistletoe had supernatural powers," he went on, voice eager and eyes wide. "It was used as an aphrodisiac and fertility herb." His chin lifted, and his gaze moved over my shoulder. We were roughly the same height, and he rose briefly onto his toes. His goofy enthusiasm waned.

"Everything okay?" I asked.

His clear blue eyes snapped back to mine, and he immediately looked away. "Mm-hmm."

I turned to see what had caught his interest, but nothing seemed amiss on the farm. I saw only clusters of smiling adults and frolicking children. In the distance, however, a blue compact SUV crunched over snow and gravel, making its way out of the lot.

When I shifted to say goodbye to Mr. Moore, he'd already turned to walk away. And he was making good time across the lot. I made a mental promise to visit his booth as soon as I could. At the moment, however, I had an ingredients report to deliver.

Mom waved wildly from a snowy field fifty yards away. A bright spot of color against the gleaming white backdrop. I smiled as I picked up my pace.

A narrow path had been worn through the snow in her direction, presumably from numerous trips she'd made while I was in town.

I raised a hand in acknowledgment, and she lowered her arms. She wore a maroon wool coat with thick cream-colored fur at the collar and cuffs. The item had belonged to her grandmother, and with a little creative seamstress work on her part, she now looked as Victorian as everyone in town.

I wasn't ready to give up my puffy coat and jeans just yet, but I was considering joining the efforts closer to Christmas Day. Very different outerwear aside, I looked like my mom. We had matching dark hair and brown eyes; ready smiles; and small, straight noses. I had about four inches on her, but she had about twenty-five pounds—and years—on me. Give or take. As with Caroline, Mom and I were identical inside, where it truly counted.

"Holly!" She opened a white folding chair from the stack beside her and placed it firmly into the snow, then turned to me with open arms. "I was so excited to see you over there! Were you able to get everything you went looking for in town?"

"I did," I said, returning her brilliant smile. "I dropped it off at the Hearth. Can I help you with anything out here?"

Mom looked at the rows of neatly ordered chairs, arranged in something akin to a wedding setup. "Nope. I've nearly finished, and Cookie's on her way to help with the fundraiser." Mom reached into her pocket and produced a small cellophane bag. "What do you think?"

A gingerbread man about the size of my palm lay inside the clear wrapping. White icing had been piped along his perimeter. Two black dots and a small, curved smile adorned his face. The number *150* had been drawn on his tummy. A tidy red and white gingham bow held the bag closed above his head. A large black tag dangled from the ribbon on a narrow piece of twine.

I caught the paper between my fingertips as it fluttered, then held it still to read the fancy script: *Commemorating 150 years. Mistletoe, Maine, home to the World's Largest Gingerbread Man.*" The tree farm's name and address were printed in typewriter font below. "I love these."

"Thank you." Mom beamed. "I'm selling them to offset the overhead costs. Purchasing all the ingredients, metal for the giant baking sheet and cookie cutter, bowls and mixers—not to mention an astronomical amount of coal and lighter fluid." She waved an arm at the field of folding chairs. "Never mind the rental fees for seating, technology, and machinery."

I didn't want to guess what those numbers added up to. I was struggling to make amends with the amount I'd spent on new snow boots this year. "Well, these cookies are perfection," I said, wiggling the bag between us. "It must've taken forever to do all this." The baking, icing, bagging, and tagging had to have taken days. "How many did you make?"

"Two thousand."

My jaw sank open and stayed there. *Two thousand* commemorative, specially packed cookies? "Mom!" I scolded. "You should've asked me for help."

She gave a politely apologetic smile and set a mitten on my shoulder. "Oh, sweetie. It's nice of you to offer, but you're already so busy with the inn and your jewelry. Besides, I had help. My friends and I have been working for nearly two weeks. We've filled freezers all over town."

She wasn't completely wrong. My to-do list was out of control. "Okay," I conceded. "But I always have time for things that are important to you, no matter what else might be going on for me."

She kissed my cheek, then smoothed it over with one fuzzy thumb. "You really are the perfect daughter," she mused. "And my very best friend. Have I told you lately?"

I rolled my eyes and grinned. "Fine. You didn't need my help because the entire town adores you, and you have a legion of ladies at your disposal. But let the record show, I am also available. Anything. Anytime."

"Noted."

My gaze traveled over the long, narrow field as she stepped away. The location she'd selected for the big bake ran parallel to the various

Reindeer Games barns and buildings, and perpendicular to Santa's Village. The area was typically a blank space, but this year it'd become yet another festive and snowy attraction.

A set of massive stainless-steel bowls sat on a bright red platform. Spotlights positioned along the perimeter pointed at the stage. Additional lights shone down from an apparatus overhead, and Dad had anchored multiple inflatable outdoor movie screens nearby. Mom's actions, from prepping the dough to preparing the cookie would be projected for onlookers in the newly erected chairs and elsewhere.

"Are those mixing bowls?" I asked, refocusing on the makeshift stage.

"Yep." She turned to admire the vessels with me. "Pretty impressive, huh?"

"They're enormous. I think we could both fit into one of them."

"Probably," she agreed. "Thankfully, your father and the farmhands are doing all the heavy lifting on this project, including operating the cement mixer for the stirring. The dump truck will be here shortly, and they've already painted the plywood props to disguise it as a massive red sleigh. Isn't that the cutest idea?"

"Adorable."

"I'm so excited," she said. "I feel like a kid, and my favorite part is that I get to share the process with all these guests." She motioned to the busy farm around us, polka-dotted with throngs of people in bright winter attire. "Finally, we can get Mistletoe some positive attention. Heaven knows we need it after all the annual chaos and whatnot."

And murder, I thought, hearing the thing she, like Caroline, was too polite to say.

Four holiday murders in four consecutive years. It wasn't exactly something to put on the welcome sign.

I looked away, forcing my thoughts anywhere else. Santa's Village bustled with shoppers. Colorful lights blinked in time to music, chasing over tent roofs as visitors browsed beneath. "Have you talked to Mr. Moore today?" I asked.

"Not today," she said. "Have you?" She turned toward the rows of tents. "He was very excited about participating in the village."

"I saw him when I got back from town," I said. "He seemed fine at first, then something changed. I'm not sure what it was, but he left without saying goodbye."

Mom furrowed her brow. "Left the farm?"

"I'm not sure. Maybe."

"Henry can be a little"—she wobbled her head—"eccentric."

A blast of icy wind tore over the land, raising a thin layer of snow into the air. I pressed my lips together and held my breath until it passed.

"Goodness!" I cried, blinking snow from my eyes.

"It's been that kind of day," Mom said.

I shivered. My intuition was rarely off when it came to people and their moods, but I supposed it was possible I'd misread Mr. Moore's sudden tension and departure, so I let it go.

"How's everything else coming along?" Mom asked. "I know you've had your hands full with the farm's holiday cards, the toy drive, your jewelry, the inn—" Her eyes twinkled. "And your anniversary," she singsonged. "I can't wait to hear all about your plans. I know you've got something lovely up your sleeve."

I forced a tight smile that felt a little maniacal.

Mom's expression grew expectant.

"Speaking of all that," I said, leaning in for a quick hug, "I should get going before the new guests arrive." I stepped back with a sigh. "The inn was cleaned this morning, so I just have to hang the new stockings and set out the keys and refreshments. I'll finish the Christmas cards after that."

"A woman with a plan," Mom said, pride thick in her voice. "Go. Do. But come back to see me later. I still want the scoop on the anniversary plans."

"Sounds good," I called, moving away with a wave. "Love you!"

"Love you!" she echoed.

My parents had dreamed of adding an inn for decades before they had the time or money to get the job done. They'd pulled the trigger a few years back, and I'd been the official innkeeper ever since. I'd spent months worried I couldn't live up to the calling, but as it turned out, I wasn't bad. I liked people enough to care if our guests were comfortable and happy, and I liked food enough to make sure everyone remained fed and fueled.

I hummed a few bars of "It's Beginning to Look a Lot Like Christmas" as I trundled along, slowed by the occasional snowdrift. I stomped on the porch and bounced my soles against the welcome mat when I arrived, knocking clumps of snow free before slipping into my home.

Scents of cinnamon and fresh pine wafted over me as I traded my boots for slippers and hung my coat on a hook in the foyer. The Victorian-inspired structure was oil-painting worthy with its wide front porch and curved bay windows. Caroline had helped me choose the exact right flooring, paint colors, faucets, and light fixtures to make the entire package come together. Mom and her friends had decorated the entire place for Christmas, and it stayed that way all year round. It really was a holiday lover's dream come true.

The perpetual holiday decor had recently been supplemented with Victorian accents to keep up with Mistletoe's town theme. Thick purple and lavender ribbons wound around the fat nine-foot fir in the parlor and the narrow pines tucked into corners of the other rooms. Evan and I had strung miles of popcorn and cranberries, our contributions to the decorating efforts. Gilded accents had been added to picture frames and mirrors. Battery-operated candles flickered from every shelf, table, and windowsill.

I turned to busy myself in the kitchen and nearly had a coronary. "Goodness!"

My rescue cat, Cindy Lou Who, sat a few feet away. Her thick calico fur pointed in every direction, and the lazy blink of her startlingly green eyes suggested I'd woken her from a nap.

"Well, how do you do?" I asked, shaking the shock from my tone. "We have new guests coming today. Have you tidied up?"

I took a step forward, and she turned, heading into the kitchen. She checked over her shoulder to be certain I followed, then took a seat before her dining area.

Dad had fashioned a custom cat-sized dining table for her, complete with elegant hand-turned legs and a stain to match the inn's woodwork. He'd cut a hole in the top and positioned a white porcelain bowl inside. Her water fountain stood beside the table, pumping tiny streams of water day and night. Above the little food station was an oil painting of Cindy in a red bonnet with white lace trim, like the ones Mrs. Claus was often portrayed wearing. The artwork and its simple white frame, stenciled with holly and berries, was a gift from my mother.

Cindy Lou Who had come a long way from the feral alley cat I'd found licking salmon droppings off my uncleaned patio grill in Portland. But her attitude remained steadfast.

"Meow."

I bent to scratch her head and stroke her fur. "You had breakfast before I went into town," I reminded her. "Dinner isn't for a few more hours, but I can give you a treat." I went into the pantry and shook a pair of green crunchies into my palm, then set them on the rubber mat beneath her table. "These help keep your teeth clean and freshen your breath."

Cindy looked at the treats, then walked the few steps to me and bit my pant leg.

"Hey!" I jumped and scolded. "No."

She gave the treats another look, then left the room.

"I love you," I called. "See you at dinner."

I checked the time and decided to set up the welcome snacks. I cued up my favorite holiday playlist before I arranged several small, decorative trays on the marble island countertop. From there, I gathered lidded containers of cutout cookies and pulled several from each bin. Soon little white inns and green trees, all neatly iced and dusted in sugar crystals, were arranged in arches across a golden tray. I added bowls of nuts, mints, and pretzels under the arch, then set a teapot with cups and a selection of teas on a second, wooden, tray.

The rattling of the back door drew my eyes to Evan, entering from the rear patio.

"Hello, beautiful," he said, shaking snow from his hat and boots.

A bolt of joy shot through me at the sight of him.

Evan was handsome every day, with his keen green eyes and thick dark hair. A slight Boston accent curled over his words. But when he was in uniform, my heart gave an extra thud. I approached immediately, tea and cookies forgotten.

The material of his coat was cold against my palms as I stretched onto tiptoes to kiss his smiling lips. "Hello, husband."

He locked one strong arm around my back and spun me off the ground before setting me onto my feet with another playful kiss. "Thought I'd stop by and check in before the guests arrived. Are you ready for a full house this week?"

"Nope." I stepped away with reluctance, thankful for his frequent drop-ins. "The Snows should be here soon. Christopher's wife and her friend are on their way too. The people from the *Guinness World Records* are going to be late." I'd prepared a detailed email with instructions for them when they arrived, so I was confident they'd be fine until morning.

"Anything I can do?" Evan asked, swiping a cookie from my arrangement and moaning with his first bite.

"No. I think I've got it under control." I reopened the lidded container of cutouts and added another to the tray.

"Are we sleeping here or in town tonight?" he asked.

"Here, I think. I want to welcome everyone in the morning and help them find their way to the Hearth for breakfast."

He nodded, ever patient, as we continued to divide our lives between his home in town and the inn. Technically, since we'd married, both homes were ours, but I'd never truly settled at the other place. And I'd been needed almost nightly at the inn since the day after Halloween.

Evan watched me closely. "Do you have anything I can take to the post office for you? Holiday cards? Jewelry orders?"

I bit my lip and shook my head. My hobby of melting glass bottles into tiny replicas of Christmas sweets, then turning those into jewelry, had become a reliable part-time income after my return to Mistletoe a few years ago. Now I had an online store and sold some pieces at the farm and other stores in town. It was a fun little business—until December, when the demand for fast turnaround quadrupled along with the number of orders. This year I'd added small gingerbread-man earrings to the lineup, celebrating the town's milestone and Mom's quest for greatness. Orders had poured in upon the announcement. Unfortunately, I couldn't make the earrings fast enough.

"I still need to package the finished orders," I said. "And I haven't had time to address the cards."

Evan popped a coffee pod into the single-cup brewer and wedged his travel mug beneath. "Well, let me know when you're ready. I'm happy to take your cards and orders with me anytime, and I'm fully capable of addressing envelopes. Whatever I can do to help."

"Thank you." I smiled, meaning it from my heart.

I knew marriage could be tricky, and not everyone married someone both willing and capable of being a true partner. I, on the other hand, had won the husband jackpot.

We chatted while I set a pot of water on the stove and dropped a few orange slices, cinnamon sticks, and cloves inside. I set a lid on top at an angle and adjusted the flame beneath. Soon, the scent would fill the rooms and add another element to the vintage holiday charm.

When Evan checked his watch, I knew it was time for him to get back to work, protecting and serving the citizens and guests of Mistletoe instead of only me. "Can I walk you to your cruiser, Sheriff?"

"You can walk me anywhere you'd please."

I snorted and wrapped him in a quick hug. "Let me grab my coat."

Outside, the temperature seemed to have dropped significantly, and a shiver rocked down my spine.

"Whoa." Evan popped the wool-lined collar on his coat. "The wind in town finally made it here, I see."

"Apparently," I said. "I hope the tents hold up."

Santa's Village stood strong for the moment, but each vinyl roof puffed and rocked with the wind.

"Is the wrapping party still on schedule?" Evan asked.

"Yep." The town donated more toys than I could wrap on my own, though I had volunteered to get the job done annually. So my friends and family spent an evening at the inn, making an assembly line of paper, tape, and ribbons. It'd become one of my favorite new traditions. "You still available?"

"Wouldn't miss it." He kissed the tip of my nose and top of my head before dropping behind the wheel of his cruiser and starting the engine.

I stepped back to wave as he maneuvered out of the little lot and onto the driveway.

He passed a trio of figures on his way toward the gate. My mom and two people I recognized immediately from their images online.

The Snows had arrived.

Chapter Three

Mom deposited the guests into my care with a kind but hasty goodbye. Folks had begun to take seats near her giant mixing bowl, and she'd been in a rush to entertain them.

"Hello," I said. "Welcome to the Reindeer Games Inn."

The Snows looked expectantly at me as I took their coats and arranged their bags at the bottom of a curving staircase to the second floor. Life-sized wooden nutcrackers stood sentinel on each side.

"Your rooms are upstairs, adjoined by a locking door so you can share the space, or not, as you prefer." I squirmed slightly when neither of the guests reacted. This was the part where most visitors mentioned how beautiful the inn appeared or smelled.

I folded my hands in wait, appraising the pair while they looked me over.

Violet Snow wore a sleek bob of blond and silver hair. Her athletic shape and perfect skin suggested she took good care of herself. Her designer clothes, bag, and boots suggested she had the money to do it well.

Her son, Elijah, on the other hand, a fortyish man with poor posture and what I guessed to be an overinflated self-worth, shifted, bored, at her side. Her style appeared to be a graceful outer showing of her inner self. His ultra-high-end attire, shoes, and watch seemed more like an intentionally crafted ad. Even the pocket square on the suit jacket beneath his unfastened coat contained his embroidered initials: EHS.

I refreshed my smile. "Your rooms are numbers one and two, top of the steps and down the hall on the left. Both overlook the farm and festivities. This is the kitchen." I led them a few more paces and opened my arms to showcase the room on my right. "I'll set out snacks and drinks throughout the day and after dinner, but you don't have to wait on me. If you get a craving for something sweet or just need a little pick-me-up, help yourself to anything you'd like. Christmas in Mistletoe can be exciting and a little exhausting." I grinned knowingly at the older woman. "You remember."

"I'm afraid I don't recall," she responded primly.

I frowned. According to locals, Violet had lived in Mistletoe until her senior year of high school, so her statement could hardly be true. I wondered again at the details surrounding her family's exit.

"A sleigh can be summoned to take you to the Hearth for breakfast and dinner. I have some cookies and treats ready now, if you're interested in something to tide you over."

Elijah sniffed. "We don't eat any of that." He motioned to the delightful spread I'd created on the countertop. "You can put it away. Sugar and caffeine are terrible for your skin, hair, and health." He looked me over carefully for the first time, then shrugged.

I wasn't sure what the shrug meant, but I wasn't going to ask. "All right," I said. "I'll leave the snacks for other guests, but I'm happy to prepare an assortment of fresh fruits, cheeses, and veggie strips, if you prefer. I also make a lovely charcuterie."

He shook his head. "Just our rooms for now."

I grabbed two keys on red satin ribbons and passed them into the Snows' hands. "Of course. I'll bring your bags up shortly."

"When was this built?" Elijah Snow asked. "Is it historic?"

I glanced at his mother, then quickly back to him. "It's only a few years old."

"And is it always decorated like this? For the holidays? All year round?"

"Yes," I said. "Mistletoe is a holiday town, and we embrace that at Reindeer Games. We do our best to make each day feel like Christmas on the farm and at the inn. You're welcome to explore at your leisure. You'll find stockings hung by the fire with care. The ones with your names embroidered across the tops are yours to keep."

His lips hitched up on one side. Amused or pleased, I couldn't be sure.

"I'm honored that you've chosen to stay here on your first trip to Mistletoe. I hope you'll truly enjoy your vacation," I said. "Maybe this visit won't be your last."

"I'm not on vacation," Elijah returned. "I'm a businessman. Work never stops because there's money to be made everywhere, if you know what I mean."

I pressed my lips together. "Of course." I understood the implication, but I could not relate. Nor did I want to relate.

I considered asking about the kind of work he did, but he'd already made it clear he wanted to go to his room.

"My family founded this town," he said, interrupting my thought. He moved in a slow arc through the kitchen, hands clasped behind his back. "We even named it Mistletoe because so many trees were covered in the stuff. We farmed the plant and the trees for generations."

"Interesting," I said.

I'd long believed Mr. Moore's family had been the only mistletoe farmers. Perhaps the Moores had bought the land from the Snows when they left?

Mrs. Snow cleared her throat. "What time is dinner?" She lifted her chin on a long inhale. "I'm feeling peckish and would like to lie down before getting ready."

"Of course," I said. I motioned to the stairs. "Go on up. The mayor is sending a car for you tonight. A sleigh will take you from the inn to the Hearth tomorrow morning for breakfast. Afterward, I hope you'll stick around to participate in the reindeer games. They're part of the experience here and a whole lot of fun."

She dipped her chin in acquiescence, then began to climb the stairs.

I sighed in relief when her arrogant son followed.

* * *

The Hearth was warm and bustling when I entered several minutes later.

I'd delivered the Snows' bags to their doors, then hurried away, eager to avoid another painful conversation with the fancy businessman.

I kicked snow from my boots and unwound the scarf from my neck as I sped across the floor to Mom.

The Hearth had been a staple on the farm since its inception, originally only serving black coffee to adults and hot chocolate to children. Over the years, however, the menu had grown, and so had the small building. Now, the log cabin–style structure had a full commercial kitchen in the back and a delightful dining area in the front, complete with eyelet lace curtains and gumdrop chandeliers. Red and white candy-striped booths lined the walls. Their chocolate-bar tabletops and black-licorice legs had all been hand carved by local artisans and my ancestors. Barstools disguised as lollipops stood before the service counter, where Mom chatted with a group of tourists.

She turned her eyes on me when the family took their leave. "Uh-oh. What's wrong?"

"Nothing." I schooled my features, feeling better at the sight of her. "I thought I'd find you with the mixing bowls, but I'm glad I found you here. Where it's warm."

"I needed to refill my thermos and check on things," she said. "Alas, all is well for me. I'm not so sure about you."

I followed her gaze to the ladies acting as waitstaff, all friends of Mom's, all excellent at making folks feel welcomed and at home. They gladly helped anytime she needed.

Evan's little sister, Libby, on the other hand, worked full time at the Hearth but was nowhere to be seen.

"How'd it go with the Snows?" Mom asked, drawing my attention back to her. The skin crinkled at the corners of her eyes. "Did you know Mr. Snow is a very important businessman?"

I barked a laugh. "You heard about that too, huh?"

Her eyes twinkled with mischief. "He told me all about himself on our walk to the inn."

No wonder she'd dropped them off and rushed away.

"I didn't know how to talk to them. Usually, guests are thrilled to be here, or at least interested in being here." The Snows hadn't appeared to be either.

"Is that the reason you're making that face?"

I tried again to straighten my features. "No. Actually, he said something that puzzled me. He said the Snows originally owned all the mistletoe in this area. I assumed the Moores always had. Now I'm back to wondering why the Snows left town. Mrs. Snow behaved as if she barely remembers living here."

Mom glanced over my shoulder, then leaned in my direction. "There was a feud." She tipped her head toward the kitchen, and I followed her through the swinging door.

"A feud," I repeated, as if that made any sense outside of 1800s Appalachia.

Mom nodded, expression solemn. "Between the Snows and the Moores."

"Over the mistletoe," I guessed.

She shrugged long and slow, then tipped her head toward my wagon. "Grab that and walk with me."

Mom donned her coat and hat, then led me through a rear exit and into the day.

I did my best to look congenial instead of on the trail of a juicy story. "If the feud wasn't over mistletoe, then what?" I whispered.

"I think it was about that at first," she said. "The families were friends and settled the land together, but then the Snows saw an opportunity to build, and moved into politics and business, leaving the Moores to manage the farms on their own. The Moores nearly went under, unable to do the work of two families, while the Snows grew rich from their new endeavors. Eventually, the Moores figured it out, the farms stayed afloat, and they made a comfortable life here, but the friendships that had led them to settle the town were irrevocably broken. The hard feelings and distrust lasted for generations. That was so long ago, I've always felt as if something else happened after that, to keep the fires stoked, but if I'm right, no one ever talks about that."

"Do you think the more recent thing is the reason the Snows left town?"

Her forehead wrinkled with thought. "They were doing well financially, and nothing significant happened as a precursor, as far as I understand. It was a shock to everyone when they left, but I was too young to be in the know, and my sweet mother never spoke of it."

My maternal grandmother had infuriatingly tight lips. She never repeated anything that might be construed as gossip. Her advice, on the other hand, rarely stopped flowing. Especially when no one asked.

We arrived at the little stage a few moments later.

Guests chuckled as Dad and Cookie made jokes and chatted with the audience. He wore a red plaid flannel shirt under a thick, sherpa-lined barn coat, looking exactly like the lifelong lumberjack he was. His jeans and boots were well worn and likely half my age. He was tall, broad and muscled, but lean from a life spent in physical labor, and had a round little belly from his addiction to Mom's amazing food. His hair and eyes were dark like mine and Mom's, but he'd allowed the grays to come in naturally, creating a distinguished, mature appearance.

Cookie was his physical opposite, comically so. Nearly a foot shorter, the top of her white hair didn't reach his shoulder, and her jazzy wool swing coat likely never spent a single day in a barn.

Dad turned to her abruptly, a microphone near his lips. "Hey, Cookie," he said, one palm turned up to the sky.

"Yeah, Bud?"

"What's it called when Frosty throws a temper tantrum?"

Cookie puzzled and scratched her head for added animation. "I don't know. What's it called?"

Dad turned to the audience, nearly vibrating with delight. "A meltdown!"

The audience groaned, and Dad cackled.

"Dear," Mom said, "he's doing dad jokes."

"Hey, Bud." Cookie pumped her brows.

Dad spun to face her once more. He moved his upturned hand onto one hip. "Yes, Cookie?"

"What does a gingerbread man need to fall asleep?" she asked.

He crossed his arms and cast his gaze skyward, feigning serious contemplation. "I don't know, Cookie. What does he need?"

"A cookie sheet!" Cookie roared with laughter as Mom made her way onto the stage.

"All right," Mom said, collecting their mics. "I'm back, and it's time to get busy."

Dad took a bow, then he hopped down and helped me move the wagon's contents onto the stage at her feet.

Holiday music played softly on hidden speakers while we worked.

"Hello! Merry Christmas!" Mom called cheerily into the microphone. "I'm so excited to see you all today!"

The crowd clapped and whistled.

"As promised, I have some piping hot chocolate to keep you warm while you keep me company." Mom motioned to a group of farmhands, and they marched forward, carrying trays of lidded, disposable cups with the Reindeer Games logo.

The workers passed out the drinks, and Mom turned back to the crowd. "Did you know the record for the World's Largest Gingerbread Man is held by a team in Oslo, Norway? And the record hasn't been broken since 2009! Three years before that, our American brothers and sisters in Smithville, Texas, held the title. Their creation, affectionately named Smitty, was twenty feet tall and weighed one thousand three hundred and eight pounds and eight ounces. The cookie in Oslo weighed one thousand four hundred and thirty-five pounds and three ounces. So, that's the bake we have to beat!"

A roar of enthusiasm poured over the crowd, and they waved their cocoas in the air.

"Today," Mom said, pausing dramatically while the onlookers settled down, "we mix the dough!"

The crowd hooted and hollered.

The farmhands swiftly traded their empty hot chocolate trays for armloads of commemorative cookies. The men moved in choreographed precision, selling neatly bagged baked goods while Mom kept the excitement going from onstage.

"Boy," Cookie said, coming to stand at my side, "who knew all those big guys could be so efficient?"

I smiled as guests waved cash at the men, eagerly trading large bills for multiple cookies.

"We might not make a world record," Cookie said, sipping what I presumed was tea from her thermos. "But we're going to have enough money to take the whole crew on a cruise!"

I laughed unexpectedly. "Win–win."

"You betcha. Maybe we'll do both!" She screwed the lid onto her thermos and unearthed a cookie from her pocket. "The local news reporter is coming tomorrow," she said, cracking the head off her treat and passing it to me. "It's going to be great publicity for the farm. Though if this place gets any busier, it might make its own record."

"Cheers to that," I said, tapping the cookie circle to the body-shaped portion in her hand.

I shoved the gingerbread into my mouth and absorbed the thrill of the moment. Whatever happened, Mom was making history, and I loved that for her very much.

"Eight hundred and twenty-five pounds of flour," she said, pointing to Dad and his workers as they upturned giant bags, dividing the mass amount equally among the mixing bowls. "Fifty-four gallons of molasses." She pointed to the jugs awaiting their turn. "Seventy-nine dozen eggs—separated!"

The crowd gasped, and she set the mic aside to begin separating eggs in a stack of cartons she'd saved for the show.

"I'd better help her," Cookie said. "That's a lot of eggs."

Agreed.

Cookie climbed back onto the platform, and I moved around to catch Dad before he was called away.

"Hey, Dad."

"Hey, sweetie." He pulled me into a quick hug and planted a kiss on my head. "Can you believe your mom is really doing this?" Pride elevated his words and brightened his smile.

"I hear she had a little help."

He looked at Mom, then back to me. "I'd do anything for her. Heck, making the two of you smile is what gets me up every morning. That and your mom's pancakes."

My heart melted a little at his words. If Evan and I were half as happy in thirty years, I'd call our marriage a wild success.

"Have your guests started to arrive?" Dad asked, looking over one shoulder toward the inn.

"The Snows are here," I said. "Violet and her son, Elijah."

Dad nodded, and I realized an opportunity before me.

"Do you know anything about the beef between the Snows and Mr. Moore's family?"

He grimaced, and I felt a little bad for ruining his good mood. "People just say it was bad blood. No one talks about it, and it was a lifetime ago."

That was true enough. Whatever happened had gone down before I was born. So why was it still a point of contention?

"I think we're all just glad to see them come back for a visit," he said.

One of the farm's horse-drawn sleighs skated by in the distance, and I tracked it with my gaze. "The Snows are having dinner with the mayor tonight. I wonder why they ordered a sleigh."

"I ordered it," Dad said, turning to watch the sleigh with me. "I asked the driver to take the Snows on a ride around the property before dinner. Your mom mentioned they were here. Maybe the experience will spark a bit of positive nostalgia in Violet."

I hooked my arm with his. "You are a kind soul with a good heart." Something about Mrs. Snow's uptight behavior had told me she could use a little positive nostalgia.

"Thanks, darling." He stepped away with a sigh. "I think I'll go over and welcome them properly before they go."

I nodded. "Oh! Make sure the driver brings them back in time for dinner."

Dad tipped two fingers against his forehead and winked, then set off through the snowy field toward the inn.

Cookie returned, wobbling slightly as she maneuvered to my side. "This world record business is a hoot. I can't wait to add this to my list of life experiences."

"You keep a real list?" I asked, always interested and rarely surprised by her revelations.

"Sure. Don't you?"

"No." I considered the possibility a moment. "A mental tally, I guess, but nothing on paper. How do you decide what to put on it?"

She lifted and dropped one shoulder. "Mostly the things that might never happen again. Also things I know are special because most people will never get to do them."

"Like driving across the country from Vegas to New York City so you could audition as a Rockette?" I suggested.

"Exactly!" Her brow furrowed. "I still think it's some sort of discrimination that those girls have a height requirement. My leg kicked just as high as any of theirs when I was young."

I grinned. I really wanted to be Cookie when I grew up.

"I'm leading the games at the Hearth tonight," she said. "That's fun, but I do it every year, so I just add hash marks on that line. Tonight, it's Christmas Karaoke, Holiday Bingo, and Bling That Gingerbread. I've been working on my accents. Folks love those. I've added Australian and South African to the repertoire."

"Impressive." I'd only heard her British accent, and that was—something.

"Accents make everything more fun."

"Definitely." I glanced at Mom, who usually smiled in complicity when Cookie had no idea she was being funny, but Mom was busy.

She set her microphone aside and pulled safety goggles over her eyes. One of the farmhands lowered a cement mixer into the nearest stainless-steel bowl, then gave a thumbs-up.

"I hope the world record people get some pictures of this crowd for the story," Cookie said, pressing her mittens against her ears and yelling over the sound of the mixer. "Have they checked in?"

"Not yet." I shook my head. "They'll be late tonight."

She frowned, then moved in closer. "Have you seen Libby or Ray?"

"Libby wasn't at the Hearth when I stopped in," I said. "Is everything okay?" My heartbeat increased with a residual pang of fear.

Libby had been through some scary stuff last year, but that was finally in the past.

"She's fine," Cookie said, "but those two love birds are tangled up tighter than the tinsel on my tree. If you ask me, there's another Christmas wedding on the way."

I smiled broadly at the thought. Evan's little sister, much like Evan, had come to Mistletoe for an escape and wound up as part of the community. They were more than a Hearth waitress and a sheriff. They were new threads in the tapestry that made our little town beautiful. And Libby's unexpected romance with Ray, a friend I'd gone to high school with, had begun at first sight. They'd been thick as thieves ever since, and I loved that for both of them. "I'd support that announcement all day."

"Me too. Some couples are just meant to be. Like your folks. Or you and that sheriff."

The whinny of an anxious horse carried to my ears, knocking the smile from my face.

Across the field Dad and the sleigh driver stood shoulder to shoulder outside the inn.

"Uh-oh," Cookie muttered. "What's that about?"

Before the two men, Mr. Moore appeared to be facing off with the Snows. Soon, voices and hands were raised, but the relentless whirr of Mom's cement mixer in a giant stainless-steel bowl made the words impossible to discern.

Mrs. Snow shot forward, stepping in front of her son, eyes wide as she spoke to Mr. Moore. A moment later, she spun to face Elijah.

Henry looked at his boots, face red, forehead creased.

Cookie tsked. "Henry looks as if someone stole his puppy."

Dad slung an arm around Mr. Moore's shoulders and escorted him away while Elijah shouted and glared at their backs.

Eventually, the cement mixer came to a sudden stop, and silence hung over the land. The faint sounds of holiday music on tree farm speakers played the afternoon score as Elijah climbed begrudgingly aboard the sleigh with his mother.

Cookie looked at me with pursed lips. "I'm going to check on Henry. This looks like a job for my special tea."

From what I could tell, I agreed.

Chapter Four

I woke early the next morning and addressed the final set of holiday cards until my hand cramped into a claw. I stuffed a dozen completed jewelry orders into bubble-lined envelopes for the post office. Then I accidentally fed Cindy a second breakfast, even though I'd already done that chore, because my coffee hadn't kicked in. "Merry Christmas," I told her when I realized my mistake.

From there, I set an array of red mugs near the coffeemaker, placed a pre-prepped tray of fruits and muffins onto the counter, and stood my pint-sized, free-standing chalkboard beside the tray. The message on the board directed inn guests to help themselves to drinks and snacks or visit the Hearth for a full and fancy home-cooked breakfast. The sleigh driver's number was permanently stenciled along the bottom.

Twenty minutes later, I was wide awake and moving briskly toward the Hearth. Frigid, biting air cut straight through me, hastening me forward. I breathed a sigh of relief when I reached my destination. No amount of caffeine would ever get me moving like a ten-degree morning.

Mom passed me a mug of steaming coffee as I climbed onto a lollipop at the counter. "You look exhausted. Were you and Evan up late?"

I wished. "I was finishing the holiday cards and a few jewelry orders." I hadn't even seen Evan before I fell asleep. "This is delicious," I said, setting my drink on the counter after a long, slow sip.

"I put a dash of cinnamon in the grounds."

"It's perfect. Thank you."

Mom slid a small white plate across the counter in my direction. A single gingerbread man rested on top. "I think this guy wants to take a dunk."

I grinned. Who was I to disappoint a cookie when no cookie had ever disappointed me?

"Can I make you something hot for breakfast? French toast? Pancakes?"

"Just the cookie," I said.

"I didn't notice Evan's cruiser on my way in this morning," Mom said. "He must've left early."

I shook my head. "We mixed our signals again. I thought he was staying at the inn, and he thought he was meeting me at the house. We talked about it, but this time of year, it's tough to keep everything straight."

Mom released a long, audible breath. "I hate this for you," she said. "You should share a home with your husband."

I did. In fact, we shared two.

"Which one?" I asked. Because it wasn't that simple. I loved his home in town, and we'd lived there following our honeymoon, until Halloween rolled past. Beginning November 1st, the inn was full most of the time, and I felt obligated to be there around the clock for guests. My parents said it wasn't necessary to be on duty every hour of every day, but I wasn't sure how to be a good innkeeper from twenty minutes away. Evan was more than willing to move into my private quarters with me, if I preferred, but the space was small for two adults, and once the winter weather kicked in, commuting to work became slow and dicey for the sheriff.

So the decision had been made, and we lived in two homes, with no signs of resolution to the situation coming anytime soon. I didn't like to think about it, so I changed the subject.

"Did Dad ever say what went on between the Snows and Mr. Moore yesterday?" I asked. The question had plagued me all night. Cookie had caught up with Mr. Moore a few minutes after the rift, but the only thing he'd told her was that mistletoe didn't have a scent, so everything at Santa's Village claiming to be mistletoe scented was a lie.

Mom tipped her head in thought. "All Bud said was that there was some sort of misunderstanding. Honestly, yesterday is a blur. I've never had so many people watching me for such a long time, and I think that cement mixer rattled my brain." She cringed and covered her ears, as if in remembrance. "I was in bed by nine, and I slept like the dead."

I wrinkled my nose at her word choice. Having been directly involved in our town's annual crime spree for the last few years, any mention of death put me on edge.

Thankfully, this year was shaping up to be different.

"How did the Snows seem when they returned from dinner?" she asked.

I thought back to the night before. "They weren't chatty, and they didn't partake in my nightcaps and cookies." I'd suspected they wouldn't, given their stance on sugar, but I'd set things out anyway. Just in case they'd at least stop to chat.

"Well, phooey." Mom pressed her bottom lip forward and cocked a hip. "How about the other guests? What's Christopher's wife like?" Her expression brightened, and I wondered if Caroline was hooking Mom on the possibility our friend and inn builder was Santa Claus.

"She didn't show," I said. "But the world record people caught an earlier flight than they'd expected and arrived just before I fell asleep. They seemed nice. Tired, but eager to explore today. They said they'd come by for breakfast when they woke."

"Excellent. I'm just sorry they missed the mixing yesterday. That was an ordeal, and one of the strangest things I think I've ever done." She laughed. "The dough didn't firm up the way I wanted, but making anything on this large of a scale is tricky," she said. "Your father and the farmhands poured the dough into the metal form and covered it after dinner. I stole a taste, and it's delicious, but thin, and more like batter than I'd intended."

I set my hand over hers on the counter. "I'm sorry." She'd worked long and hard preparing her recipe and figuring out the measurements.

She managed a small smile. "I'm not opposed to baking the world's largest gingerbread man–shaped cutout cookie, but I'd have to look up the current record holder on that. And don't get me started on how I'm supposed to make enough icing."

I laughed.

"Wait until you see the crane lift the tray onto the dump truck's bed," she said. "Have you seen the truck yet? It really looks like a giant sleigh with the decorative wooden panels around it. You wouldn't believe how much charcoal a truck that size holds."

"I might," I disagreed. "That thing is huge."

Mom smiled. "I haven't baked over an open fire since you were in that wilderness explorer group as a child. Your father was a leader. Do you remember? He had to wear that silly cap with the antlers. What was that called?"

I wasn't sure the hat had a name, but the group did. "Mini Mooseketeers."

Mom laughed. "That's right! You camped so often that summer, I started going with you so I wouldn't be alone."

"And you baked," I said.

"And you read." She chuckled. "Your father planned all sorts of informative wilderness lessons for the group, but you had your nose in a book."

"I'd already heard all of Dad's wise words," I said. "I'd only signed up for the adventuring and maybe looking for moose. You became the real hit. You were a genius with the campfire cooking." A flood of delightful outdoor memories returned in an instant, all highlighted by unbelievably good food.

"I enjoy a challenge," she said. "I show people love with food."

"You don't say." I cast a pointed glance to the window. The coal-filled dump truck where she'd bake the world's largest gingerbread man–shaped cookie visible beyond.

She followed my gaze. "I just hope the drastic temperature drop last night won't affect anything. It wasn't supposed to get that cold. I'm not sure what's going on with the weather lately. I feel badly for the poor meteorologists—they never get it right."

"Do you need any help with anything today?" I asked.

"Nope. I've got plenty of staff on hand, and Cookie's going to take shifts keeping an eye on the gingerbread man as it bakes. She's bringing Theodore and his wife to hang out in the barn with the horses."

I dunked the last bit of cookie into my coffee before tucking it into my mouth and savoring the sweet flavors. "I've heard she's a wild driver when pulling that animal trailer."

"People get out of the way, that's for sure," Mom said. "Locals and the regular tour bus drivers recognize her. I'm not sure what the average tourist must think when she's headed their way."

The images I conjured were cartoon worthy. Then something related came to mind.

"I heard Cookie on the phone, and it sounded as if she was looking for a new house. Do you know if she's having any luck?"

Mom's amused expression pinched. "Not yet. Finding a place to accommodate one goat was tough. Finding someplace she can keep two is going to be tricky. If the happy couple has kids, that'll be a whole other ball of wax. She's trying to get prepared."

Cookie lived in an adorable cottage in a snooty HOA community where there were strict rules about everything from the number of cars permitted to be visible in her driveaway to how long her trash bins could sit at the roadside after the weekly pickup had been completed. The HOA had sniffed about Theodore before, because livestock technically required a permit and a larger plot of land than Cookie's postage-stamp yard. But Cookie was a staple in our community, and no one on the neighborhood board or the council wanted to insult her by calling the goat livestock.

I supposed adding a second goat and talking proudly about the possibility of kids was the motivation her HOA needed to draw a line.

The Hearth door opened, and a gust of icy wind whirled inside.

I turned to see Libby and Ray knocking snow from their coats and boots.

"It's really coming down out there," Ray said. "I hope this won't interfere with the baking."

"Good morning," I said, raising my mug to our friends.

Mom hustled to the nearest window. "It wasn't supposed to snow today! It wasn't snowing five minutes ago!" She groaned and turned her back to the window with a sigh. "Good morning. Oh! You two look cute."

The couple approached wearing matching ugly Christmas sweaters. Each featured a large gingerbread man on crutches, one leg missing, and the words "OH SNAP!" stitched in capital letters over the poor guy's head.

Ray was tall and thin, with sandy hair and a boyish smile. He had the disposition of a Teddy bear and dreams of becoming an official *Mistletoe Gazette* reporter. He'd even earned a byline or two this year, but his official title was still newspaper photographer. "Funny, right?" he asked, glancing down at his shirt.

Libby moved confidently beside him. She was strong and stylish, a little sarcastic, and a lot of fun. She was everything I'd expected Evan's sister to be, once I'd known she existed.

I loved having her as my sister too.

Ray stacked their coats on a stool and gave my mom a hug. "Don't worry. I'm sure the snow won't amount to much. The important thing is that we passed the news crew in town, and I think they're headed this way."

Mom perked. "So soon?"

Libby slipped behind the counter and donned an apron. "I'm guessing they need time to set up before the crowd arrives and the baking begins."

Ray pulled a lanyard with his newspaper credentials from one pocket and hooked it over his head. "I'm here on business too. I'm compiling a series of snapshots and video clips to create fresh online content. When you succeed, the *Gazette* can use the material annually to reach new holiday lovers."

Mom beamed.

Libby dipped into the kitchen and returned with a large tray of commemorative gingerbread cookies. She set them on an empty table, then ferried a container of plastic bags, ribbons, twine, and tags to the tray.

Ray took a seat across from her. "I'm on bag and wrap duty until it's time to take pictures."

Mom pressed a palm to her heart, then delivered mugs of coffee to the couple.

I watched as they created a two-person assembly line, stuffing, tying, and tagging the cookies.

Libby rolled her eyes when she caught me smiling. "I know. I know. I used to bartend every night and harass catcallers by day in Boston. Now I live on a Christmas tree farm and work in a giant gingerbread house." Her accent clung thickly to each word. "Somedays I still can't believe it."

"But are you happy?" Ray asked.

Her flat expression turned light and silly. "Very."

Mom cupped her hands over her heart. "Aw."

Ray laughed. "I plan to hide the pickles in the trees for you when I finish with the cookies and the pictures," he said. "What's the prize this year? In case I want to go back for one." He winked.

Find the Pickle was one of my favorite games. Anyone who discovered a pickle in the tree they bought won a gift package from the Hearth, and it never disappointed. Seeing folks peer between the branches, hoisting children onto their shoulders to check up high, or sending them underneath to make sure they didn't miss something down low, was always fun. The occasional, unsuspecting tree buyer who came to us perplexed as to how their tree grew a pickle was absolutely hilarious.

Mom moved a pair of reading glasses onto her nose and checked a clipboard with her primary list of prizes. "Looks like winners get a six-pack of Santa's snickerdoodles, a commemorative cookie, and a canning jar with all the makings of my caramel cream hot chocolate," Mom said. "But I've got plenty of that for you anytime you want it. No pickle necessary."

"Appreciated, Mrs. White," he said.

The Hearth's door opened again, and Cookie blew in on a cloud of snowflakes. "It's like Jack Frost's wrath out there." She tugged off her mittens as she hurried toward our little group. "Theodore wouldn't even go outside, and he has a nice coat and beard to keep him warm. I had to back the trailer all the way up to the barn, then lure him in with a carrot."

"Good morning, Cookie," we called in near unison.

"Oh good." She stopped to look us over. "The gang's all here. I get hot coffee *and* a chat!"

"You certainly do," Mom said, pouring a fresh cup of coffee.

"Speaking of Theodore"—I spun to face her as she climbed atop the lollipop at my side—"you said something about moving yesterday?"

Cookie frowned and explained the gist of her dilemma. I'd hit it on the nose with my guess. Her neighbors weren't thrilled with a second goat or her plans for more. She needed more room for Theodore's growing family.

Mom patted her hand.

"Being a married man has changed everything for Theodore," Cookie explained. "And having his wife around changes the dynamic at home. I'm not the only woman in his life anymore."

I pressed my lips tight to suppress a laugh and a number of sarcastic comments.

"Theodore is welcome to stay on the farm," Mom offered. "You know he's well loved here."

"I know," she said. "I just can't imagine being that far away from him."

Ray and Libby exchanged looks but didn't share whatever they were thinking.

"Well," Mom said, "I'm sure it'll all work out. Everything always does."

The look on Cookie's face suggested she wasn't convinced.

A sudden whoop of wind whistled around the door and window frames, and a collective shiver passed over our group.

"Goodness!" Cookie called.

"Criminy," Libby complained.

Mom turned for another look through the window. "My dough will be frozen solid if this keeps up." She checked her watch again, then went to flip the sign from "Closed" to "Open" in the window. "It's a good thing we'll be starting soon."

Cookie wrapped her small hands around the steamy mug Mom had delivered. "Maybe this is a job for Christopher."

"The weather?" Libby asked. "Or the giant cookie man?"

"No. My housing." Cookie's eyes flicked to Mom. "Carol has the cookie under control, and there's nothing to be done about the temperature."

"Does Santa do housing?" Libby asked, humor curling her pink lips.

"Christopher definitely does," Cookie said.

Unexpected laughter rocked through me a heartbeat before another chill raced down my spine.

I spun toward the door on instinct, though I hadn't heard it open or close.

Two women stood inside the threshold, warm smiles on their faces. The taller of the two wore a red wool cloak and hat. Her eyes were blue and bright, crinkled with mischief at each side.

Her friend stood a step behind. Taller and thinner, her serious eyes were dark against ivory skin. Long white hair fell over her shoulders, and her coat seemed far too light for the current temperatures.

"If you're talking about my husband," the first woman said. "No job is too big, or at least that's been my experience."

The four of us stared.

"I'm Gertrude," the woman continued, unphased by our collective silence. "But you can call me Gertie. This is my dear friend, Jacqueline. Most folks just call her Jackie or Jack."

"Oh!" I set my coffee aside, finally finding my tongue. "Welcome." I stood and made quick introductions on behalf of my group.

Still speechless, Cookie nodded, thin white eyebrows climbing into her hairline.

I rushed to grab my coat, unsure what Cookie might say about the appearance of a woman who looked very much like the traditional portrayal of Mrs. Claus. "I'm so sorry if you tried the inn first. I usually hop over to see Mom before the days officially begin. I wasn't expecting you to arrive so early."

"It's no trouble," Gertie said. "Jackie and I are early birds. We had a little stroll around the grounds while everything's still quiet. Christopher says this place really gets hopping as the day goes on. He loves to talk about your farm."

Mom reanimated at the compliment. "He does?"

"Oh yes. So much so, I had to check it out for myself. Sometimes I think he'd move here if he could."

Cookie's eyes narrowed slightly. "He would?"

"Absolutely," Gertie said. "I'd have brought him with me for this little getaway, but he works such long hours this time of year."

Cookie's gaze flicked to me.

I gave my head an infinitesimal shake in warning.

"Jackie and I decided to make it a girls' retreat instead," Gertie said. "We try to have an adventure of some sort every year."

Mom took a step in the guests' direction. "I hope the snow and wind didn't give you any trouble."

"No," Gertie assured. "We love this weather, and we're made of heartier stock than you might think."

Mom chuckled congenially.

I felt an eyebrow cock as I imagined the women having a stroll in the brewing blizzard. "With a little luck the sun will be out soon," I said.

"Goodness." Jackie spoke for the first time, her expression of utter distaste. "I should hope not."

Cookie made a strange, strangled sound, and I turned to see Mom pat her back.

"Are you okay?" Gertie asked, gaze hung on a reddened Cookie.

"Mm-hmm." Cookie cleared her throat several times. "What's the weather like back home for you? Where did you say you live?"

Gertie folded her hands before her. "We're from up north. Our weather is much like this."

Jackie's sly grin gave me the impression she had something to add but wouldn't.

That was probably for the better.

"Well," I said, making a show of threading my arms into my coat sleeves, pulling all eyes back to me before things got any stranger, "I'm excited to show you to your rooms. Fires are already going in your fireplaces, and I can have a sleigh bring you back for breakfast once you're settled."

Gertie and Jackie stepped aside so I could lead the way.

"Don't worry about the sleigh," Gertie said, stepping into the snow behind me. "We brought our own."

"Own what?"

The answer whinnied before me.

I stopped abruptly, my brain short-circuited a little.

The women moved toward the tall white stallion and matching gilded sleigh waiting only a few yards away. Two large, old-timey, steamer trunks were strapped to the back. A thick crimson blanket lay across the rear seat, barely touched by the falling snow.

"Sleigh," Gertie answered. "Can we give you a ride?"

Jackie climbed into the driver's seat, and Gertie patted the space beside her in back.

I joined them in silent awe and marveled at the sleigh bells when we all began to move.

Beside us, eight wide eyes peered through the Hearth window as we zipped away.

Chapter Five

Later that morning, when Gertie and Jackie were settled, and the farm was officially open for business, I headed out to see the spectacle of a giant unbaked gingerbread man—or gingerbread man–shaped cookie, whichever the case might be.

I made it as far as the porch before additional work found me. I side-eyed the giant box beside the front door, wrapped as a faux gift and full once again with unwrapped donations to the community toy drive. "Fine," I told the mountain of plushies, dolls, and action figures. "I'll take you inside, but only because you're so cute, and I don't want this wackadoodle weather to ruin any of you."

Also because the overflow of offerings was fast becoming a tripping hazard.

Three armloads later, I'd moved everything into my office. I'd never been so thankful for the annual wrapping party. Though this year I wasn't convinced one night would be enough as I heaved a sigh and surveyed the narrow path to my desk.

Across the foyer, Cindy leaped onto the bay window's sill, slinking smoothly between a showstopping Christmas tree and the glass.

"I'll be back in time for your lunch," I promised, wiggling my fingers in goodbye.

Her tail flicked in agitation as I slipped back outside. She missed the aimless prowling of her youth. She'd tried returning to her roots a couple of years back, but all that had gotten her was stuck in a tree. These days she was indoors in perpetuity, thanks to an expensive but necessary electronic indoor barrier.

I bounced merrily down the steps and along the walkway to the farm road. The sun was out, and the world around me was picture-perfect. I loved winter, the outdoors, and this holiday. Growing up at Reindeer Games probably had a lot to do with that, but at age thirty-two, the joy I felt in all those things had only grown.

I'd hoped to be early for the big show, but people had already filled the seats before the stage, and many others were standing nearby with steaming cups in hand.

A reporter from the local paper chatted with Dad near one of the outdoor movie screens.

Excitement danced along my spine as I hurried toward the merry music and contagious energy. My mom was about to make baking history, and I didn't want to miss a thing.

Marcy and Caesar, the duo from the Guinness Book of World Records chatted on the fringe as I approached. Marcy was young and serious, probably in her early twenties, with short, curly brown hair and wide brown eyes. She hadn't returned my smile or been big on eye contact during our initial meeting. I'd presumed she was simply exhausted at the time, but she wasn't smiling now either. I supposed she might find my inability to stop smiling a little strange. I attempted to rearrange my features and look less enthused but failed. Caesar was closer to my parents' age, tall and broad with salt and pepper hair and dark brown skin. He wore a thick red scarf around his neck, and he was definitely the more enthusiastic of the pair.

"Good morning!" I called, stopping first to greet my guests.

Caesar smiled. "Hello! We were just talking about you."

"All good, I hope. Morning, Marcy." I offered a small hip-high wave.

"If there's anything I can do to make your time on the farm more enjoyable, just let me know," I offered. "It's a small town, and folks love granting a holiday wish or two."

Marcy nodded. "We like it here."

"I'm glad." My smile widened at her affirmation. All of my favorite people loved this town. "Have you been to the Hearth for breakfast?"

"Yes." Marcy pulled a small doggy bag from the pocket of her oversized down coat. "Your mom sent us away with extra goodies. Will we eat the gingerbread man?"

Caesar's brows rose. "That's an excellent question."

"It's the plan," I said, "and one of the reasons she worked so long on the recipe. She wanted it to be something everyone would enjoy afterward. The idea of wasting all the ingredients by throwing the finished product away isn't her style."

Caesar smiled. "I love how community-centered the residents of this town are. People aren't like that everywhere."

"It's nice," Marcy added.

I agreed.

The quiet bustle of farm guests making their ways to the rows of folding chairs grew as the crowd thickened. Excitement snapped and crackled in the brisk morning air.

"We were lucky to have caught an earlier flight," Caesar said. "The colleagues we'd traveled with to our last location are all stuck at the airport today. Apparently, a major cold snap came through not long after our flight left."

My gaze slid to the massive covered cookie tray. Hopefully Mom's world record attempt wouldn't be foiled by the unpredictable weather. Baking the world's largest anything wasn't exactly something she could easily try again. I hated the thought of her disappointment.

Caesar turned in a new direction, chin lifted. "Looks like the local news station is getting into position."

As promised, a cameraman and crew, complete with boom mic and fashionable female reporter strode along the periphery in search of a good place to set up their shot.

Marcy turned to me. "Tell me about the dump truck."

I grinned. "My parents did their best to make it look like a giant sleigh."

Some of the boards attached to the front of the truck, covering the cab completely and depicting the front seat of a red sleigh instead. Painted gifts piled on the hand-drawn seats. Shorter boards, depicting the sleigh's runners, had been arranged to cover the wheels.

"The bed is filled with coals," I said. "They'll start the fire and then a crane will move the tray with the cookie onto the bed."

We watched as Dad lit his electric torch and tipped it into the coals. Live footage of the action played on inflatable screens. The crowd oohed and aahed as fire slowly spread, and a mirage of heat rose in the air.

Caroline and Libby caught my eye from a distance, moving swiftly toward the crowd.

I set a hand on Caesar's forearm and nodded to Marcy. "I'll see you both again soon. Enjoy the show."

I headed in my friends' direction, excited to share this moment with them.

Caroline made a beeline for Mom, giving her a tight hug before waving to Dad, Cookie, and me as I reached the group.

"Thank you for being here," Mom told her. "It means a lot."

"I wouldn't miss this," Caroline promised. "I hate that I'm late, but I had to help my staff through a big rush. Have I missed anything?"

Mom shook her head. "Not yet. The crane's getting the cookie sheet and dough now."

"How was dinner last night?" I asked Caroline, eager to know if her impressions of the Snows aligned with mine.

She rolled her eyes and glanced around before answering. "Zane went with me, and we were iced out by my parents, as usual. I suppose the upside was that he didn't mind, and we had fun anyway."

Caroline had met her boyfriend, Zane, last Christmas, when Evan hired his security team for the season. The state ballet was in Mistletoe to perform *The Nutcracker*, and yet another murder had occurred. She and Zane had immediately hit it off, and he fit in well with our friend group. We later learned that he and Caroline had a lot in common. He'd grown up in a similarly small, tight-knit town, and his mother was in local politics. I liked Zane for a number of reasons, but my favorite thing about him was how happy he made my best friend.

"My parents talked about the Snows as if they were royalty for the entire hour before their arrival," Caroline continued. "Then they paired up at the table. Mom monopolized Mrs. Snow, bragging about all the time and attention she'd put into the town-wide Victorian theme, while Dad talked Elijah half to death about random business ventures. Meanwhile, I had a nice quiet meal with my boyfriend, so I can't complain."

I gave her an apologetic smile. I hated that her parents didn't see her for the high-value, brilliant, kind, and talented human she was. I hoped regularly that one day they'd wake up and see what I saw.

Cookie straightened at the sound of a nearby engine chugging to life. "That's my cue!" She hastened onto the platform, a cordless microphone in hand. Her red velvet swing dress, black boots, and tights gave a distinct Mrs. Claus vibe. The crown of white hair and matching red cape sent the look into full North Pole territory.

She tapped the mic, and the soft thump-thump registered from speakers at her feet and attached to nearby light poles. "Hello, hello," she began in her merriest of British accents. "Welcome to Reindeer Games. My name is Delores Cutter, but everyone around here calls me Cookie. I got that nickname from my beloved late husband because I love to bake."

I smiled as a round of gentle laughter rolled through the gathered crowd. I'd called her Cookie Cutter for at least ten years before I'd understood the joke.

"Today I'm going to be part of the biggest baking event this town has ever seen, and you are too. So, get comfy, grab a hot drink from the Hearth or from one of the helpers coming around in a jiffy, and prepare to see history made! Oh, and don't forget to buy a few of those commemorative gingerbread cookies. They're delicious!" She motioned for several of Mom's friends and a couple of farmhands to begin circulating with the drinks and sweets. Then she added, "Let's get this party started!"

Mom grabbed my hand and squeezed as a crane motored into view.

A series of metal chains connected to a covered cookie sheet swinging gently from the machine. The edges of the thermal cover lifted on the breeze as the crane trundled forward, coming into full view in person and onscreen. The tray and batter-filled cookie cutter had been stored in a pole barn overnight, protecting it from as much of the wind and elements as possible. Now, bright morning sunlight glinted off the reflective silver surfaces.

Mom exhaled a long breath. "I'm so glad this morning's weather straightened up. I was worried about—"

A gust of icy wind whipped over the land and through the trees, stopping her mid-sentence. A gasp rose from the crowd.

I burrowed low into my puffy coat and squinted against the frigid air.

"Goodness!" Mom released me to hold the hat on her head.

Caroline pulled blond hair from her glossy lips and tucked the locks behind her ears as the gust settled. "This weather has been nuts for the past twenty-four hours. I don't know what's going on."

"Merry Christmas," a familiar voice called, turning us all in the direction of the sound. Gertie marched through the field to our sides, her friend Jackie in tow.

Mom extended her hand and offered words of welcome.

Gertie pulled her into a hug. "Thank you. This is incredible." She motioned to the rows of seating. "Tell me about it."

Mom began an overview of today's process. Unveil. Bake. Measure. Eat. And hopefully win a world record.

Meanwhile, the crane carrying the enormous cookie tray stopped a few yards from the dump truck and settled its engine for the big reveal.

"Here we go," Cookie announced into the mic. "Carol, Bud, let's get a look at yesterday's work."

Gertie, Jackie, and Caroline took seats in the front row, where Mom had placed little signs stenciled with the word "Reserved."

Mom and Dad moved to stand together on one side of the covered tray. She'd linked one arm with his. Their images were projected, larger than life, onto the inflatable movie screens, along with the tray and dump truck in disguise.

"Holly!" Mom waved her free hand at me. "Take the other side!"

I moved quickly to join them, hating the thought of being in the spotlight and on the giant screens.

I felt the collective gaze on me as I reached for the edge of the thermal cover.

Cookie raised her free arm in the air. "Everybody ready?"

The crowd clapped and whistled.

The news crew adjusted their positions for the best shot.

Mom spoke softly to Dad, and he kissed her head, responding with quiet words of his own.

"Three," Cookie called.

The crowd joined in on two.

"One!"

Mom, Dad, and I turned in unison and began to drag the cover away from the form's feet, up its legs and over its abdomen.

The dough resembled a thick batter, just as Mom suspected. Nothing like the dough I'd helped cut a thousand gingerbread cookies from as a child. I hoped Mom wasn't too disappointed by the results, and I wondered how much icing I could make or find while the cookie baked. Icing the big guy would be easy compared to all the prep work.

Ray came into view behind my parents, a wide smile on his face as he snapped shots of the official unveiling.

Cookie rose onto her toes for a better look as the cover made its way toward the top of the form. "It's awful lumpy," she said, narrowing her eyes at the image projected onto the screens. "We should probably fix that so the batter bakes evenly."

Mom frowned, and I suspected she was thinking the same thing as Cookie.

On second inspection of the cookie, however, my gaze fixed on something dark in the batter. My feet slowed and my hands clutched the thin thermal cover. My stunned brain scrambled to make sense of what I saw. Was it an undissolved hunk of brown sugar? A frozen glob of molasses?

"I think that's a shoe," Cookie said, lowering her arm and the mic as she moved to the edge of the stage.

I let my gaze travel from the lump in question to several others nearby.

"Oh my stars!" Mom's panicked voice pierced the air and my heart.

The crowd began to murmur and shift. Someone screamed.

The unmistakable shape of a human body lay in the center of the makeshift cookie cutter, arms and legs gently parted, every inch covered in batter.

Chapter Six

Emergency lights drifted in ominous carousels over the brilliant white snow. An unmarked van I recognized as the coroner's rolled slowly into place beside Evan's cruiser. I'd called to let him know about the body in the batter the moment I realized what I was seeing. Based on the uncharacteristic string of naughty words he'd unleashed, and the ferocity of his typically faint Boston accent, he hadn't been happy.

No one was. Most of all, I suspected, the person whose body had nearly been baked on the back of a dump truck.

Additional cruisers crept silently up the lane, parking thirty yards short of the crime scene. Uniformed deputies climbed out and got to work, pushing back knots and clusters of confused onlookers. Tree farm guests understood something was horribly wrong, but many hadn't yet processed what they'd seen or heard about the unveiling.

Evan had escorted folks from their seats and moved them to the Hearth for interviews.

Dad had stopped the camera from sharing to the big screens, and Ray had cut the livestream he'd established after breakfast, isolating the crime scene as much as possible given the amount of footage already shared.

Still speculation was spreading fast, and given our annual holiday homicide, it hadn't taken more than a few minutes for tree farm guests to begin recording whatever they could with their personal devices.

I crossed my arms over my chest and rubbed mitten-clad hands up and down my sleeves, fighting a chill that had nothing to do with the wintery air. A chill that seemed to start in my gut and seep into my bones.

Movement caught my eye along the edge of Santa's Market, and I turned to watch the podcasters make their way in my direction. They'd completely avoided the crime scene tape and deputies by using the collection of merchandise-filled shops as cover.

I frowned, delivering my most no-nonsense expression.

The taller man grinned. Then winked.

My jaw dropped. *The audacity!*

He stopped several feet short of me and turned to face his partner, microphone in hand.

"This is Tate the Great, with *Dead and Berried*, your favorite true crime and baking podcaster, coming to you live from Mistletoe, Maine, once again. Today we're on the infamous Reindeer Games tree farm at the site of what looks to be this town's annual homicide."

Tate looked expectantly at the man before him.

"That's right, and the timing couldn't have unfolded better if we'd planned it," his partner returned. "I'm Harvey from the Harvest, midwestern farmer turned true crime podcaster, here to share in this stroke of lethal luck. A body in what would have been a twenty-foot cookie man? I'd say this murder pairs well with a hot gingerbread latte."

Tate bobbed his head, smile wide. "I can think of one guy who could use a little something to thaw him out."

I pressed my lips tight, livid and appalled. What would their mothers think of their behavior? Who did things like this? Why? For likes? For listens? Awful. Awful. Awful.

Snow crunched beneath my feet as I marched stiffly to their sides, fingers curled into frustrated fists.

"Holly!" Evan's voice rang clear and sharp through the distance. My footsteps faltered, and I turned to clock him headed my way. His expression was hard, serious eyes flicking to the podcasters.

Both men turned to watch his approach.

I stilled, fighting a smile. They were in trouble now.

Evan touched my coat sleeve briefly, an action I recognized as a check-in. He wanted me to know he was here as my husband and friend, not just the sheriff. He leveled me with a pointed stare and raised his brows slightly. A silent question. Was I okay?

I nodded. I knew that look well. Evan had a number of specific expressions that I'd tuned into years ago. He said the same about me. We sometimes joked that we could hold entire silent conversations this way, but nothing was a good replacement for hearing his voice.

And I couldn't wait to hear him tell the creeps in front of us to get lost.

The podcast bros grinned, and their eyes lit, having absolutely no shame for their presence or purpose at the crime scene. Probably also hoping the sheriff would lose his temper and give them something more to talk about on air.

Tate offered a hand before Evan could address them. "It's Sheriff Evan Gray in the flesh. I've been waiting nearly five years to meet you. The minute I heard about the murder of a little old lady in a holiday town, mere days before Christmas, her body left in a sleigh on a tree farm, I knew it would be my true crime tale of the year. And you, my friend, did not disappoint. I'm Tate the Great from *Dead and Berried*, the web's most popular true crime podcast."

"That's debatable," I muttered, earning a side-eye from my husband and a frown from Mr. The Great.

Evan exhaled a patient breath. "I'm afraid I'm going to have to ask you both to relocate." He pointed to the crowd behind the yellow tape, monitored by his deputies.

Tate waved a hand, disregarding Evan's words. "No, thank you. I'm pretty sure the story is right here, and we aren't causing any trouble. In fact, we're going to get to the bottom of this year's kill, and we're bringing our audience along for the ride."

I gaped at the complete show of disrespect, both for our town sheriff and for the loss of life only a few yards away.

In the space of that breath, Tate extended his microphone to Evan, and Evan reacted with lightning speed. I blinked, unsure what I'd seen, but the aftermath was perfection. Evan held the microphone in one hand. Tate's back pressed against Evan's chest, Tate's arm bent between them, secured by Evan's grip.

"Hey!" Tate protested. "That hurts! Abuse! Misuse of power!"

Harvey gaped, eyes wide, body still, and mouth silent.

Evan's lips twisted, fighting a grin.

I shook my head, knowing he sometimes missed the physical parts of the job he'd left in Boston. Chasing assailants. Disarming gunmen and such. He rarely had on-the-job cause to get handsy in Mistletoe.

"You shouldn't point anything at a lawman," Evan said merrily. "Tends to incite a reaction. Now, as I was explaining politely—" He pushed Tate gently forward, maintaining the hold. "I need you and your partner to stay behind the established perimeter. If I see you on this side of the tape again, I will arrest you for obstruction of justice. You can see and hear everything you need for your podcast from right over there."

"We can't see or hear anything from way over there," Harvey protested, shuffling along behind Evan as he steered Tate to the waiting deputies.

"Perfect," Evan answered. He dropped the offenders off and returned to me, smile widening.

"Have fun?"

He shrugged. "A little."

I slipped my arm behind his back, and the fabric of our ice-cold ski coats quietly swooshed.

"This town is so pleasant all year long," he said. "Why on earth do we have to deal with chaos every Christmas? It's nuts and bananas."

I smiled at his Mistletoe-quality curses. "I'd like to know the same thing."

He glanced at me. "You ask a lot of questions."

"You don't answer most of them, but you once told me crimes are statistically more likely to happen around Christmas in this town because tension is historically high around the holidays, we're flooded with tourists, and you are short-staffed."

He rubbed his forehead, then smoothed a vein that had begun to throb visibly at his temple. "That sounds very reasonable of me."

I laughed.

"But why does it always have to be murder?"

"Maybe it wasn't foul play this time," I suggested.

Evan turned wary eyes on the dump truck, crane, and massive cookie cutter full of batter. "I'm not sure how that could've been an accident, but I'm willing to hope."

"Maybe someone got drunk and fell in," I said.

Evan took my hand and led me toward the dump truck. He raised one of my mitten-covered hands to his lips and pressed a kiss there. "Here's to hoping this was just bad luck."

Cookie met us as we walked. Her eyes were bright with elation. "I saw the way you took the mic from that podcaster," she said, vibrating with excitement. "You looked like a movie cop, disarming him and locking him against you like that." She threw a few wild air punches. "He never knew what hit him. I'll bet that teaches those guys a lesson."

I doubted we were so lucky. In fact, I suspected the exiled podcasters would only double down on their mission, but that was a problem for another time.

Evan gestured to my parents, and they moved closer. "Any chance there's security footage of the area where the cookie tray and batter were stored last night?" he asked Dad.

"I don't keep surveillance on the pole barn specifically, but a couple of the other cameras might pick up movement on this section of the property if it's within their periphery."

"I'd like to take a look at last night's footage from all of those devices," Evan said.

Dad nodded, and I caught his eye.

"When was the last time you made your rounds out here?" I asked. He typically made a trip around the property before heading to bed. "Did you look at the batter while you were out?"

He shook his head. "I made my final rounds on the four-wheeler at about ten o'clock. I didn't check under the cover."

"What do you mean?" Mom asked. "Didn't you cover the batter."

"I didn't."

Mom frowned. "Who did?"

"I thought you used the thermal as a way to manage the dough's temperature through the night," Dad said.

"No." Mom shook her head. "The plastic wrap I wanted to use kept blowing off with the slightest wind. I assumed you swapped it for the thermal cover." She looked to Evan. "We bought both, because I wasn't sure which would be best. Ultimately, the dough was too thin, and I opted for the plastic. I assumed Bud didn't realize and used the thermal."

"Interesting," I said. Did that mean someone else had covered the body after Mom's thin plastic wrap had blown away? Was that person the killer? My wheels had only begun to turn when I felt Evan's body press against my side. I looked up to find him staring down, another trademark scowl in place.

"Do not," he said.

"What?" I repeated.

"Whatever you're thinking in that big brain of yours—just don't. Everyone knows you can figure this out if you start digging, but no one wants that. Especially me."

"And me," Mom said.

I winced internally at her heartbroken expression.

"Or me," Dad said, echoing the sentiment. "You nearly get yourself killed every year, and I'm not getting any younger. My heart can't take it."

"Let Evan handle this," Mom pleaded. "It's all I want for Christmas."

My eyes moved from parent to parent, then to Evan, who looked a little too pleased. "I wasn't thinking anything." Except that the coroner could probably place the time of death between ten last night and now. Also, that unless someone staying in town was reported as missing, the person in the batter had to have been on the farm last night. That left us, my inn guests, the farmhands, or a stowaway. "Are all of your farmhands accounted for?" I asked Dad.

And were there footprints to examine, or had the night's storm covered them before dawn?

His expression turned curious. "I believe so. Everyone who was on the schedule for this morning is here. Why?"

"What about everyone working last night. Are they all here too?"

Dad paled. His gaze darted to the cookie tray. "You don't think—"

"Holly," Evan warned.

Mom pleaded with her eyes.

"I'm just wondering," I complained. *Jeez.* "Has anyone been reported missing in town?" I asked Evan. "A tourist who didn't make it back to their hotel or bed and breakfast? A local who never returned from an errand or party?"

Evan gave me a painfully bland expression.

"I think I've heard from all the farmhands," Dad said belatedly, looking distinctly relieved. None of his men were frozen inside a giant cookie man.

The coroner set a tablet onto the stage and climbed up. He was bundled in white from his all-weather boots to a tightly cinched hood. He motioned the crane to lower the tray into the space before him. A moment later, he moved carefully around the giant metal cookie cutter. A camera hung from a short strap around his neck.

I turned in a small circle, shivers cascading over my skin beneath the suddenly icy coat.

In the distance, Mr. Moore came into view, his knit hat clutched in his hands. He made his way along the front of the crowd. A tuft of gray hair lifted from his head on the breeze. Worried eyes focused tightly on the coroner.

Relief washed through me, then shame. I was indescribably thankful to know he was okay, but whoever lay in the batter was decidedly not.

A jolt of fear and realization hit next. I'd asked Dad about the farmhands, but I hadn't taken a full headcount of my guests. I'd spoken to Marcy and Caesar, Gertrude and Jackie, but I hadn't seen either of the Snows.

A horror-film worthy scream jerked me from my thoughts. In the distance, Mrs. Snow raced down the inn's steps.

On the cookie sheet, the coroner had removed the batter from Elijah Snow's face.

Chapter Seven

Paramedics tended to Mrs. Snow, who'd stopped crying abruptly, then gone into shock. Mom ushered them into the Hearth and away from the crowd. Most of the folks initially sequestered there had since given their statements and been dismissed.

I imagined Mrs. Snow in a booth, a red wool blanket wrapped around her shoulders, a cup of tea before her, Mom and the paramedics covering her in compassion and care.

Violet and Elijah were the last of the Snow family line, but I hoped she had someone who would come to Mistletoe and comfort her. A friend or neighbor. A cousin or former coworker. Anyone who loved her and wouldn't want her to be alone.

Not after losing her only child.

Forbidden from "interfering" with the crime scene or approaching emergency responders with questions, I decided to check on Mr. Moore, who hadn't moved a muscle since I'd first noticed him in the crowd.

Caesar and Marcy had climbed onto the inn's front porch, staying clear of the crime scene while retaining their view. I made a mental note to prepare warm drinks and snacks for them as soon as I could.

I crossed into Mr. Moore's line of sight and offered a small smile. "Hey," I said, cautiously. "Are you feeling okay?"

His cheeks and hands were red. The knit cap in his grip had been wadded into a ball. I worried about the possibility of windburn or frostbite. "I came to open my booth," he said.

I nodded. "I think Santa's Village and Reindeer Games will be closed the rest of the day."

I selfishly hoped both would reopen before Christmas, but I couldn't be sure.

Moore's gaze moved past me and into the distance. "Was that—" He glanced at me, then quickly back to the dump truck. "Was it—" His clear blue eyes flickered again to mine. "I saw her scream, so I thought it might be—" His darting gaze made a circuit. The Hearth. The dump truck. Me.

"I think so," I said quietly, hoping I'd interpreted his question correctly. "But I can't confirm."

He closed his eyes briefly, then reopened them with a devastated expression. He stretched his crumpled hat onto his head. "She would know."

A mother knows, I thought. My mother had said those words a thousand times for a thousand reasons, but this one hit like a sledgehammer to my gut. "Yeah," I agreed. "I guess she would."

A sharp whistle cracked the icy air, and I spun in search of the sound. Across the field, Evan raised an arm overhead. Deputies jogged in his direction, and my curiosity spiked.

"I should probably see what that's about," I said, turning to excuse myself from Mr. Moore.

He nodded before pushing his way back through the crowd.

I hurried in Evan's direction, eager to know what had caused him to call for his deputies.

Mom's path met mine as she exited the Hearth. "They're taking Mrs. Snow to the hospital for evaluation. She said she's had heart problems in the past, and this is a big shock, so they want to be sure she's okay."

I wrapped my arm around Mom's waist, and she leaned her head on my shoulder as we walked.

"Any idea what that's about?" she asked, her gaze fixed on Evan.

"Not yet."

He transferred something small into an evidence bag, and I moved a little faster, desperate to see what they'd found.

"You doing okay?" I asked Mom.

"No." Her voice cracked, and I pulled her tighter against me. "But I'm not alone," she said. "And my baby is right here." She kissed my cheek. "Go ahead. I'll find your father."

I nodded, then released her.

The deputies were on their way across the field and moving in the opposite direction.

My shoulder accidentally bumped against the man carrying the evidence bag, causing him to misstep. "Goodness!" I gripped his arm to steady myself and took the opportunity to steal a long look at the contents of the bag.

"Whoa," he said. "Careful there."

"My fault," I said. "This day has me off-balance."

His expression turned apologetic. "You and the whole lot of us. Take care now."

"You too."

I bit my lip, reminding myself that this was a new year. I was a married woman now. Happy. Healthy. And in no sort of headspace to jeopardize any of that. *Even if the small commemorative pin in that deputy's evidence bag looks exactly like the one I saw on Mr. Moore's lapel yesterday.*

A pin that had been missing when I'd spoken with him only minutes before.

* * *

Following a solemn dinner at the Hearth, Marcy, Caesar, Gertrude, and Jackie made their way back into the night. Mom, Cookie,

Caroline, and I polished off a tray of sweets and two pots of cinnamon tea. There simply weren't words to make sense of what had happened to Elijah Snow, Mom's dream, or her giant gingerbread man.

"It's last year all over again," Cookie said, uncorking her thermos of schnapps and Earl Grey. "And the year before. And the year before . . ." She trailed off, repeating herself two more times.

Mom stifled a whimper.

I patted her hand. "I'm sorry this is happening again."

Her fingers curled around mine. "It's not your fault, sweetie. I'm just sick for Mrs. Snow. If I lost you—" She covered her mouth and shook her head, unable to continue the thought.

"I'm right here," I promised. "And Evan's out there sorting the details. He'll get justice for the Snow family."

I cringed inwardly as I thought of my husband. The last time I'd spoken to him, I'd confessed to peeking at the evidence bag. Then I'd reminded him about the argument between Mr. Moore and the Snows before mentioning I hadn't seen Henry's pin on his lapel today.

Evan had left the farm for about an hour after that, and I'd been waiting on pins and needles to speak with him since his return.

My heart said Mr. Moore was a sweet old man, incapable of harming a fly, let alone committing murder, but I'd learned a lot these last few years. The lesson I hated most was that people sometimes did things in the space of a few minutes that they'd regret for the rest of their lives.

The sky was deep blue beyond the windows, sprinkled with countless stars. Behind our closed gate at the bottom of the lane, people had gathered with candles and united voices to pay respect to the loss of life that occurred here. They sang hymns and carols. Sometimes there was only endless eerie silence.

I wondered if Mrs. Snow knew the crowd was there and what she thought about it. I longed to help her somehow, but I also knew enough about loss to understand the best thing I could do was be available for anything she asked.

Cookie removed the napkin from her lap and eyeballed the mostly empty tray of treats we'd shared. "I'm never eating another gingerbread man," she said, draping the white linen over a trio of the cookies in question.

Mom moaned. "That's bad news because I baked thousands in commemoration."

Caroline wrapped an arm around Cookie's shoulders, then looked over her head to me. "I wish we could just ask Gertie to make this all go away. Maybe she can get Christopher to rewind time and protect Mr. Snow."

It took a moment for her words to make sense. Then I rolled my eyes. "She's not Mrs. Claus, Christopher isn't Santa, and the Clauses don't grant wishes," I said. "They deliver toys to children."

Cookie took a long pull on her tea. "I agree. We'd have to find a genie if we wanted a wish granted. That fellow, Dr. Who, is good at time travel."

I met Caroline's gaze and smiled.

"I knew a genie once," Cookie continued. "I was passing through LA, and she played one on TV."

Mom offered Cookie a glass of water and screwed the cap onto her thermos.

I grabbed my coat. "I'm going to see if I can catch Evan before he leaves."

Hopefully, he'd gotten the chance to speak with Mr. Moore. I'd been worried about the older man since his abrupt departure. I also worried Evan might interpret yesterday's exchange between Henry and Elijah as something sinister. In my opinion, the heated conversation only proved that Mr. Moore knew the Snows, and that information could be valuable to the investigation.

For example, if Henry knew Elijah, he might also be aware of someone with reason to want to hurt him.

I plunged into the frosty air on a mission.

Evan noticed me immediately and headed my way in response. His cheeks were rosy from the cold, but the look of determination on his brow told me he wouldn't go inside until he'd done all he could for Elijah Snow. "I was looking for you earlier," he said. "I worried when I didn't see you badgering the farmhands or deputies."

"Funny," I said. "I had dinner at the Hearth. Were you able to catch up with Mr. Moore?"

He nodded. "That's what I wanted to tell you. He was struggling to breathe when I found him at his car. I took him to the hospital for evaluation. Apparently, he has some known health conditions and was admitted for observation."

"Goodness!" I'd had no idea, and I hadn't pushed when he'd said he was fine, even though I could tell he wasn't.

"I don't see him as a flight risk," Evan said. "The hospital staff predicted I'd find him there later tonight if needed, so I'm doing what I can here first."

I sighed. "He's not going to leave town. When I told you about the exchange between him and Elijah, I hadn't meant to insinuate—"

"Holly." Evan cut me off. "Your dad and the stable hand who drove the sleigh already told me about the argument. I'd planned to talk to him anyway. I just hadn't realized Moore was at the farm today until you mentioned it."

"Oh." I dashed the toe of my boot against hard-packed snow. "Did my dad tell you what they were arguing about?"

Evan cocked a brow. "I'm not answering that."

I crossed my arms. "Then tell me how they know each other."

"Moore and Violet grew up in Mistletoe together. I haven't gotten the whole story yet, but apparently the beef between the families goes back long before either of them were born," Evan said. His smart green eyes turned hard as they bore into mine.

"Their families were friends once," I said, repeating the information Mom had shared. "Back when they settled the town." I didn't see how a falling-out so long ago could have anything to do with a death today.

"I don't want you getting involved in this. I mean it. I've had enough holiday scares with you to last a lifetime. Ten lifetimes," he amended. "The last thing I need this year is for you to get mixed up in some hundred-year-old feud, or whatever this was."

I followed his sweeping gaze to the crime scene. "As long as you believe Mr. Moore didn't do this," I said. "Feud or not, I saw the look on his face tonight. He was as horrified as the rest of us."

"Maybe," Evan said. "But the pin I found looked an awful lot like the one Mr. Moore likes to wear on his coat."

Chapter Eight

I headed into town when Evan and the deputies wrapped up for the night. The inn guests were in their rooms, and I'd set out a spread of snacks and drinks before leaving. Cindy Lou Who was snoozing in my private quarters, tucked safely away from the countertop treats.

Despite the piles of work awaiting me in my office, and my husband's requests, I couldn't stay away from Mr. Moore tonight. He didn't have any family, and I wasn't sure who knew he was at the hospital. If he had called anyone to sit with him, I wondered if they'd be apprehensive, given the situation. News of Elijah's death had surely spread through the locals by now, and Moore's family feud with the Snows was common knowledge.

I'd felt the same apprehension five years ago. These days, however, I was significantly more resilient and less concerned about spending time in jail for meddling. Hopefully Evan would understand that I couldn't live with myself if poor Mr. Moore was sick, scared, and alone after his earlier trauma.

If Cookie or one of my parents were in the same situation, I'd hope someone would be there for them too.

The hospital parking lot was quiet as I parked my truck beneath security lighting and climbed out. My breath floated in steamy puffs as I made my way to the sliding glass doors outside the emergency room. A bevy of locals filled blue plastic chairs along the walls inside. A short line had formed at the check-in desk. Pink-cheeked children gazed listlessly at a television anchored in the corner while a cartoon grinch rode a sled into Whoville. Other kids played chase around a ratty-looking plastic tree with paper ornaments hung on pipe cleaners. More than one of the adults looked as if they wouldn't mind being admitted too, if it meant getting a little sleep.

"I told him not to sled at night," a woman explained to the intake nurse while a pint-sized boy cried at her side. "Even with our motion lights, it's just too difficult to see."

A second child, not much bigger than the first, looked frantically from the woman to the nurse. "I couldn't help it," he pleaded. "The path was clear until Marvin tried to stop me!"

The first kid wailed. His nose and mouth were smeared with blood, and he held an ice pack to his forehead. "It was my turn, and you knocked out my front teefs!"

I pressed my lips together and hurried past.

A doctor carrying an X-ray through the waiting room spoke quickly with a nurse in holiday-themed scrubs. "Looks like another ankle fracture," he said. "Everyone thinks ice skating is great until they realize they don't know what they're doing."

"Or the ice breaks," the nurse said. "Let's be glad it's just an ankle. Those heal."

A group of carolers in Victorian garb roared in behind me, falling against one another in laughter. A scent I associated with Cookie and her peppermint schnapps arrived with the group.

"He stuck his tongue to a light post," one of the group members called.

I slipped into the wide hallway beyond the waiting area while everyone was distracted. HIPPA laws would stop anyone on staff from helping me find Mr. Moore, so I'd have to do that on my own. Thankfully, I had a plan.

I checked my watch before climbing into the elevator and pressing the button for the third floor. Holiday tunes played softly as I climbed.

A moment later, the silver doors parted, and I hustled into the cafeteria, hoping I hadn't missed Mom's friend, Mona.

Like everything in Mistletoe, the large dining space was decorated for the holidays. Another sad plastic tree stood in the corner. Shiny red and green garlands outlined the windows, and Christmas cards taped to the wall formed the shape of a big star.

"Holly White!" Mona cried the moment I turned the corner. "What are you doing here?"

"Hey, Mona," I said. Though my name was legally Holly Gray now.

I'd considered hyphenating my last name with Evan's, but Holly Gray-White and Holly White-Gray sounded equally silly, so I'd stuck with tradition. My left thumb traced the wedding band Evan had given me the year before, and I smiled.

Mona tipped her head curiously. She wore her dark hair in big curls, teased to within an inch of their life, a look left over from her days as a pageant queen, no doubt. She'd been a cafeteria worker at the hospital for years, and her name tag had a worn Santa sticker in the corner. "Everything okay?" she asked. "Your parents? Cookie?"

"Oh yes, we're all fine."

Mona visibly relaxed. "Thank heavens. I heard about what happened at the farm today. I planned to call when I finished my shift."

"Mom will appreciate that," I said. "She's pretty shaken. We all are, but I'm here looking for Henry Moore." I pulled a lidded container of pastries from my bag. "I heard he was admitted for observation."

Mona looked at the wall clock. "Visiting hours aren't over just yet, but you'd better get moving."

I wrinkled my nose and leaned in her direction. "If you had to guess, where do you think I'd find him?"

She considered me for a moment. "What brought him in?"

"Shock, maybe. He was at the farm today."

She nodded. "I'd start with the fourth floor."

"Thank you." I fished a commemorative gingerbread man from my pocket and passed it to her. "Merry Christmas!"

She beamed at the cookie, and I hurried away.

I took the elevator up one floor and hoped Evan hadn't posted images of my face behind the nurses' station, with instructions to send me away.

Mistletoe Memorial Hospital was big, and I wasn't sure which way to turn after stepping onto the new floor. I read the signs and quickly ruled out Labor and Delivery as well as the wing designated as Urology. That left one hallway to explore.

Men and women in festive scrubs moved in double time, dodging families and other visitors toting balloons and gift bags.

I tried to blend in. I peeked through every open doorway until Mr. Moore's balding head came into view. He was on his side in bed, staring forlornly through the window at the night sky.

I rapped my knuckles against the door frame. "Knock knock."

He looked over his shoulder in my direction, then rolled onto his back. "Holly?"

"Hi." I slipped inside and closed the door. The room smelled faintly of coffee and antiseptic. "I wanted to make sure you're okay. I brought treats from the Hearth." I extracted a pastry bag of cookies from my pocket and extended the offering in his direction.

Emotion swam in his eyes. "That's very kind. Thank you."

"It's no problem." I set the container on the nightstand when he didn't reach for it. Then I took a seat in the chair at his bedside. "How are you feeling?"

"Tired," he said.

"I won't stay long," I promised. "I just needed to know you were okay, and I wanted you to know my family is thinking of you."

He sighed deeply, looking significantly older than his years.

"How long are they keeping you here?" I wondered, hoping he'd be home for Christmas next week. "Have you let anyone know you're here?"

"No need. They're sending me home tonight. I'm just waiting for the paperwork."

I blinked, initially surprised by the news. Then I noticed he wasn't in a hospital gown. He'd stretched the blanket over himself, but the collar of his sweater was visible at his neck. His coat hung on a hook near the door, and his shoes were lined up beneath it.

He was waiting to leave.

"Do you need a ride home," I asked. "I can drive you if you don't have another plan."

"I'd appreciate it," he said. "An ambulance brought me. I've been trying to decide who to bother."

"It's no bother," I promised. "I'll stay and wait with you, if that's okay."

His eyes were glossy with emotion when he nodded. "Did you know mistletoe is poisonous?" he asked quietly. "And it's invasive."

"You mentioned," I said.

I hoped for Mr. Moore's sake Elijah's cause of death wouldn't be poison.

"Once mistletoe infests a tree, it's really hard to get rid of," he said. "But it's not all bad." A measure of hope crossed his wrinkled face. "It's medicinal too."

I wondered if he was trying to tell me something, perhaps drawing an analogy? If so, I couldn't guess the true meaning.

"Alternative healers use mistletoe for treating headaches, arthritis, seizures—"

The door opened, interrupting his words.

I saw my life flash before my eyes, afraid Evan had returned to speak with his only suspect, and caught me snooping.

Instead, a young nurse appeared. "Oh, hello," she said, visibly startled to see me. "I wondered who had closed the door."

I wiggled my fingers at her. "Hello. I'm Holly."

Mr. Moore creaked upright, pushing away the blanket and turning his legs over the bed's edge. "May I go home now?"

"Yes." The nurse passed him a tablet. "Take a minute to review the release, then initial and sign, please. It says you agree to set a follow-up visit with your primary care physician within seven days and that you should rest. I know that's hard to do this time of year, but you need to try. Return to the ER if you experience chest pain, dizziness, or shortness of breath. I'll get a wheelchair for your discharge and be right back."

Mr. Moore looked vacantly at the tablet.

After the nurse had gone, I stood. "Do you need help with that?"

"I just want to go home."

"I know," I said softly. "Here." I dragged a fingertip down the screen, scrolling to the line. "Use your finger like a pen. Initial there. Sign below."

He scribbled illegibly, then set the tablet on the bed. He shuffled toward his coat and shoes.

"Are you sure you should be going home?" I asked. In my opinion, he looked as if a night or two of observation was in order.

"I'm okay," he said. "They ran the tests, and I'm still kicking."

I bit my tongue against asking for more information about his health. I presumed he had a heart issue, based on his age and the nurse's instructions, but I didn't know enough about health or medicine to think of anything more specific. I supposed it didn't matter what ailed him. Only that he was okay.

As promised, the nurse returned to collect the tablet and deliver a wheelchair. I walked along beside her as she pushed him to the elevator.

When the doors opened on the first floor, a familiar pair of faces came into view. Tate and Harvey, the true crime podcasters leaned against a wall at the edge of the ER. They spotted me before I could get my hood over my head.

Tate smiled a wide grinchy grin as we approached the hospital's exit. "Well, well, well. If it isn't Mistletoe's infamous local sleuth." He pushed off the wall and took a step in my direction. "I don't make a habit of pairing desserts with encounters, but I'd say this one goes with some kind of fruit cobbler because it's juicy."

"Gross." I said, wrinkling my nose before looking pointedly away.

"You know, Harvey," Tate said casually to his partner, "I'd say I'm surprised to see Holly with the town's number-one murder suspect, but we both know I'm not."

The nurse gasped.

Harvey chuckled.

Moore made a strangled sound.

I forced a smile and turned pointedly away from him. "I'll bring the truck around," I told the nurse. Then I leaned into Moore's view. "I'll be right back. Please ignore these two awful people." I hooked a thumb in the podcasters' direction, then hurried to get my truck and return.

Two minutes later, I pulled my truck up to the automatic doors and shifted into park.

Tate and Harvey were speaking with the nurse when I reached them once more.

"Go away," I told them when I climbed out. "Kick stones. Buzz off. Goodbye."

The nurse's eyes were wide and her grip on the wheelchair handles, white.

"This way," I told her. I rounded the truck's hood and opened the passenger door for her patient.

Thankfully, she complied, and Moore was quickly loaded into the cab.

"I-I didn't—" he began, head shaking. His hands trembled as he reached for the seat belt.

"Ignore them," I repeated. "They're looking for a story, and they don't care if it's true."

"You're the story," Tate called from behind me.

I wasn't sure if he meant me or Mr. Moore. Either way, I didn't care. I closed the passenger door and went back to the driver's side.

"But I didn't—" Moore tried again when I climbed behind the wheel.

"Don't listen to them," I said, shifting into drive.

Outside, Tate and Harvey stared at the soft blue glow of a phone screen, possibly videotaping or, worse, livestreaming our escape.

* * *

I turned onto the lane at the base of Moore's property several minutes later. An old carved-wood sign announced "Mistletoe & Moore" in gilded letters, a play on words I'd always enjoyed. The stout driveway was lined with trees and shrouded in shadow as we crept forward. Multiple sets of tire tracks were visible in the snow. I shifted into park beside his little white pickup truck, outside a home straight from the pages of a storybook.

Beside me, Mr. Moore gazed through the windshield, looking distant and a little sad. "Birds and animals make mistletoe nests," he said as the truck's engine settled. "It makes wonderful homes for woodland families. Some of the nests are big. Up to fifty pounds." He unfastened his safety belt and opened his door. "It kills the trees, but it redeems itself in that way by protecting other creatures. Don't you think?"

He closed the door before I could answer.

I didn't particularly love the direction this little trivia session had gone, and I had no idea what to say about it. So, I took my time joining him on his porch.

I'd always loved Tudor-style houses like his, with their steeply pitched roofs, regal wooden beams, and gorgeous stonework. Set back among the trees, topped with snow and outlined in twinkle lights, Moore's home looked downright enchanting.

He unlocked the heavy wooden door and stepped inside. A small lamp had been left on in the corner, illuminating the space.

"Come in," he said. "Would you like some tea?"

My gaze traveled the tidy space, catching on the myriad of motionless animals on every flat surface. A set of squirrels on hind legs, arranged in a cluster and dressed in mauve Victorian garb, stopped me in place. Their little fingers were curved around tiny sheet music, their mouths open in song.

"That's the Mistletoe Holiday Choir," he said, moving back in my direction. "They sang at your engagement. Cookie is part of the group." He pointed to a singer with a crown of white hair. "There she is."

I dragged my gaze to him, but it jumped back to the pack of squirrels. "Are these real squirrels?"

"Taxidermy," he said. "Look. All of Mistletoe is here." He flipped a switch on the wall, and a buttery light bathed the room. "It helps to pass the time during our offseason. It's a lost art. My grandfather was much better, but I try."

My mouth dried as I processed the sights before me. Frogs with snowshoes and hiking sticks stood near the covered bridge where Evan had proposed. A blond chipmunk held a tray of cupcakes outside a wooden shop. Squirrels dressed as mail carriers and shopkeepers. A little town square with a blinking, decorated tree.

"I wasn't sure where to put you," he said. "I thought it made sense to leave you there." He pointed to a brown squirrel in a white parka outside what I guessed to be the Reindeer Games Inn. Beside her, a black squirrel in a tiny sheriff's jacket held a gift wrapped in red. "There's a marble in the box."

"What?" I hadn't had any real expectations of what the inside of Mr. Moore's home might look like these days, but taxidermied wildlife dressed as Evan and me wouldn't have been on the list. The displays had not been present in years past when I'd visited with my dad.

"I thought about putting a ring in the box, but all I had was a marble." He hung his coat on a hook and moved through a nearby archway. "I'll make tea."

He was gone before I could protest, and I was thankful for the moment alone.

Aside from the squirrels, his home was lovely. Neat and tidy, if sparsely furnished. A bookshelf near a rocking chair overflowed with well-worn novels and photos of people through the years. The Christmas tree in the corner was about my height, with white lights and an abundance of what I presumed was mistletoe. I thought about his warnings that the plant was poisonous and decided to keep my distance.

When I didn't hear any movement in the house, I went in search of my host. "Mr. Moore?"

He looked up at me from a chair in the kitchen. The exhaustion on his face made me wonder again if the hospital had been right to send him home.

"Are you feeling okay?" I asked.

"Tired," he said. "I don't think I can make the tea."

"It's okay. Let me help you to your room. I'll lock up behind me when I leave."

He nodded, and I helped him stand.

I made a pot of tea while he changed for bed, but when I carried a steamy mug to him several minutes later, I was met with the sounds of gentle snores.

I traded the hot tea for a glass of water and left it on his bedside table. "I'll be back to check on you when I can," I whispered. "I'm sorry you fought with Elijah Snow yesterday. I know how bad that seems, and how terrible you feel about it, but this wasn't your fault. I'll do everything I can to help you. I know you'd never hurt anyone."

I turned for the door, knowing Evan would be upset, but I couldn't stay out of this. Not when a sick old man, and lifelong friend of my family, was the prime suspect.

"I loved her."

My muscles tensed as I looked over my shoulder. Mr. Moore's eyes were closed, his features soft. For a moment, I thought I'd imagined the words.

Unable to resist the intrigue, I took a step toward him once more. "Who?" I asked.

He'd never married, as far as I knew. At least not in my lifetime, and like the Snows, his family line had diminished, if not dissolved completely.

I rolled my eyes when he didn't respond. Moore was asleep, and I'd read one too many mystery novels.

I stepped into the hallway, doorknob still in hand when the answer came.

"Violet."

Chapter Nine

I waited nervously in the kitchen the next morning, unsure what to expect from my rising guests. The last time something similarly awful had happened on the farm, most of my guests had rushed to check out.

Surprisingly, Mrs. Snow was the first to make a morning appearance. Her sleek, bobbed hair was hooked behind her ears, and her expression was expectedly vacant. She wore an off-white tunic over matching flare-legged pants, and slippers on her feet.

"Good morning," I said softly.

She raised her eyes to mine but didn't speak.

"I hope you were able to find a little rest," I said, unsure if anyone could truly sleep after losing their only child so suddenly. So bizarrely. *How did he die exactly?* I wondered, realizing I hadn't asked Evan, and he hadn't volunteered the information. He also hadn't slept at the inn again last night. Was he up late following leads? Or had he chosen to stay at our home in town because the podcasters had ratted me out?

I shook away the worry and refocused on the woman before me. "Can I make you a cup of tea?"

She moved silently to the counter and took a seat on one of the tall stools.

I set a cup before her, but she didn't reach for it. "Will you be going to the Hearth for br—"

She shook her head.

"No problem. If there's anything you need or want, just let me know. If I don't have it here, I can get it for you."

She curved her hands around the mug before her, and I returned to my work.

I set out an array of fruits and cheeses, pastries, and yogurts, then lined up small glasses beside clear pitchers of cold juices. The coffee had brewed, and a kettle was ready for tea.

"I should be wearing black," she said.

I stilled and met her eyes, though she seemed to look through me.

"I only packed for parties and holiday dinners."

"Oh." I pressed my lips together and took a small step in her direction. "I have a black cardigan," I offered. "You're welcome to it, and I'm happy to pick up anything you'd like in town." I'd have offered her more of my things, but I was significantly taller and broader. "If you'd prefer to shop for yourself, I can drive you."

She shook her head again. "You're very kind. The Whites have always been that way."

I nodded because that was true. If my family had any legacy beyond our tree farm, it was our kindness and generosity. Both had been instilled in me from a very young age and reinforced every day by my parents' and grandparents' examples.

"Elijah is with the authorities," Violet said. "The sheriff promised he would be in good hands and that I could see him again soon, but"—she swallowed a ragged breath—"he won't be released to return home with me for a proper funeral until the coroner has finished."

My heart sank deeper with her every word.

"Who would do this?" she asked, finally seeming to see me. "I'd only returned to this town for a single day, and this is what happened?"

"It's not the town," I promised. "Everyone in Mistletoe has been looking forward to your return. You're beloved here. Most of the people I've spoken to didn't understand why your family ever left."

A crease formed between her eyes. "Didn't they?"

"No," I said, befuddled. "No one seems to know what happened or why you've stayed away so long. What made you change your mind about a visit after all this time?"

"Elijah." She spoke her son's name with the intense love and adoration of a mother. Her lips twisted, stuck somewhere between a prideful smile and utter heartbreak. "I did this for him. He was glad to come. He's a very talented businessman. He had meetings set up in the area. Projects and dreams of making a mark on this place. Now he'll never have the chance."

I fought the urge to pat her hand or otherwise physically console her. I didn't want to cross a line or scare her away. I offered her a box of tissues instead.

The sounds of footfalls on the staircase drew my eyes to Marcy and Caesar. The duo chatted excitedly as they moved into the foyer.

"I'll be right back," I told Mrs. Snow.

Caesar passed a coat to Marcy from the hooks near the doorway, and she threaded thin arms into the sleeves. Caesar followed suit with his own black wool coat.

"Good morning," I called. "Would you like a sleigh ride to the Hearth for breakfast?"

"It's already on the way," Caesar said. "We heard you in the kitchen with Mrs. Snow and didn't want to bother you. I called ahead to the Hearth, and your mother arranged the ride."

"Well, then I hope you'll have a lovely day. Let me know if there's anything I can do to make your time at Reindeer Games more enjoyable."

"Don't worry about us," Caesar said. "We've got plenty to keep us busy."

Marcy dipped her chin in silent affirmation. "A number of people in town have asked us to review their submissions to the *Guinness Book of World Records*."

I smiled. "I can't wait to hear all about it."

A sleigh arrived, and the duo made their way outside.

When I returned to the kitchen, Mrs. Snow had helped herself to a cinnamon roll, and it was already mostly gone. "I haven't eaten carbs in years," she said, looking more than a little guilty. "And I avoid sugar as much as I can." She forked a massive bite into her mouth and chewed. Her eyelids fluttered. "This is amazing."

"My mom bakes them fresh daily," I said. I refreshed her cup of tea and pushed a napkin in her direction.

"I gave up everything for my son," she continued. "Absolutely everything so that he could have all the best chances at happiness. I wanted to live forever. Or at least as long as humanly possible so I wouldn't miss a moment of his life." She took another bite and chewed aggressively. "Now what will it matter?" she asked. "I can do whatever I want because I'm the last living Snow. The lineage ends with me, and what a sad ending it will be." She finished the cinnamon roll and reached for another.

I poured a mug of coffee and got comfortable. "Why do you say that, Mrs. Snow?"

She gave a humorless laugh. "Call me Violet."

Hearing her name triggered the memory of Mr. Moore's sleepy face. "What kinds of plans did Elijah have here?" I asked. Showing an interest in her son and listening to what was on her mind was the least I could do, I assured myself.

I wasn't being nosy. I was being kind.

"He was making more rental spaces for Mistletoe," she said. The distant look in her eyes made me wonder if she was still in shock. I was sure I would be if I were in her shoes.

"Places for visitors to stay," she continued, "shop spaces to rent—you name it. He knew those things would be assets to the community as well as a source of revenue for everyone, not just the owners of the rentals. More people in town means more money spent on tourism. Everyone would've been happier."

I nodded, easily following her logic. My family's inn was generally booked every night from Halloween through New Year's Day, and all the weekends. More places to stay would be great for folks wanting to spend time in town during the holiday season. The perplexing part was where he'd planned to create those spaces.

I pictured the downtown area, then tried to imagine anywhere that wasn't already occupied. Nothing came to mind. In fact, our little town was relatively full in every sense of the word. Homes rarely went on the market, and those that did were purchased before the "For Sale" sign made it to the yard. Shops downtown stayed for decades and changed hands without ever being officially on the market.

Violet sucked a blob of icing off one fingertip, then surveyed the pastry tray for her next selection. "I'm not sure. He had a few meetings set this week."

I frowned. "Do you know where or with whom?"

She wiped her lips on a napkin. "Not really. There was someone named Weible and another named Lincoln. The investor was Hamish Hunter, utterly pretentious. I heard them on a video call while we were at the airport."

"Interesting." I levered myself upright and refilled my mug. I added a little cream to my beverage and slipped a cinnamon stick in for merry measure. Meanwhile, my mental wheels began to turn.

Mr. Weible was a retired electrician with a small handyman service. He lived in the building with the art studio where I sometimes sold my pieces. I suspected he was also the superintendent, because I'd seen him fixing things from time to time. I didn't know the other names Mrs. Snow mentioned.

But I could find out.

I pushed the thought away, determined to behave, wanting to give Evan and Mom the Christmas gift of not worrying them sick this year. "Did you tell the sheriff about this?"

Mrs. Snow frowned. "Why? Elijah's gone. There won't be any meetings now."

I chewed my lip, unwilling to point out that those big business plans of his might've been the reason for his death. I could tell Evan for her, but he'd be grumpy because it would look as if I'd been snooping when I was only being friendly. "Sheriff Gray is an incredible detective," I said, trying again. "I think you should share as much as you can with him about your son and your trip. Even the smallest detail might be the thing he needs to find out what happened that night."

Her expression fell, and she shivered violently.

I felt the chill a moment later and hoped none of the fires had gone out or that furnace hadn't failed, which would be even worse.

Mrs. Snow loaded an apple cinnamon Danish onto her plate.

"Good morning," Gertie called, startling me as she padded into the kitchen with Jackie on her heels.

I rose and went to grab two more mugs. "Morning. Come. Sit. Can I get you some coffee or tea? Will you be having breakfast at the Hearth?"

Another chill slithered down my spine as I spoke, and I paused to shiver, then checked the lock on the back door in case it had come open.

"We're going to walk," Gertie said. She exchanged a sly look with Jackie, who smiled in return. "If you need anything, let us know. We're happy to help."

I glanced at Mrs. Snow, then to the women at her side. "Help with what?"

"All your work of course," Gertie said. "We saw the piles of donated toys in your office. You need them wrapped before Christopher's man picks them up, and we are excellent gift wrappers. And I know you're stuck with all those commemorative gingerbread men. We're happy to pass those on to Christopher and his men as well if you'd like. He has quite a large work crew this time of year, and they love all cookies indiscriminately."

I smiled certain my mom would adore the idea.

I thought of Christopher and his work crew of relatively short men, then of Caroline's steadfast belief that he was Santa. His wife, clad in yet another crimson dress and black boots, her white hair arranged neatly on her head, didn't exactly work against the notion. Her friend, Jackie, however, didn't fit my idea of an elf.

Jackie was tall and willowy, and her white hair hung low over her shoulders and seemed perpetually in disarray, as if she'd just walked through a windstorm.

"Don't worry about the presents," I said, forcing the strange ideas from my head. "You should relax, spend some time in town, shop, eat. Enjoy the getaway. I know that pile is intimidating, but I invite all my friends over every year to help me wrap. It will be fine. No need to worry."

Jackie moved to the island and selected a chocolate croissant. She looked at Mrs. Snow with a sympathetic expression. "We're very sorry for your loss."

The other woman's eyes brimmed instantly with tears. She returned her fork to the plate before her. "Excuse me." Violet's voice cracked on the words as she slid onto her slippered feet and turned for the steps. Her sobs echoed through the house as she darted back to her room.

I rushed in her direction, but Gertie caught me by one arm.

"Let her go," she said. "She needs time to cry. I'll check on her later."

I jolted when a door slammed upstairs.

Gertie released me and clasped her hands at her middle. "Right now, you need to put that big brain of yours to work."

My jaw dropped. I hoped she wasn't a mind reader, because I wanted more than anything to know every ugly detail of how a full-grown man had wound up in the batter of a twenty-foot gingerbread cookie. "What do you mean?" I hedged.

"You need to decide what you're getting that handsome husband of yours for an anniversary gift. Have I mentioned how much I appreciate your Christmas Eve wedding? Christopher told me all about it. I'm sorry to have missed such a magical ceremony."

"How do you know I haven't bought a gift yet?" I asked.

Her lips pinched into a tiny smile. "People talk, and I like to listen."

I thought of Caroline again. Did Gertie hear things, or did she *know* things?

I nearly groaned at my silliness. Caroline's Santa Claus theory was getting to me. I lived in a very small town where everyone knew my business, and Gertie was staying at the farm where everyone loved to talk about my business. It stood to reason that she'd heard about my life and problems.

A sudden and incredible clatter stunned us all into stillness.

"Goodness," Jackie said. "What was that?"

"I think someone's on the front porch," Gertie answered.

"Doing what? Breaking dishes?"

I sprang into action, rushing into the foyer to see what was the matter. Had I absentmindedly thrown the lock behind Marcy and Caesar, accidentally locking them out? "Coming," I called.

I imagined my mother, arms loaded with baked goods, struggling to open the door. Or Cookie, carrying who-knew-what and attempting to let herself inside by the tips of her fingers.

Whoever it was, I wanted to help them in from the cold as quickly as possible.

I swung the door open with a smile, but no one was there.

"Uh-oh," Gertie muttered from behind me, having clearly followed along.

It took another moment for my eyes to find the thing she'd already seen.

A gingerbread man the size of a dinner plate lay in pieces on the welcome mat. Its arms and legs were broken off, and a boot print crushed its head.

Chapter Ten

Evan's cruiser appeared twenty minutes later.

I hurried from my post at the front door, where I'd been peering through the window, impatiently awaiting his arrival. I'd been prepared to defend the crime scene, if needed. Thankfully no one had come to the door.

His green eyes found mine as he climbed the steps to the porch. Then he pulled me into a tight embrace. "You okay?"

"Yeah, just a little shaken," I said. "I could be overreacting, but I thought you'd want to take a look to be sure."

He kissed my head before releasing me. "Is it under the foil?"

I nodded, then crouched to gently remove the layers of aluminum foil I'd formed into a coverup. I'd used piles of snow from the porch railing to weigh down the ends. Luckily, the wind cooperated by not blowing the cover away. "I wanted to protect the cookie from anyone who might stop by." Especially lookie-loos and podcasters.

"Good thinking." Evan lowered into a squat at my side, then took a long look at the mangled dessert in question.

"I was in the kitchen with Gertie and Jackie when we heard a clatter," I explained. "Mrs. Snow had just gone back to her room, and I rushed to the door. I'd suggest that someone threw the cookie at the door, but—" I pointed to the boot print smashed into the cookie's head.

He raised his phone to snap a few photos, then pulled an evidence bag from his coat pocket and moved the broken pieces inside.

I stretched upright once more. "Can I get you a cup of coffee?"

"That sounds good."

Evan followed me into the inn, through the foyer, and past the staircase to the kitchen.

I fixed two cups of coffee and passed one to Evan. "What do you think about the dismembered gingerbread man?"

He frowned. "Hard to say. I suppose anyone wanting to cause some trouble might've left it there."

"Podcasters?"

"Maybe." He looked me over carefully. "Do I have any reason to think another killer is warning you to butt out?"

I sipped my coffee, shaking my head slightly and trying to look innocent. "I missed you last night," I said instead, redirecting the conversation. If Evan didn't think the cookie was a threat, then who was I to dwell?

He ran a hand over his hair and sighed. "I missed you too. I was up late running leads and just didn't have it in me to make the trek back out here. It started to snow around midnight, and the roads were bad. The crews and salt trucks were out, but they concentrate on the roads in town first, so I just called it a night."

"I understand," I said. "I wouldn't have wanted you driving longer than necessary when you're that tired, especially when the roads are slick."

Evan nodded. "How are things around here?" he asked. "Besides the cookie."

I offered a sad smile. "Not great, but they also could've been worse."

He raised his mug to his lips with a sigh. "True."

"Will the farm be closed for long?" I asked. "I know that sounds insensitive . . ."

Evan waved me off. He knew me well enough to know my intentions weren't heartless. He also knew the week-before-Christmas sales often determined whether or not my parents struggled throughout the next year.

"I'm working on that," he said. "My deputies and I had time to do a thorough review of the crime scene yesterday, and it was far enough away from the Hearth, and other frequented stops on the grounds, to avoid a lot of traffic. I'd like to work with your dad and the farmhands to quarantine the area. If that pans out, I'll post a man near the scene to keep watch, just in case anyone attempts to tamper with anything."

I wet my lips, attention stuck to his use of the words *crime scene.* "What exactly was the crime?" I asked.

Evan froze, mug halfway to his lips. His sharp eyes narrowed. "Murder."

"I mean how?" I asked. "Are you sure it wasn't an accident? Could he have had one too many spiked eggnogs and fallen into the batter, then frozen to death?"

"I suppose, but it seems unlikely."

"How can you be sure?" I leaned closer, eyes widening despite my best efforts to look casual and barely interested.

"That's what I'm figuring out. Mr. Snow's body showed evidence of head trauma, but ultimately, the coroner believes he froze to death."

I grimaced. "If he fell and knocked himself out, why do you still suspect foul play?"

Evan sucked his teeth. "If I tell you, will you drop this and have coffee with me as if we're a normal couple?"

I nodded quickly.

He rolled his eyes. "We've confirmed the pin found near the crime scene belongs to Henry Moore."

My heart kicked painfully, and I pressed a palm to my chest. "That feels inconclusive. How can you be sure the pin belongs to

Henry? There must've been hundreds of those pins created. Half the town and hundreds of visitors probably bought one."

"And each one had a serial number," he added. "Guess who purchased this one?"

I felt my eyelids shut. "Well then, who's to say that pin didn't change hands a dozen times in all these years?"

"A number of people who spoke with Henry at Santa's Village on the day of Mr. Snow's death recall the pin on his lapel. As you know, Mr. Moore no longer has that pin."

I bit my tongue. Clearly there was a reasonable explanation for this. "Henry has a booth at Santa's Village. Maybe he was walking the grounds, and the pin fell off his coat."

"The backing is still on the pin," Evan said. "Both Snow's and Moore's prints were found on the enamel. And let's not forget someone covered the batter after Snow fell in. He wasn't alone out there."

I felt my shoulders sag.

"What else is new?" Evan asked, blatantly changing the subject.

I locked my gaze with his, temporarily stumped. It was hard to think of much else when a man had drowned in the batter of a twenty-two-foot cookie only a day before. "Not much. Have you finished your holiday shopping?"

Something wicked flashed in Evan's eyes, there and gone before I could consider the reason. He schooled his features and nodded. "I have. How about you?"

"I'm almost finished for Christmas," I said. "I'm still struggling to find the perfect anniversary present for you."

He grinned. "Are you looking for ideas?"

"Not that idea," I said, laughing. "Be serious."

"Oh, I am very serious."

I looked away, mentally fanning my heated face. "You always find the perfect gift, and I give you something perfectly pedestrian." Birthdays, Valentine's Day, Easter—whatever the occasion—my gift never measured up. "I want to be the most thoughtful giver this time."

Evan worked his brows, and I cracked up.

"Stop it. This is important to me."

He lifted his palms in surrender, then rested one against my back and rubbed gently. "Okay. I hear what you're saying, but you should know I love all your gifts, and it's not a competition."

I pulled away for a better look at him. "You love getting puzzles of kittens in Boston Red Sox jerseys?" I asked. "You love all the boring flannel button-down shirts? The socks with goofy sayings on the soles?"

He snorted lightly. "'Feet up for football,'" he said, quoting one pair of socks.

I set my mug aside, deeply thankful our friend group had decided to draw names for a Secret Santa this year. I'd only underwhelm one person instead of six or seven. And I'd save a lot of money.

"Please tell me what you want," I said. "You can't imagine how badly I want to do a good job."

He kissed my head. "I have everything I've ever wanted," he said. "And a goofy little holiday town I never knew I needed."

"That makes me happy, but it's not very helpful."

Evan's phone buzzed, and he set his coffee aside to check the screen. He was on his feet in the next heartbeat. "Duty calls," he said. "Thank you for the coffee."

"Hang on." I hurried along at his side, determined to walk him to the door. "Will you let me know what you learn about the broken cookie?"

"Absolutely." He scanned the door and frame. "We really need to get one of those doorbell cameras for this porch."

"That's a no-go," I said. "Inauthentic." In a historic town like Mistletoe, maintaining appearances was mandatory. Doorbell cameras and keypad locks were forbidden by the Historical Society.

Anyone daring to go against the rules was promptly fined. "You know the rules."

He rolled his eyes, then kissed my lips. "Then a nanny cam in a teddy bear that we position in the front window. No one will ever know, and I'll rest easier."

I nodded in approval. "Not bad."

"I know," he said, tapping a finger to his temple. "Be safe, Gray."

A smile popped onto my face at the sound of our last name. "Back at ya."

I closed the door and turned for my office.

Cindy Lou Who was asleep on my chair.

"Hey you," I said. "Scootch."

She cracked one eye open, then closed it.

"Come on," I said. "I know you're awake."

She craned her neck and twisted her body until her feet were in the air.

I ruffled the fluffy fur on her stomach. When that didn't work, I angled my arms beneath her and attempted to raise her to my chest.

"Meow!" She spun, claws extended and thrust away from me, parkour style.

"Ow!"

She hit the ground running and exited the room with a screech of complaint.

I fell onto my chair. "You get coal," I called after her.

I checked myself for bloody scratches or puncture wounds and determined I'd survive. Then I booted up my laptop.

Dozens of new jewelry orders had been placed through the night. Too many to fill before Christmas, and almost all were for tiny replica gingerbread men earrings, or charms for bracelets. Thankfully, the pieces I'd advertised didn't mention Mom's attempt at the world record, but I couldn't help wondering if all the new orders were a result of what had happened yesterday. If so, I needed to take the item off my website.

I dropped my head against the chair back and turned to look through the window. I considered visiting the gallery that sold some of my jewelry, to see if they needed more. While I was there, I could ask about Mr. Weible, then maybe knock on his door. I could ask him about the business meeting with Elijah that Mrs. Snow had mentioned. Very few people in town knew Elijah, so it only seemed reasonable that one of those who did was the one who wanted him dead.

My suspect list was short and sweet. It had to be Weible, Hunter, or one of the creepy podcasters always looking for a story. Maybe they'd go to any length for a hit show.

As if on cue, four figures came into view outside my office window. Small from the distance, Caesar and Marcy were easy to identify with their drastic height differences and Caesar's bright red scarf. The podcasters, Harvey and Tate, strolled along at their sides.

Chapter Eleven

My reflection in the glass suddenly looked as if it had sucked a lemon. I pushed onto my feet, silently promising the computer screen full of waiting orders that I would be back.

I grabbed my coat and boots and headed outside, determined to rid myself of the podcasters once and for all. "Hello," I called, waving my arms overhead and interrupting whatever the group was saying.

The foursome looked in my direction, and I picked up speed.

"Caesar, Marcy," I said. "I was just on my way to find you. My mom's been baking at the Hearth all day, and with the farm closed, she has a plethora of treats to share."

Tate crossed his arms. "You just keep popping up," he said. "I don't usually side with killers, but I'm beginning to see how you get under their skin."

My eyes narrowed and I turned to face him. "Did you forget my husband is the sheriff?" I asked. "He just left the inn, which means he's still nearby, and you are trespassing."

I motioned for Caesar and Marcy to change directions, then hurried them toward the Hearth, where I could lock the podcasters out.

"Why so rude?" Tate asked. "We were just getting to know the recordkeepers."

"No, you weren't," I said. "You were just leaving."

Harvey muttered something behind us that I couldn't understand.

"Fine," Tate said far too loudly. "We'll see ourselves out for now, but I'm positive we'll see you again."

"Not if I see you first," I called over my shoulder.

"I think I'll pair the game we're playing with chocolate rum cake," Tate said, "because I can't get enough." He tapped a finger against the brim of his black ballcap, then ducked into the tree line, with Harvey on his heels.

"This is not a game," I called, but they were already gone.

"I don't think the Hearth is open," Marcy said. "The farm is closed, and I got the impression your mom was only available for breakfast and dinner."

"The café stays open for inn guests, farmworkers, and friends," I said. "From sunup until around nine every night, you'll find folks gathered there. Did you have fun in town?"

"We did," Caesar said. "Everyone is so clever. A nice-sized crowd tried to create the world's largest group of carolers by singing for us at the square."

I raised my brows. "That's fun. How'd they do?"

"A great job singing," Caesar said. "But the largest group of carolers is around one thousand eight hundred and eight. There were only a few hundred folks at the square."

"Bummer," I said.

He lifted and dropped one shoulder.

"A man at the pie shop tried to eat the most pie in a single sitting," Marcy added.

I hoped that hadn't been my husband because I could easily beat him at any eating contest.

"The record is thirty-five slices in eight minutes," Marcy said. "But the gentleman making the attempt barely finished ten slices before getting sick."

I felt my features bunch on instinct.

"That's what I thought," Caesar said, chuckling at my expression.

"Well, here we are." I kicked snow from my boots and reached for the door to the little café. "Welcome."

Mom and Libby turned expectant faces our way.

"Hello!" Mom rubbed her hands against her apron as she hurried to meet us. "How are you? Come. Sit." She moved Caesar and Marcy to a booth, then pressed a kiss to my cheek. "I'm so glad to see you. Can I get you something warm to drink? Perhaps a little pick-me-up before dinner?"

To her delight, both guests agreed to sample anything she put in front of them, and Mom glided away, looking as if she'd won the lottery.

I took a seat at the counter beside Libby, who faced off once again with masses of gingerbread cookies. This time, however, she wasn't bagging them up for distribution. She was editing the tags. "Wow," I said. "How long have you been doing this?"

"Six years?" she guessed, dragging a wide-tipped permanent marker across the brown paper, effectively redacting the words "home to the World's Largest Gingerbread Man."

"Do you have another marker?" I asked, grabbing a bagged cookie from the pile.

She produced one from her apron pocket, and I got to work beside her, heartsick for Mom's disappointment.

Mom reappeared a few minutes later, ferrying a golden platter to her only booth with guests. "I'm calling this my cookie charcuterie," she said. "Whatever you can't finish, I'll package up to send with you. I've included a sampling of all my favorite sweets. From the left you've got Santa's snickerdoodles, whoopie pies, Christmas tree cutouts, almond pizzelles, seven-layer bars, peanut butter blossoms, Kris Kringle cookies, snowballs, and thumbprints. I made the jam myself." She clasped her hands before her, delighted. "I've got a pot of cinnamon tea on for you, and a slow cooker full of homemade hot cocoa. I'll bring you each a cup of both." She danced away before they could try to stop her.

I leaned back on my stool, catching their wide eyes. "This is her love language."

Caesar released a deep belly laugh.

Marcy blinked.

"Consider me in love," he said, lifting a snickerdoodle from the tray.

Marcy watched as he ate, apparently undecided about the strange situation.

A round of chatter arose from the kitchen, and Libby smiled. "Your mom's friends are back there helping prep for when the farm opens again and filling orders from folks who want cookies but can't get up here to purchase direct. The ladies will deliver for her when they leave."

My heart swelled. "Mom has really great friends."

"So do you," Libby said, nudging me with an elbow.

"Very true."

The kitchen door swung wide, and Mom followed her friends into the dining area. They approached Caesar and Marcy, setting steamy mugs before them, then two small gingerbread houses.

Mom beamed. "We thought you'd like to play one of our reindeer games. I don't know how long the farm will be closed, or how long you can stay, and I hate to think you've been here and missed out."

"We'd love to play," Caesar said amiably. "What do we do?"

The ladies beamed as Marcy looked on, bewildered, and Mom explained the rules. "The game is called Bling that Gingerbread, and you have five minutes to decorate your house. When the time is up, we vote on the best design and use of materials."

Mom's friend Evelyn set a pair of small trays on the table. "There's icing here," she said, pointing to a small pot on each tray. "And all the sprinkles, candies and gumdrops you need."

Caesar and Marcy took the small trays and each selected an undecorated house.

Mom pulled two handkerchiefs from her apron. "You decorate blindfolded."

She passed the thin red material to each player, and Caesar gamely tied his on.

Marcy looked abashed. "I don't like blindfolds."

Mom took the offering back. "How do you feel about the honor system?"

Tension visibly drained from Marcy's features, and she nodded.

Mom counted down, and the recordkeepers got to work.

"I love Bling that Gingerbread," I said, blacking out another row of text.

"Yeah, but this is nice," Libby said, tipping her head toward the players, Mom, and her ladies. "A bright spot in a pretty dismal day."

I couldn't disagree.

When the time was up, we all clapped for the contestants. They were both declared winners, and Mom carried the finished houses to the counter for display.

"If you had fun, there's more where that came from," Libby warned, her tone light but dry, much like her sense of humor.

"Tell us more," Caesar said. "Unfortunate matters aside, we're having an incredible time in Mistletoe. The town is gorgeous, and we love the Victorian theme. The broad dedication to the look is inspiring. Not to mention the camaraderie here. Everyone we've spoken to has been equally excited to see us. They offer tips and tricks to get the best parking, the best meals, deals, and photographs. All the shop owners seem just as proud of the other shops as they are of their own store."

"That's the Christmas spirit," I said. "It runs thick around here."

"It's lovely," Caesar said.

Marcy watched as we spoke, then interjected when the opportunity arose. "What are the other reindeer games?"

I grinned. "You probably noticed Build a Big Frosty outside." I hooked a thumb toward the window. "We do blindfolded sled racing, team hat tosses, and slip and slide games in the field near the snowmen. A lot of games happen in here too, like Christmas Karaoke, Holiday Bingo, and Gingerbread Goes to Hollywood. There's a formal dance we call the Snow Ball in the big pole barn. Everyone dresses up, and there's always a theme. This year's theme is Victorian Christmas, of course. We decorate and then auction Christmas trees to raise money for charities. Oh, and the Snowball Roll on Christmas Eve morning is the capstone event of the season. If you're still here, definitely check that out. The whole town shows up. There are food trucks, music, and a ton of fun."

"That's a lot," Marcy said.

I couldn't tell by her expression if she thought an abundance of games was a good thing or a bad one. I decided not to ask.

"How are you doing?" Marcy asked, still looking my way. "With what happened yesterday."

The room stilled, and for a moment, I forgot to breathe.

Mom made a soft gasping sound.

"I think what happened yesterday was a terrible tragedy," I said. "I absolutely hate that things like that ever occur, much less so close to Christmas and so publicly." I'd forgotten to check the newspaper this morning, but I was sure Elijah's death had made headlines.

"But how are you doing with your case?" Marcy asked.

Caesar let his eyelids drift shut for one long beat, then wrinkled his nose apologetically.

"I'm not sure what you mean," I said.

Marcy looked at her partner, then back to me. "When we researched the town after being given this assignment, we found all the previous cases like this one and all the online articles about your involvement in the capture of the killers. I'd initially assumed you were a private investigator. You aren't."

"No," I agreed. "I'm definitely not."

Libby chewed her lip, fighting a smile. "Holly doesn't find the killers as often as they find her."

Somewhere behind me, Mom moaned.

"Do you think it was the mistletoe farmer?" Marcy asked. "People are saying there's evidence pointing in his direction and that you were seen with him last night. Were you questioning his whereabouts at the time of the murder?"

I opened my mouth, but nothing came out. This was the most I'd heard Marcy talk at one time, and everything she said stunned me further. They'd researched me? I was seen with Mr. Moore? They knew about the evidence?

"The *Dead and Berried* podcasters are saying you were at the hospital last night," Marcy said.

So that was where she'd gotten her information.

"Holly?" Mom asked.

I spun guiltily to face her. "I just wanted to be sure he was okay. They discharged him while I was there, so I drove him home."

Mom pressed a palm to her heart, presumably in approval.

Wait until she heard about the squirrels.

I turned back to Marcy, hoping to look much calmer than I felt after being called out and put on the spot. "Tate and Harvey are looking for a story. They need to stay out of this and let the sheriff sort it out." Mr. Moore was as innocent of murder as I was, but I wasn't so sure about Mr. Weible or the businessman Elijah had been in town to see. And I wasn't ready to write off the podcasters either. If their whole livelihood depended on getting a good story, and they made their living studying crimes like this one, how could I be sure they wouldn't try to get away with murder?

She stared. "They're very good," she said eventually. "Engaging and entertaining. If you like true crime stories. They're calling you the Gumdrop Gumshoe."

Libby barked a laugh, then slapped a hand over her mouth.

"Is that right?" I asked, shooting my sister-in-law a look.

"Yes," Marcy assured. "You don't like the name?" she guessed.

"I do not."

Chapter Twelve

I shoveled snow off my truck and pumped up the heat to melt the ice on my windows. I needed to find the perfect anniversary gift for Evan, and I was running out of time. As a bonus, shopping would take my mind off the troubles at the farm, at least for a little while. I hated that Reindeer Games was under scrutiny by law enforcement again, the site of yet another holiday murder. Mom's deep disappointment was a secondary kick in the gut for everyone who loved her. She rarely did anything for herself, and she'd worked so long and hard in preparation for the world record attempt. Then someone had taken her joy, along with a man's life and his mother's heart, all in one fell swoop.

The fact that it had all happened so close to Christmas made things infinitely worse.

The truck's cab was toasty warm when I shifted into drive. I couldn't help Mrs. Snow with her grief, and Mom didn't need me while the farm was closed, so focusing on something I could do, like surprising my husband, seemed like the way to go. Unfortunately, every time I thought of Evan, I wondered if he'd made any progress on the murder investigation.

Thinking of Elijah's untimely death set my mental wheels in motion, despite my best efforts to think of anything else. I couldn't stop wondering about the men Elijah had planned to meet and where they'd expected to put more shops and rentable rooms. I still had no idea why he'd argued with poor Mr. Moore or why he had his pin.

The familiar winding road into town seemed to reflect my meandering thoughts. Who would hurt Elijah? And why? He hadn't been in town twenty-four hours. How many enemies could he have had here?

Slowly the rolling hills and forest dissolved into valleys and tree-dotted fields as I rolled along. Homes popped onto the horizon as the miles passed, independently at first, then in clusters when downtown drew near. Dark puffs of smoke rose from red brick chimneys, and inflatable snowmen stood on elaborately decorated lawns. Mechanical elves waved at motorists by light of day, and multicolored string lights chased patterns over roofs and around windows from dusk until dawn.

I pumped up the radio and bopped my head along to the local station, playing holiday tunes nonstop through New Year's Day.

Brake lights slowed my progress nearly half a mile from downtown. Tour buses and other traffic crept slowly forward as an added security team rerouted all motorized vehicles to designated parking areas. In support of Mistletoe's trip back in time, folks were forced to park at one of the high school's athletic fields' lots, then shuttled back to the square. I refused to do either.

I followed the bus before me under a twisted iron "Welcome to Mistletoe" sign, then a short distance farther, guided by a man in reflective gear and earmuffs. He swung a plastic flag in circles, indicating the direction we should go. I broke away at the first available alley, knowing he couldn't follow me without giving up his post. A few turns later, I lodged my pickup alongside a dumpster behind a set of shops and hopped out. I stuck a receipt that I hoped looked like a parking ticket, under the wiper, then hurried away from the scene of my crime. With any luck, if someone saw the truck and the paper, they'd assume I'd already been punished and keep moving.

It was easy to blend into the mass of shoppers when I reached the mouth of the alley, bustling forward as if I'd been there all along. I wondered idly if I'd run into the podcasters again today. Their presence at the discovery of Elijah's body bothered me more each time I thought about it. I wasn't a believer in coincidence, and I'd checked their podcast's website while waiting for my truck to heat up. The number of subscribers had quadrupled since their arrival in town. The biggest spike occurred while they'd been live at the uncovering of the body in the batter. I'd say that paired well with stinky cheese and undercooked fish.

Tate and Harvey had been pointing fingers at me, but they'd also been at the hospital when I went to visit Mr. Moore. And they were interviewing everyone who'd talk to them. Considering how much they had to gain, I'd call that behavior suspicious.

How could I be sure one of them hadn't attacked Elijah Snow for the sake of launching their midlist show into the atmosphere?

I rounded the corner onto the square several paces later and nearly collided with Ray and his mom, Fay.

"Holly!" Fay pulled me into a hug. "How are you? How's Carol?" She released me and shook her head with sympathy. "I just hate what happened at the farm. I wanted to check in on you both, but Ray said the sheriff closed the whole place down. Horrible."

"Thank you. We're hoping to reopen soon. Dad's working with his crew to quarantine the crime scene, and Evan's posting security."

Ray crossed his arms. "Any news about today's threat?"

I tented my brows.

"I heard about the broken cookie on your doorstep," he said. "That was definitely a threat, right?"

"How did you—"

"Police scanner. You should get one." He snapped his fingers. "If I draw your name in the secret Santa next year, I know what I'm buying."

I smiled. Evan would positively hate that, but Ray knew me well. "Heard anything else?" I asked.

"Nothing useful. Why? You aren't . . . you know . . ." He opened his eyes comically wide.

I returned the goofy face when he didn't relax.

His mom laughed. "Stop. People are staring."

Ray and I eased into matching smiles.

"I don't know why you're making that face, but no, I'm not doing anything."

He continued to watch me without speaking, and I folded like cheap giftwrap. "Fine." I stepped a little closer and lowered my voice. "Henry Moore had a verbal spat with Elijah and Violet Snow outside the inn the day before Elijah died. Any idea what they might've had to fight about?" I flicked my gaze to Ray's mom. "I hear their families have a long history of feuding."

She glanced around nervously, then leaned in my direction. "That's town folklore at this point. I believe Henry's the end of his line, and I don't recall him having an issue with the Snow family, or anyone else, in all the years I've known him. Of course, he has a couple of decades on me, and I try my best to stay out of these sorts of things."

I absolutely could not relate.

"What does Henry say?" Ray asked. "I hear you took him home from the hospital."

My thoughts returned to that night, and I heard Henry's sleepy voice saying he loved Violet. Was that a motive to murder her son? Surely not. It should be the opposite. "He was confused and tired when I last spoke with him," I said, answering Ray's question. "But I plan to check in again soon, make sure he's eating and getting enough rest."

Fay's skin suddenly paled. "Sweetie, no. He could be dangerous. You should keep your distance until all this is sorted."

Ray snorted, then straightened his features when his mom shot him a pointed look.

"Mr. Moore didn't do this," I said, pulling her attention back to me. "I understand it looks bad, but I know him. He used to pull me around his farm on a plastic sled while Dad helped him harvest mistletoe and cut firewood. He taught me the names of the birds, and we placed bets on the squirrels playing chase."

My stomach flopped as I recalled the squirrels in his living room, all stuffed and dressed as my friends and fellow citizens. "He's upset," I said. "He's all alone and not well. No one should be any of those things at Christmas."

I hoped Mrs. Snow wouldn't be alone much longer either, but I feared she might. So far no one had shown up at the inn to stay with her. Hadn't she told her friends about what happened to Elijah? Didn't she have anyone to tell?

A quartet of carolers in top hats and long wool coats stopped to sing beside us, and Fay wrinkled her nose.

"I think that's our sign to stop loitering in this beautiful Victorian village," she teased.

I nodded. I hadn't meant to keep them for so long. "Have fun today. Merry Christmas!"

"You too," she called, already on the move.

"Holly." Ray caught my sleeve and I turned. Caution mixed with concern in his big blue eyes. "Be careful."

"I will."

He held my gaze another long beat before releasing me, then jogging to catch his mom.

I headed for the pie shop.

Evan's cruiser wasn't parked outside, thanks to the vehicle ban, but I could see his handsome face through the window.

I breezed inside, immediately enveloped in the mouth-watering scents of fresh-baked pies and sweet caramel lattes. I smiled at the hostess dressed in a pink-and-white retro waitress ensemble, complete with ruffled holiday-print apron. "I'm meeting my husband," I said, pointing to the back of Evan's head.

The teen's eyes widened. "Nice."

"Thanks."

She gathered a menu and a set of silverware from the wooden stand, then led me to his booth. "We started the twelve pies of Christmas," she said. "Today's special is Victorian vanilla. It's a custard pie baked with brown sugar and cinnamon."

I took a seat on the bench across from Evan and smiled. "I'll just have coffee for now."

The waitress set my placemat and napkin-wrapped silverware onto the table before me. "I'll be right back with a mug and carafe."

Evan rose immediately in her absence and leaned across the table to kiss me. "This is a nice surprise. How are things at the inn?"

"Quiet," I said. "A little sad and very dull."

He cocked a brow. "Have you finished addressing holiday cards? Wrapping toys? And handling your jewelry orders?"

I fixed him with an absolutely bland expression, and he chuckled.

"Maybe Santa can do all my work for me as a Christmas gift," I said.

"I think he's got his hands full for the next week or so. Are you in town for Christmas shopping?" Evan asked.

My knee began to bob. "Kind of." My thoughts circled back to the podcasters. To poor Mr. Moore and Mrs. Snow.

"What?" he prompted.

I bit my lip.

"Out with it, Gray."

I grinned.

He frowned.

"Well," I started, "it's hard to concentrate on the things I know I should do, because my mind is thinking about—" I narrowed my eyes, willing him to fill in the blank.

The moment his expression went from curious to bored, I knew he'd gotten the message. "Oh." He clasped his hands on the table. "Don't think about that."

I imagined flicking his forehead.

"I can't just turn it off. You know my curiosity is insatiable."

"Here's the thing," he said, shifting forward on his seat. "You get to decide what you think about. The same way you decide what you do or don't do."

I deflated at his polite scolding, and my body went boneless against the seat. "Blah."

He smiled. "I didn't get to say it earlier, but I missed seeing you last night. I've been thinking about our living situation for months, especially since the holidays began. Living at the house in town January through September, then at the inn October through December isn't working out the way I'd imagined, and it's kind of a bummer. I want a place where we live together all year round. Someplace we can make memories and call our own. I think we should sell the house."

"No." I straightened. "You love that house." He'd told me repeatedly over the years how proud he'd been to buy his first home, and he'd put uncounted hours of sweat equity into making it gorgeous in every way. He'd repainted everything from ceilings to cabinets, torn out old carpets and refinished the floors. He'd landscaped the front and back yards, updated the light fixtures throughout, and made a rec room over the garage. He'd loved every second of it. And I loved the results, but only a fraction as much as I loved him.

"It's just a house," he said. "You're my wife. I want to be with you, not living across town from you three months a year or trying to remember which place we're sleeping at on which day. I can barely remember where I put my cell phone most of the time."

"We'll figure it out after Christmas," I promised. "That's only eight days away. The tourists will go home. The crowds will be gone, and we'll have all the time we want together."

He sighed. "We have to make the decision together by the end of January, or I'm selling the house in town."

I lifted my palms in peace. "Agreed." I'd genuinely believed the arrangement made sense when we'd started, though I'd missed the farm and my family desperately on the days I wasn't there. But I hadn't anticipated how much more I'd miss my husband during the holidays, the most special of days.

Evan sized me up for a long moment. "Now we should probably talk about why you were at the hospital visiting Mr. Moore after I asked you so nicely to leave this case alone."

"Who snitched?"

"There are pictures of you leaving the premises with him on the *Dead and Berried* website."

I rolled my eyes.

"Holly. Moore is a murder suspect."

"He's not," I said, leaning across the table and lowering my voice. "He loves her."

Evan frowned. "Who?"

The waitress reappeared with the mug and carafe as promised. "Here you go. Can I get you anything else?"

I shook my head, eyes fixed on Evan.

She waited another beat before leaving us to our chat.

"Mrs. Snow," I whispered. "He was all doped up from the hospital when I took him home, and before I left, he said he loved Violet. He had to mean Violet Snow, right?"

The switch between protective husband and cop mode was seamless. Evan's features flipped into the unreadable expression I hated, and his eyes narrowed, assessing, evaluating. "If he loved the mom, why kill the kid?"

I lifted my shoulders to my ears. "That's what I'm saying."

Evan tapped his thumbs against the tabletop. "What do we know about her husband?"

"He's dead."

"Besides that?" Evan asked.

"Nothing."

He shot his hand into the air, catching the waitress's attention. "Can I get the check, please?"

"Where are you going?" I asked, still pouring my first cup of coffee.

"To talk with Mr. Moore."

"Wait for me." I raised my cup for a sip, then set it aside. "Besides, there's more."

Evan stilled. "What else?"

"For starters, stop listening to that podcast. They don't need any more followers or support."

"I'm interested in what they're hearing and seeing around town. I can only be one place at a time."

"You don't like it when I do what they're doing," I protested. "And how do you know they aren't making up everything they say on that show?"

He tapped a fingertip to the shiny silver sheriff's star on his lapel.

I forced a sweet smile, hating when he pulled rank. "Mrs. Snow came down for coffee this morning and told me that Elijah had meetings arranged in town."

Evan's jaw clenched and released.

"Maybe one of the people he planned to meet with didn't like his proposal," I said. "Maybe they lashed out, and it ended poorly." I took another sip of my drink, enjoying the steamy, bitter liquid on my tongue, savoring the warmth before I headed back into the cold.

Evan waited.

"You knew," I accused.

He pointed to his badge again.

I puffed my cheeks. "Do you know the names of the people he had plans with? His mom mentioned Mr. Weible and someone named Hunter." I couldn't remember the third name.

"One is a retired electrician," he said. "The other is a local investor. He also had an appointment with the Historical Society."

I frowned. I hadn't been to the Historical Society in several years, and I didn't know any investors. Investor didn't even sound like a real job. I had a connection with Mr. Weible through the gallery, however, so I would have to start there.

"I'm handling this," Evan reminded me.

The waitress delivered our bill, and he placed a twenty on top.

"Have you decided when the farm can reopen?" I asked, sensing the subject of Elijah's murder was closed again for now.

"Give me another day or two. I want to be diligent, and I can't afford to slip up when I have a personal interest in the case. People will say I rushed the job to please my wife's family."

My jaw dropped. "Who would say that?"

"People. Voters. I like my job, and I want to get reelected."

"Overachiever."

He grinned. "Don't forget it."

My cheeks heated, and I cleared my throat. "Any word on the broken cookie at my door?"

"Not yet." He set his hat on his head and relaxed while I finished my coffee. "Have you talked to my sister and Ray lately?"

"Sure. Why?"

"I think they're up to something," he said. "I don't know what, but I don't like it."

I chuckled. Cookie had said something similar, but I hadn't noticed anything odd about Ray or Libby. "I'll see what I can find out."

"Excellent." He stood and kissed me. "See, these are the times I can appreciate your uncanny ability to learn things. Investigate the lovebirds. At least if they catch you, they won't try to kill you."

"Depends what they're up to," I said.

"Touché."

Chapter Thirteen

I parted ways with Evan outside the pie shop after ordering a slice of the holiday apple cinnamon to go. He headed for his cruiser, and I turned toward the gallery where I often sold my jewelry. I hadn't spoken to Mr. Weible more than a handful of times, but I knew him well enough to strike up a conversation.

The sights and sounds of the town overcame me within seconds, pulling me out of quizzical citizen mode and tossing me back in time one hundred plus years. The abundance of pine greenery on lampposts and windowsills had doubled since last year, and gone were the traditional twinkle lights, replaced with flickering faux candles. Large wooden ornaments, small glass trinkets, and an abundance of fruits took the place of more modern Rudolph and Frosty replicas. Everything smelled of cinnamon, cloves, peppermints, and chocolate.

I purchased a stiff paper cone of warm candied pecans and a bag of kettle corn before reaching my destination. I fanned out my canvas tote, emblazoned with the Reindeer Games logo, and tucked my goodies inside, resting my precious container of pie on top. I loved the merry music rising from carolers on corners and the smiles on passing visitors' faces. Their cheeks were kewpie-doll pink from too much time in the biting wind. Bus tour guests were marked with name-tag lanyards, color coded to keep them from boarding the wrong ride home. Their arms were heavily laden with shopping bags and sweet treasures for Christmas Day.

The art gallery was dark as I approached. The large brick building was only a block and a half away from the square and had been built at the turn of the previous century. The structure had been home to everything from a paint and wallpaper factory to an all-girls' school, to a halfway house during the Great Depression. In my lifetime, the building had been apartments and a series of shops. Currently the art gallery was the only remaining storefront, but there were still a handful of apartments, including Mr. Weible's.

I'd often seen him working on things around town, adding replica faux gas lamps to storefronts or fixing the historic clock on the town square.

Tiny spotlights illuminated my jewelry in the gallery's window display. The pieces were arranged on smooth wooden tiers and ornately framed mirrors alongside blown glass cardinals, hand-carved nutcrackers, and knitted cashmere throws—further proof that Mistletoe was flush with gifted artists of every kind.

A small red sign on the door showcased three short words: "Be right back."

I had no idea how long the sign had already been in place, so I retrieved my phone and found the number to the gallery in my contacts.

My call went straight to voicemail.

I cleared my throat as the phone beeped, allowing me to leave a message. "Hello, this is Holly White. Gray," I amended. "I have more one-hundred-and-fiftieth anniversary charms ready if you need any. They're going fast online and at the farm. I didn't want you to run out. Give me a call and let me know when I can stop by with them. Merry Christmas!"

I put the phone away and walked a few yards farther, bypassing the gallery door, positioned at the corner of the building, and entering the large historic structure through a centrally located set of double doors instead. Mr. Weible's name was the only one on the bank of mailboxes. Announcing his exact location seemed unsafe to me, and it seemed the other tenants felt the same. But Mr. Weible was a man from another generation. His concerns about being abducted were likely not as great as mine. I climbed the steps to his loft, each of my soft footfalls echoing in the silence. The muffled merriment outside the door diminished further with each passing flight. I stopped at the top floor, overheated and out of breath. Only one door appeared on this level, and I wondered at the size of his apartment.

I unzipped my coat and used one end of my scarf to wipe sweat from my brow. Five flights of stairs wrapped around a central empty cavity, showcasing the black and white checkered floor below. I didn't want to think of carrying groceries up here every week. Or moving furniture.

Yikes.

When my body temperature returned to normal, I knocked on the door, jostling the festive wreath. My gaze clung to the mistletoe wound through the holly and ivy. I shook away the strange sensation climbing the back of my neck into my hair, then knocked again before finally trying the bell.

Mr. Weible was apparently out and about with the rest of the town.

I opened a browser on my phone as I trudged back down the steps. I dialed the number for Mr. Weible's small handyman service, then bundled up as it rang. I left a voicemail letting him know I had some questions and wondering if we could meet for coffee when he was available.

I had mixed feelings about my dual intentions in town. Evan had so clearly asked me to leave this alone, and I wanted to be the woman he wanted me to be, but I also knew that would never happen. In fact, sometimes when I tried to fall asleep, I thought of Libby saying she'd like to leave the waitressing business and become a private investigator. I was pretty sure that would be the thrill of a lifetime. And it would also cause Evan six consecutive strokes.

A heavy wind pressed against the door as I forced my way onto the sidewalk. Once free, I thanked my lucky stars I was headed in the same direction as the gust, not against it. My next stop was Oh! Fudge, and I shifted back to shopping mode with a groan of internal disappointment. My spirits rose as the delectable scents of molten chocolate and rich, melted peanut butter circled my head. I picked up my pace, delighted by spirals of white confectioner's boxes tied with red ribbons in the fudgery's window. Each set of boxes formed a three-dimensional triangle, sweet gifts in the shape of a tree. An array of cake stands were positioned in between, all piled high with squares of chocolates and fudge. My stomach grumbled with desire.

I tugged open the door and floated inside like Fred Flintstone on a whiff of brontosaurus stew. The line to the register was as long as always this time of year. I took my place at the end, in eager anticipation of all the gorgeous displays and sampling stations I'd pass on my way to the counter.

Before I knew it, someone called my name.

I wiped chocolate from my lips as Jean, a tall, willowy woman, smiled from behind the counter. She co-owned the fudgy enterprise with her best friend, Millie, who was currently operating the register beside Jean's. "We were wondering when we'd see you."

The duo had dressed in hooded, fur-lined cloaks and long dresses, with little lace-up boots, keeping nicely with the town's theme. Millie's ensemble was largely a muted rose color, while Jean had opted for mauve. The differences between pink and lavender undertones were subtle, but somehow the distinction felt right. The ladies had plenty in common, but like everyone else, they were far from the same. Millie was small but mighty and full of feminine energy, while Jean, though larger in stature, was much lighter in *oomph* and far less excitable.

I checked the corners of my mouth for evidence of my gratuitous sampling and smiled. "I'm running behind as always," I said. "But I can't forget Cookie's special fudge. Please tell me you haven't sold out."

"Of course we have!" Millie chirped. "We were out of that last week." She handed her customer change and a receipt, then fished a box from beneath the counter and set it before me. She motioned the woman behind me to approach her next.

Jean tapped on her register screen. "We saved a pound for you and Cookie. We're catching on to the fact that you're routinely behind."

"Chronically," Millie interjected. "Next!"

A bearded man moved up to take the previous customer's place.

"I had to take that right out of some woman's hands!" Millie said, pointing to the box.

"At least this time it wasn't my mother," Jean added, and the twosome broke into laughter.

The man looked around, visibly confused.

Millie rang him up and bagged his chocolates.

I grinned. "You're both very thoughtful, and this is much appreciated." I opened my wallet to search for cash. "Buying Cookie's fudge has become a tradition I enjoy." I held a twenty in Jean's direction.

"Don't be in such a hurry," she said. "We want to know what's been going on at the farm. This place is too busy for us to get away for a visit."

I raised cautious eyes to hers, then glanced carefully around before speaking. "You heard about Elijah Snow."

"Honey, everyone's heard about that," Millie said. "We want details."

"Well, the farm's closed for now, but Evan is working with my folks to help us reopen soon."

"And?" Jean asked.

"And what?" I asked, unsure I should say more in a crowded shop.

Throngs of guests came and went so often the door rarely closed. Beyond the window, a sea of shoppers filled sidewalks. Goose bumps raised the hair on my arms as I recalled being followed once. Paranoia told me I could easily be followed again. With so many bodies in the crowd, I'd never know who was minding their business and who was minding mine.

"Where are you in your investigation?" Jean's voice pulled me from the horrid thought. "It's been two days. You must have a pile of suspects by now."

"And a few wild stories!" Millie added.

I cringed, and her customer gave me significant side-eye on his way out of the store. "I'm not doing that anymore."

The women laughed. Loudly.

Millie motioned another customer in her direction. "Next."

Jean leveled me with a get-serious look. "Honey, you're a leopard, if I've ever seen one, and leopards don't change their spots."

"No," Millie corrected, passing a receipt and bag to the woman before her. "She's the Gumdrop Gumshoe."

They broke into laughter again, and the shop around us seemed to go silent. Everyone inside had probably recognized the silly name, and now they'd have my face to go with it. Assuming I wasn't already featured on the podcast website.

Heat shot to my cheeks, and I pressed my palms to the counter. "Please do not listen to *Dead and Berried*. Those guys are awful."

"They're hilarious," Millie corrected. "And they have wonderful recipes."

I clenched my teeth.

"They were in here yesterday," Jean said, "asking all sorts of questions. We told them we were new in town and still getting to know folks, so we didn't have much to add."

The tension in my body eased. "You did?"

"Of course."

A bubble of excitement formed in my chest, wiggling through me as the implication reached my heart. "You know something," I whispered, seeing the confirmation in her eyes. "What?"

Millie cast me a cat-that-ate-the-canary look before moving on to the next person in line.

Jean pinched her lips into a tiny smile. "Are you sure? I mean, if you aren't investigating—"

"I lied," I said, quietly interrupting. "Please tell me."

"Excellent." She traded a satisfied look with Millie. "Violet was a friend of ours once upon a time. She had plans to run away on the day her family up and left town. I guess they beat her to it. Took Violet and everything they owned along with them."

"She was in love," Millie added, her voice a lithe singsong. "It was a real Romeo and Juliet situation. Except everyone lived," she amended.

"Not everyone," I muttered.

Jean widened her eyes. "You knew."

"Knew what?" I hedged, careful not to say more than I should.

She shook a finger at me. "You're good. No one ever spoke of it. We all kept her secret, because we knew how bad it could be for her if we didn't."

"She told you?" I asked.

"It's a small town," Jean said. "It was even smaller then. We speculated a lot. She gave very few details, but we knew it would take a real scandal to send a whole family running, and that narrowed the field."

"I suspected Coach Wiseman," Millie said with a cackle. "I assumed it had to be someone too old or too married. Otherwise, why not just make Violet break it off?"

Jean sobered with a deep sigh. "She was in love. The real, heartbreaking, long-suffering kind. I don't think they could've made her, and they didn't want to lose her, so . . ."

I covered my mouth. What would it have been like to love someone so deeply and know it was forbidden? So much so that her family uprooted generations of life in this place to take her away from him. I couldn't imagine the pain of losing Evan that way, and I was a grown woman in another era. To be a woman—and just a teenager—a half-century ago, would mean having very little control over anything. The helplessness alone made me want to weep.

"She wrote letters to her friends for a little while," Jean said. "Basic updates that were passed around by word of mouth. Where they'd moved. What the house and school were like. Boring tidbits, but everyone talked about them. She claimed the move had been in response to some sort of job opportunity for her father. He was a businessman. They owned one of the biggest homes in town."

I thought back to my first impressions of Violet and her son. They'd certainly appeared as if they were from money.

"That's all we know," Jean said. "I hope it helps."

I nodded absently, lost in a blizzard of thoughts. Mr. Moore had said he loved Violet. Had he confronted her for moving on without him, when he'd never married or had a family of his own? Had it hurt him to meet her son and know she'd been able to have the life they'd dreamed of with someone else? Had Elijah stepped in to protect his mother from the hurtful words?

I hated that scenario. It painted Mr. Moore as angry and vengeful, and I'd never known him as anything other than sweet, if a little odd. Could Mr. Moore have felt badly about the tiff outside the inn and returned to talk things over with Violet, only to wind up in another kerfuffle with her son?

Jean rang me up and made change, then packaged my fudge and set a big box on the counter. She opened it to reveal a dozen chocolate-covered strawberries drizzled in white stripes. "An anniversary gift for you and Evan. We know you'll be busy on your anniversary, it being Christmas Eve and all, so we wanted to give these to you when you stopped in for Cookie's fudge."

Emotion welled in my eyes at the unexpected gift, and I rounded the counter to hug her, then Millie. "Thank you."

They pulled back with curious expressions. "They're only strawberries," Millie said. "Are you okay?"

I wiped my eyes and sniffled. "I'm just worked up about finding the perfect gift for Evan, and it feels as if everyone else knows exactly how to choose the thing that will mean the most."

Jean pushed out her bottom lip, then gave me a second squeeze. "Here." She plucked a tissue from a box beneath the counter and passed it to my hand. "Chin up. You know him better than anyone, and for that reason you will find the exact right thing. Whatever it is, you'll know it right here"—she pressed a fist to her middle—"when you think of it."

I nodded, hoping she was right and that I'd think of something in the next seven days.

I said my goodbyes, stuffed my sweets into the canvas tote, and headed back into the day.

My phone chimed with an incoming message as I reached the sidewalk. I read the words with a smile. Mr. Weible was glad to hear from me and had agreed to meet me for coffee tomorrow morning.

The sun warmed my cheeks as I made my way through happy holiday shoppers toward Wine Around for my mom's annual Christmas gift. A smile curved my lips as I thought of how quickly things change and how much my day had improved. A surprise anniversary gift had arrived just moments before I'd secured a chat with someone who knew all about Elijah Snow's business plan. The way things were going, I wouldn't be surprised to find the wine club memberships at half price.

The Wine Around storefront was quirky in all the best ways. The former century-old home had been converted into a gorgeous wine shop featuring blends from all over the world. Deep purple paint covered the aged cedar shake exterior, punctuated with matte black trim around the window and door. A wave of visitors exited upon my approach, causing the decorative leather strap of sleigh bells to swing. I took a moment to admire the window boxes, overflowing with holly and fresh pine, before slipping inside.

Wine Around's interior was equally charming. Wide planked floors ran beneath wooden shelves painted in rich earthy tones. Displays of bottles, openers, holders, and accessories were thoughtfully arranged throughout. An impressive, hand-painted mural of a vineyard adorned the wall behind a long service counter stretching the length of the shop. Each aisle and section of the store was labeled by country, region, and wine type. A meticulously organized masterpiece.

I ran my fingertips over the Christmas tree covered in holiday cards and well wishes near the entrance. Each card was addressed to the store's owner, Samantha Moss. She'd strung white twinkle lights through the branches and tied the cards onto limbs with red ribbon. The tree's base and stand were wrapped in burlap.

I bebopped to the counter on the beat of my favorite holiday tune, playing through hidden speakers. Then I waited while Samantha poured wine samples into tiny plastic cups for customers to taste.

She turned to me a moment later with a wicked grin.

I wiggled my fingers.

Samantha was tall and lean, with dark hair and eyes. She was gorgeous and dressed like a fashionable New Yorker. Her sleek black body suit, wide-legged dress pants, and heels were undoubtedly from a store I couldn't afford and would never willingly walk into. She'd paired the ensemble with a ruby-red lipstick and nails. Both matched her small glass gumdrop earrings, a gift from me last Christmas.

"Two annual membership renewals, please," I said.

Mom and I had joined the monthly club on Cookie's advice a couple of years back. Samantha lovingly called the group her Winers, and she introduced us to new vintages by pairing them with amazing charcuterie creations. I wasn't much of a drinker, but I'd never met a cheese I didn't like, and I adored the nights out with Mom and Cookie.

Samantha moseyed in my direction and selected two blank certificates from a folder on the countertop. She wrote my name on one and Mom's name on the other before slipping each paper into a festive crimson envelope.

"You're unusually quiet," I said, picking up on a strange energy as she worked.

Much like Cookie, Samantha was a wild card, and I rarely knew what I was going to get when she stopped talking for too long. Cookie usually hit me with crazy stories after too many sips of her forty-proof tea. Samantha, on the other hand, had previously tried to hit me with whatever was within reach. More than once.

"What? No questions about the dead guy in your mom's cookie dough?" she asked. "It's been two days. This is usually the point where you've peeved off a killer and had a few threats come your way."

"Funny," I said. "As a matter of fact, I haven't upset anyone, and I'm just here to maintain my membership, and my mom's, in your stellar wine club."

"Mm-hmm." She pushed the envelopes across the counter in my direction, then rang them up on her register. "So you don't care that those podcasters were in here this morning asking about you."

I bit my tongue against my many thoughts about Tate, Harvey, and their shameless endeavor. "Nope."

"Okay," she said, nodding. "That's good, because I just remembered they weren't looking for you. They were asking about the Gumdrop Gumshoe." Her eyes widened merrily while she waited for me to lose my temper. "Oh, wait. You are the Gumdrop Gum—"

"I am not a Gumdrop Gumshoe," I snapped.

A dozen faces turned in my direction.

"Sorry," I apologized, raising one palm and wrinkling my nose. I passed Samantha my credit card, then quickly signed the slip when it printed.

Samantha's smile was wide when I returned my eyes to hers. She leaned a slender hip against the countertop. "I told them they were barking up the wrong tree, because you're my friend, and I get territorial when people mess with my friends."

I leaned back an inch, reminded of her incredible throwing arm. "Yeah?"

"I might've also suggested they not continue to talk about you online by any name. It's libelous and mean. I don't like that either."

"Thank you."

She batted long, thick lashes at me. "Of course, but if they continued to harass you and force me to make good on all my promises, I hope you'll keep this conversation to yourself."

I stilled, unwilling to ask what she'd promised them, specifically.

"One more thing." She turned smoothly, breaking the tension so swiftly I wondered if I'd imagined it. "I nearly forgot. This is for you and that sexy sheriff you call a husband." She placed a box on the counter, the lid still in her hand. A bottle of champagne lay nestled in a cushion of white silk. A golden ribbon was tied around the bottle's neck. "You're going to love this with the cheese you bought at our holiday meeting. It'll also pair well with the chocolate-covered strawberries from next door. Millie, Jean, and I coordinated our gifts."

I smiled, recalling the berries in my bag. "Thank you."

"Don't mention it. I knew you'd be busy Christmas Eve, and I wanted to make sure you had it early. What are you getting Evan this year? A Christmas gift and an anniversary gift is double the pressure."

"Hopefully the perfect gift." I didn't comment about the pressure she'd mentioned, because I was sure if I did, my head would explode. Instead, I thanked her for the champagne, then slipped away when the wine tasters at the other end of the counter required her assistance.

I took a moment to rearrange the items in my canvas bag before heading back outside. I had no idea what to buy Evan, but there was time to think it over. I couldn't do any more shopping without making a trip to my truck. The tote was at maximum capacity and straining under the weight.

A ringing phone stopped me before I reached the crosswalk. The small device danced and vibrated on the park bench nearby, playing a beloved holiday tune. I immediately hummed along, childhood nostalgia dancing in my mind. *"You'd better watch out, better dah dah."* I smiled as I headed for the lonely device. I thought of my mom, perpetually in search of her phone, left on a counter, in the car, or occasionally in the refrigerator. Dad and I were in charge of calling it so she could listen for the ring. Once she called me for this purpose, only to realize the phone was in her hand. She'd used it to call me!

The owner of this device was probably on the hunt for it right now.

I swiped the phone to life without need of a passcode. One more stroke of good luck. "Hello?"

"I see you, Holly White," a strained, whispering voice announced.

My muscles seized, and my gaze darted around the busy square. "Who is this?"

"You're up to your old tricks again," the caller continued. A dark chuckle followed the words, and an avalanche of chills cascaded over my skin and into my boots.

I scanned the merry crowds. Carolers and street vendors. A passing horse and sleigh. Hundreds of pedestrians, shoppers, and passersby.

No one paid me any attention.

"I want you to hear me, Holly. I want to make this very clear," the menacing voice continued. "Stay out of my way, before there's another . . . accident."

Chapter Fourteen

I called Evan with news of the red cell phone, then went to wait for him at Caroline's Cupcakes. I hadn't seen Caroline in two days, her shop was the first place that came to mind when Evan told me to meet him someplace safe.

Caroline's Cupcakes was a precious little space filled with mouth-watering scents of warm vanilla and spun sugar. Caroline had decorated in creams and whites with enough pastel pinks and blues to make guests feel like they'd walked into a dream. Her cupcakes were light as air and heavenly good—the perfect balance of cake and frosting in every bite.

I felt my tension ease as I stepped over the threshold and into the delightful shop.

A line of customers stretched from the service counter to the door. Every table and chair was filled with guests. Some people were forced to stand near seated family members and friends, but no one seemed bothered. In fact, the whole room chatted merrily, oblivious to my recent threat and inner turmoil.

Caroline took one look at me and left her post.

Her workers filled the void, seamlessly stepping in as she rushed to my side.

The concern on her perfect features drew tears to my eyes.

"Glory!" she whispered, clasping my arm and pulling me toward a door marked "Employees Only." "What on earth happened?"

I raised the red cell phone in a trembling mitten-clad hand. "Can I borrow a baggie?"

She frowned at the device, then quickly released me in a storeroom lined in white shelving. "Stay right here. I won't be a minute."

Dozens of pastry boxes waited with me. Each wore a golden seal with a Caroline's Cupcakes logo and a pink receipt taped to the lid.

She returned quickly, as promised, a gallon-sized freezer bag in hand. "Come on." She motioned me into the smaller, Pinterest board–worthy, space that was her office. "Sit."

My knees bent on command, and I fell into an overstuffed pink velvet armchair across from her polished white desk. I fumbled the offending telephone into the bag and tugged off my mittens. My trembling fingers struggled to seal the plastic zipper.

Caroline opened a small refrigerator beside a bookcase of recipe books and passed me a water bottle. "Can I get you anything to munch on?" she asked.

I shook my head before I downed half the water.

"Tell me about this." She pointed to the bagged phone.

I finished the water, then filled her in.

Caroline gasped. Her thin blond brows pinched in offense. "Rude."

"I know," I said. "Evan's on his way. I asked him to meet me here."

"Good." She rubbed my shoulder, then gave it a squeeze. "I've been meaning to check on you after the murder, but business has been absolute bananas around here. No matter how much I bake, I'm always sold out before dinner, which really upsets my usual customers who work nine to five or own a shop like me and can't get away. I started taking orders through the night, filling them in the morning. and storing them for pickup in the evening, but that means I'm out of product even sooner for my business-hours shoppers." She released a long sigh, then stiffened. "Oh my goodness. this is not about me!"

I laughed. "It's okay. I'm sorry you're overwhelmed. It sounds stressful, and I know how much the success of your store means to you."

Her expression softened. "At least no one is threatening to drown me in dough, or whatever that caller was insinuating."

Right.

She handed me another bottle of water. "I'll be right back. I want to let the staff know they should send Evan to my office when he arrives."

I took a series of steadying breaths to gather my wits in her absence, reminding myself that I was safe with each exhalation. My heart rate was less frantic when she returned.

Caroline's gentle smile warmed me as she stepped back into view, a white pastry box in hand. "I made something for you." She perched on her desk before me, and I gazed at the little box. The plastic window on top revealed a series of white frosted cupcakes with a variety of sugar crystals and patterns.

My eyes misted with tears. "These are the cupcakes you made for my wedding."

She nodded. "I thought they'd make a nice anniversary gift."

I set the box aside so I could hug her. Tears rolled over my cheeks. "They're perfect."

Caroline released me, looking proud. "I'm glad you think so. You're not an easy person to buy for. From the outside looking in, you already have everything you want."

That was true, and the view was much the same from where I stood. "I will always want more of your cupcakes," I promised.

"Stop. Now I'm going to cry."

We laughed though a mini round of tears, then fell into a moment of silence as we looked at each other. I wasn't sure what I'd do without Caroline in my life, and I knew she felt the same.

"So," she said, straightening and wiping the pad of her thumb beneath each eye. "How are you and Evan doing? Since the murder, I mean. He must be freaking out."

I wrinkled my nose. "Not really. I don't think he minds the murder. Not that he wants anyone to be murdered." I backpedaled and she laughed. "It's just that sometimes I think he misses working in Boston. Chasing real criminals and putting killers in jail."

"He doesn't want crime to happen anywhere, but when it does, he's excited to facilitate justice," she said.

"Exactly."

"That makes perfect sense," she agreed. "He's very good at his job. He proves that to the town every year. How are the two of you managing all this?" She circled a finger in the air, not seeming to indicate anything in particular, but I knew better.

"My snooping?" I guessed.

She shrugged, too kind to say it aloud.

"He doesn't like it."

She smiled and lifted her brows. "Yeah."

"Yeah," I echoed sadly.

Elijah Snow's murder had been the first since Evan and I had exchanged vows last year. Until now, things between us had been wonderful. A perfect eleven-and-a-half-month honeymoon phase.

"I'm unintentionally provoking him," I said.

Caroline sighed. "I think you're intentionally provoking a killer, and that worries your husband. It could be worse. Imagine marrying a guy who didn't care about that."

I couldn't imagine it, and I didn't want to. While we were on the subject—"Tell me more about the dinner you had with the Snows at your parents' house," I said.

She considered my request for one long beat, then crossed her legs and met my eyes. "Dad and Elijah talked all night, excluding the rest of us as soon as the greetings and niceties were over. Then

Mom squared her shoulders and decided to pretend she didn't notice by consuming Mrs. Snow with endless conversations about the town, our Victorian theme, her time here, and so on."

"Your mom knew Mrs. Snow before?" I asked.

Caroline nodded. "Apparently, she babysat my mom. I had no idea."

"What was said about Violet's time here?"

"Just that it had been hard to leave in the moment, but it all worked out because she met her husband soon after the move, and they married right away. He was a soldier home on leave. They fell in love. He was deployed." She rocked her head side to side. "They were together forty-five years before he passed."

"Interesting."

She frowned. "*Romantic* was the word that came to my mind, but okay." She shook her head, amused. "Zane and I sat at the other end of the table, completely ignored. It was awful, but also kind of nice. My parents insisted I be there, and that frustrated me, but Zane agreed to keep me company, and he makes most things better, so I can't complain too much. Plus they served chocolate mousse, and we both asked for seconds just to get under Mom's skin."

I laughed.

She checked her watch. "All right. Evan will be here any minute, so you might as well tell me where you are in this investigation and see if I can help."

It was pointless to play dumb with Caroline. She knew me too well, and I'd already started the conversation by asking about dinner. Also, what was taking Evan so long? I hoped he was okay and that everyone else in town was too.

"Elijah had meetings set with people in town this week," I said, refocusing on Caroline's request. "His mom says he was trying to create more rentals for tourists or new shops."

"Where?" she asked, looking as baffled as I felt. "The Historical Society would never approve a new building anywhere near downtown, and there isn't any room anyway. Even home builders have to jump through hoops to meet the criteria on their own land."

"That's what I thought, but Mrs. Snow said he was meeting with Mr. Weible and Hamish Hunter. Evan said he had an appointment on the books with the Historical Society too."

Caroline tapped red manicured nails on the desk. "My dad worked with Orrville Lincoln at the Historical Society while he was arranging the partnership with the Chamber of Commerce. It's a long shot, but it might be worth checking out."

"Ever heard of Hamish Hunter?"

"Uh, yeah," she said, eyes wide. "He's the multimillionaire with that big house on the hill. It has all those rectangular floor-to-ceiling windows and multitier decks. The one that looks like a Swiss chalet."

I flipped mentally through all the biggest homes I could think of, but none fit the description she'd suggested. "Where?"

"Near the ski resort. The house overlooks town, but that guy's never there. I think he just keeps the house as a tax write-off."

"A multimillionaire, a Historical Society employee, and a retired electrician. I guess the first two make sense. Elijah would've had to work within Mistletoe's guidelines to create rentals." There were strict parameters and major fines for anyone daring to disregard the rules that kept us on the National Register of Historic Places.

"I think Mr. Weible works with the Historical Society from time to time," Caroline added, interrupting my thoughts. "He has a lot of experience working on the really old properties. There aren't a lot of people in Mistletoe who are qualified to repair century-old machines and gadgets. My dad thought he'd have to fly the clock from the square to another state when it quit working. The costs for shipping were astronomical, and the risk of further damage was even worse. Then someone recommended he ask Mr. Weible about it, and Weible had the clock running again in no time. His hourly rate was negligible when compared to the alternative, and he thanked my dad for the opportunity to work on something so rare."

I warmed at the sweet story.

Heavy footfalls echoed on the floor outside the office, pulling my eyes to Evan's as he appeared in the open doorway.

He was crouched before me in the next instant, cold palms on my hot cheeks. "Are you okay?"

I nodded, suddenly emotional again.

He glanced at Caroline. "Thank you."

She nodded. "Anytime." She offered me a little-finger wave, then saw herself out.

Evan scanned me head to toe before easing back. "I'm sorry it took so long to get here. I forgot the roads were closed, and I had to find somewhere to leave my cruiser. I considered using my lights but suspected the town wouldn't see this as an emergency since you, thankfully, aren't in danger. I decided not to make any enemies, and parked a couple of blocks away, but then I had to navigate the crowd."

I blinked back building tears. "I'm fine, and I know you got here as soon as you could." I raised the bagged phone.

Evan rocked onto his knees and set his forehead against mine for a long moment. I ran my fingers through his messy hair. From the looks of it, he'd been doing the same before his arrival.

"I'm sorry," I whispered, stomach tensing with regret. I hated anything that caused him distress. Knowing I was the reason he'd fallen to his knees was gutting.

He shifted back into a crouch and met my eye. "Last year I promised you, myself, your parents, and everyone in this town I'd always love you exactly as you are. I promised I'd do my best to keep you safe." He lifted my hand to his lips and pressed a kiss to my knuckles. "No one thought for a second you'd make that easy."

I grinned. "You're not mad?"

"At whoever threatened my wife? Hell, yes. At you, no."

I kissed him.

"All right," he said, pulling away too soon. "I see you already bagged the evidence."

"I did."

He raised the red phone, crinkling its plastic sheath. "Cute. The sheriff's department's bags don't have all these little pink hearts and cartoon cupcakes."

"Caroline makes everything truly adorable," I said. "And she recreated the cupcakes from our wedding as an anniversary gift. Would you like one?"

He followed my outstretched finger to the box on her desk, then he opened lid with reverence and selected a sweet. He peeled the pastel paper away on one side. "You first."

I took a bite and stifled a moan of pleasure.

Evan pushed the rest of the cake into his mouth and chewed. His shoulders drooped and the tension fell from his features. "Magic."

"Truly," I agreed.

He stretched onto his feet and assumed the frustrated husband stance I knew well. One hip cocked, one hand on his waist, the other in his hair. "I love you to the cosmos, but you're going to be the death of me. You know that, right?"

I nodded regretfully, desperately hoping the second part wasn't true.

Chapter Fifteen

Evan took the phone with him when we parted ways. He insisted on walking me to my truck and seeing me safely inside before returning to his cruiser. I was thrilled he hadn't been upset with me about the threat. Maybe he really had accepted me for the curious human I was. The possibility made me smile.

I rubbed my palms together as the truck heated up. A seemingly endless stream of traffic being directed away from the square blocked the intersection at the end of the alley, holding me in place. I dialed the Hearth while I waited my turn.

"Holly?" Mom answered on the first ring. "Everything okay?"

"Yep. Just waiting on a couple of tour buses to get out of my way. Do you need anything from town while I'm here?"

"Nope. I'm good. Everyone's warm and fed," she said. The smile in her voice lightened my heart.

"Oh yeah?"

"Mm-hmm. Marcy and Caesar were so full when they left, they let me call them a sleigh." She giggled. "Then Gertie and Jackie stopped by and sampled all my sweets. I had to turn the thermostat up twice. I think the heating system is on the fritz, but other than that, it's been a fabulous morning."

"I think the temperature is testing everyone's system," I said. It'd been unseasonably cold the past few days, and shop hours were extended through Christmas, which meant increasing demands on HVACs all over town. "I'm glad you got to feed the inn guests. Have you seen Mrs. Snow?"

"No, but I sent a care package to the inn with Caesar. He promised to deliver it for me. I wasn't sure which of my soups she'd like best, so I went with chicken noodle. Something about it soothes the soul. I added a sandwich that will hold up in her mini fridge without needing to be heated. The soup's another story."

"You're very kind and thoughtful," I said. "I don't tell you enough."

"I try," she said. "But I'm often outdone by my daughter. Oh, hold on." Her voice grew distant as she spoke with someone in the background. "I hate to do this," she said, returning to the line. "I have to go. Your father and his crew are erecting a white wooden fence around the area Evan wants monitored. It's blending into the snowscape nicely, but they're all getting a little hungry. Drive safely."

"I will," I promised, finally inching forward to merge with traffic.

"Love you! Duty calls!" Mom disconnected the call, and the screen on my dash returned to the radio.

I turned away from downtown a few moments later, glad to be rid of the road congestion and alone with my thoughts. Part of me wanted to obsess about the scary red phone and threatening call, but the rest of me knew that was of no use. Evan would find out what he could about the device and call log, then fill me in. The most I could do in the meantime was stop answering random phones.

I didn't feel like shopping anymore. Not when I was clearly being watched. Someone had known I was inside Wine Around. They'd planted the phone at the right place and time for me to find it.

My skin prickled with goose bumps, and I pumped up the heat inside my truck.

Signs for Reindeer Games appeared at the roadside, but my mind wandered a moment too long, and the next thing I knew Mr. Moore's farm came into view. Since I was already there, I decided to turn around in his driveway, and if I happened to see him, I'd be forced to say hello, because Mom hadn't raised me to be rude.

My tires crunched loudly over gravel at the edge of the road and along the frozen path to Mr. Moore's home. No one had shoveled the new fallen snow, but there was a blue SUV parked near his porch.

I thought of the vehicle that had distracted Mr. Moore the day before Elijah's murder. I couldn't be sure this was the same SUV, but if it was, who did it belong to? And what was it doing here? He certainly hadn't been glad to see it at Reindeer Games.

I parked beside his guest and went to knock on the door. My muscles tensed, and my nerves jangled. My mind raced with ugly scenarios. Maybe Mr. Moore was in trouble. Maybe I was also now in trouble. Maybe the SUV belonged to a killer.

No one answered when I knocked, so I tried the bell.

Just like Mr. Weible's apartment, no one seemed to be home.

A gust of wind blew through the trees, rattling the windowpanes and whistling around the door.

I burrowed deeper into my coat and peeked through the glass.

An array of old photobooks had been pulled from the bookcase and opened in piles on the coffee table and couch. A roll of wrapping paper, tape, and scissors lay on his chair.

I hated the thought of anyone being alone at Christmas, and wondered where Mr. Moore usually spent his time. He didn't come to my parents' place as often as he had when I was small. Did he have a best friend? Someone to talk to or play cards with? My gaze caught on a stuffed squirrel, and I frowned at the possibility she and the other forest creatures in tiny Victorian garb were his friends.

"This feels like a job for Cookie," I said, realizing she'd know how to get him plugged in and surrounded with people. Mr. Moore was a tad eccentric, but so was Cookie. It was a wonder they weren't already friends.

I straightened and scanned the world around me. The forest was silent, save for romping wildlife and the blowing wind. Maybe Mr. Moore had taken his guest somewhere in his pickup? Unfortunately, his garage didn't have windows, so I couldn't confirm or dismiss the theory.

Instead, I climbed back into my truck and watched his home for a long moment. Then an idea came to mind. I called Mr. Moore.

Just when I thought the call would go to voicemail, he answered. "Hello?"

"Hi, Mr. Moore. This is Holly. I'm outside your house. I thought I'd stop by and check on you. Everything okay?"

I waited through an extensively long pause. "Mr. Moore?"

"Oh, um, yes. I'm fine. Just . . . taking a bath."

I looked at the SUV beside my truck and considered asking who was visiting, but suspected that was too much. "Well, okay. If you don't need anything—"

"All righty," he said. "Have a good day."

The call disconnected.

Dissatisfied, I opened a browser on my phone and typed Hamish Hunter, the multimillionaire's name, into a search engine, along with the name of our town. A number of responses returned to me, and I clicked on the one with a local number.

"Luxury Real Estate," a smooth female voice answered.

"Hi." My mouth opened and closed a few more times without any additional sounds. I hadn't made a plan before selecting the call feature. A rookie mistake.

"Hello?" she said. "How can I be of assistance?"

"Um . . ." I blinked at the screen, then gave myself an internal kick or two. "I'm looking for my next luxury property," I said, attempting to mimic her soft, unhurried tone. "I'm hoping to discuss the matter with Mr. Hunter."

The familiar click-clack of fingernails on a keyboard carried across the line. "I'm afraid Mr. Hunter is on holiday until January third. Would you like to arrange an appointment for some time that week?"

"Holiday?" I chewed my lip. "No. We're old friends, so I'd hoped to see him before Christmas. I won't be in town long and hate to miss him."

The responding silence pulled my shoulders to my ears. I'd accidentally mixed my stories. First I wanted a luxury property, five seconds later, a visit with an old friend.

"I can forward you to his voicemail," she offered. "If he gets the message, the two of you can sort that out. If you're in a rush, you can try his home or cell number. I assume you have both." Her tone implied she knew I didn't have either.

"Yep," I said. "Sounds good." I shook off the embarrassment of being busted, and reminded myself that the woman had no idea who I was. I left a message for Mr. Hunter, returning to my original ruse. He obviously knew we weren't old friends, so I claimed to have interest in purchasing a luxury property in town.

Leaving a message for Mr. Weible had earned me a quick response. I could only hope the same would prove true for Mr. Hunter.

I cast a final look at Mr. Moore's home before pointing my truck down the driveway. I'd have to catch up with him another time.

* * *

I arrived for my coffee date early the next morning. The Cup of Cheer café was positioned outside historic downtown, making it easier to access than most things on the square, in theory anyway. I'd wasted ten minutes navigating one-way streets and snowy roads with cars parked on both sides. If a more direct route existed, I'd be sure to identify it before making a return trip. Thankfully, there was an empty spot in the attached parking lot once I arrived. I held the shop door for a family in matching outerwear. The toddler's hair stood tall in a style reminiscent of Cindy Lou Who's in Whoville.

"It's a plastic cup," the woman behind her said after catching me staring. "We put the cup on her head like a hat, then pulled her hair up to hide the plastic and tied the bow on top. She loves Cindy Lou Who."

I grinned at the woman, then the little girl. "Me too." I told her. "If you meet a grinch, be patient. Some folks just need a little extra love this time of year."

She nodded solemnly, as if in complete understanding.

"Merry Christmas," the woman said. She winked as she steered the child away.

I moved into the café and searched the dining area for an open table. I'd been meaning to try the place for lunch since it opened a while back, but hadn't yet made the trip. The overall color scheme was white on white with pale blue and gold accents. The floor was shiny, reflective marble. Giant snowflake-shaped piñatas hung from rafters, which were wrapped in twinkle lights and strewn with a garland of Sweden's national flag. Christmas trees filled corners and alcoves, each adorned with a multitude of straw ornaments, many of which appeared to be goats.

I wondered if Cookie had visited the café and what she thought of all the tiny Theodores. Not that all the straw goats were meant to represent our favorite local pygmy—there was only one goat who mattered in Cookie's world.

A small whiteboard on the hostess podium advised: "Free cup of cheer with every mandelmusslor purchase." I wasn't sure what either of those things were, but the hand-drawn images beside them suggested the former was a hot cup of coffee and the latter looked a lot like a dessert, so I was game for plenty of both.

A woman popped into view, her long blond hair hung over one shoulder. "Welcome to Cup of Cheer," she said. "Would you like to sit inside or outside?"

I frowned. It was roughly twenty degrees outside, until the wind blew; then it was easily ten degrees cooler. "I'm not sure," I said, carefully, following her gaze to an opening door in the back. A group of people entered the building in brightly colored coats, carrying take-out bags. "I'm meeting a friend."

"Are you Holly?" she asked.

I blinked. "Yes."

"Jerry just grabbed an igloo and let me know you were on the way. Follow me."

I obeyed, intrigued by the prospect of igloos out back. I was only slightly disappointed to find an arrangement of massive clear plastic domes with internal heaters, glass tables, and white chairs.

Mr. Weible rose as we entered. I wasn't sure I remembered ever hearing his first name before the hostess spoke it. A small knit cap sat on the empty chair beside him. His thick gray hair rose in messy tufts. "Holly. Welcome. Thank you, Alice."

"Of course," she said, setting a menu and silverware on the table for me. "What can I get you started with?"

I took a seat across from Mr. Weible, and he lowered onto his chair as well.

"The sugar plum cream cheese bars are bliss," he said. "But I think I'll go with the special. Mandelmusslor and a cup of cheer."

"Sounds good," I said. "I'll take that too."

Alice smiled. "Cream or sugar?"

I looked to Mr. Weible. I liked my coffee black, but I wasn't clear on the exact contents of a cup of cheer. "Both, please."

Mr. Weible nodded. "Same."

"Be right back with that," Alice said before darting back into the café.

"Did you have any trouble finding the place?" he asked. "It's a bit tucked away."

"It is," I agreed. "I didn't realize how residential the area was. The café kind of pops up out of nowhere."

"That's how things used to be," he said. "Folks opened shops in densely populated places to capitalize on customer convenience. When most people traveled by foot, it made sense to frequent the nearest stores."

I smiled.

"I love this place," he said. "I helped with the wiring."

My brows shot up, and I leaned forward, accepting the easy segue as a Christmas miracle. "I think you've worked on everything in this town."

He chuckled. "Somedays it seems that way. Alice was on a budget, so I worked out a deal with the community college and borrowed a few students in the electrical program. They got extra credit and real hands-on experience. Alice cut her labor costs in half." He looked like a proud grandpa telling his story, and I warmed to him instantly.

"Alice?" I asked, glancing in the direction the blond woman had gone.

He nodded. "She opened the café to honor her grandmother after her passing."

I warmed immediately to Alice. "This place is lovely."

"I try to come here a couple of times a month. It's good to support small business owners who can't afford a place downtown."

"I've been lucky enough to sell my jewelry online and in existing shops, like the art gallery near the square," I said. "I can't imagine trying to find my own retail space."

"The gallery is in my building," he said. "I've lived there longer than you've been alive."

I grinned, not bothering to tell him I knew exactly where he lived. "It's a beautiful structure."

"All original masonry," he said. "Updates have only been done as needed and with painstaking care. I like to stick my nose in whenever

I see something needs done." He smiled a bit sheepishly. "It's important to prioritize historical accuracy over speed, especially in a town like ours."

"I've heard there will be a few more rentals coming to the area soon," I said as casually as possible. "A push to create additional space for shops and overnight guests. Will you be involved in any of those?"

Mr. Weible held my gaze for a long moment, then turned his attention to the world beyond our igloo. "You've been talking to Hamish Hunter, I see."

I bit my tongue, wondering if he'd say more or less if he knew I hadn't been able to reach the wealthy investor.

"Hamish bought my building earlier this month," Weible said. "The ink's not quite dry, but it's as good as done."

I did my best to school the surprise from my features. "Was it a good deal?"

He smiled. "Lifetime rights as an occupant, along with a small cash incentive to pad my pension."

I inhaled deeply, hoping the gentle buzz of the space heater masked the sound. This was the story I'd come for.

"Here we are!" a merry voice sang.

I started as Alice set a mug of light-brown coffee and a plate with several small tarts before me.

"Can I get you anything else?" she asked.

"No, thank you," Mr. Weible said.

"Wait." I lifted a smile to Alice. "Tell me about the mandelmusslor."

Alice folded her hands in front of her, an eagerness in her pretty blue eyes. "They're very popular in Sweden, especially this time of year. These are my favorites." She pointed to my small plate with two samples. Each tart had a dollop of what I suspected was cream cheese–based substance and a drizzle of something else. "Chocolate and strawberry. Try them. You'll want more."

"I have no doubt," I said as the inviting scents rose to my nose.

Someone called Alice's name, and she glanced toward the sound. "I'll be back in a few minutes to see what you think."

I took a bite and felt my mood brighten. A heartbeat later, I recalled the conversation at hand.

Mr. Weible had sold his building to the wealthy investor, a man I'd recently left a voicemail for. A man Elijah Snow had planned to meet with while he was in Mistletoe.

Another thought pushed the rest from my mind. Mr. Weible had owned the building where he lived? That had to be worth a small fortune. How much had Hunter paid him?

I brushed a napkin against my lips and pulled my gaze to Mr. Weible. "Sorry. You were saying . . .?"

I took another bite, savoring the perfect mix of textures and flavors, then followed that with a sip of coffee. "Mmm."

"They put cinnamon in the grounds," he said.

"So does my mom." I returned the mug to the table, then did my best to appear casual. "You owned the building where you live?" I asked, opting for the direct approach when he didn't pick up our earlier discussion, as I'd hoped.

"For many years. I got lucky when the market took a dive about thirty years ago, and the previous owner was underwater with the bank. I had a little nest egg, and it saved my home."

"That was lucky," I said.

"Karma is powerful. I was able to purchase the property for the balance on the loan, and the other guy didn't have to file bankruptcy. A real win–win."

"Then you made another great deal with Mr. Hunter," I said, repeating what I'd learned for added clarity.

Weible's features tightened. "I'm not sure anyone ever gets a great deal when working with someone like Hunter, but I got enough money to spoil my granddaughter, and I get to grow old right where I am."

I forced a smile. "Did you know Elijah Snow?"

"We had plans to meet, but—"

I nodded in understanding. "He had plans to meet with Mr. Hunter this week. I wonder if the sale of your building was the reason?"

"Without a doubt," Weible said. "I've heard they had interested parties lining up. Someone mentioned Soul Cycle and a microbrewery. Snow and Hunter probably had plenty to discuss."

I took a minute to process the news. Soul Cycle was a fitness chain delivering high-intensity indoor cycling classes. Mistletoe didn't welcome chains of any kind, in an effort to preserve the overall aesthetic, but I couldn't help wondering if the businessmen had a plan to tuck the enterprise inside the existing building and thereby skirt town guidelines. We also didn't have a microbrewery, which also sounded like fun.

"I'd hoped to introduce myself on the night of Snow's arrival, but he had plans with the mayor, and I had plans with my daughter's family. Our schedules didn't align."

"It's a busy time of year," I said, taking another sip of the sweet coffee. "I'm sorry things didn't work out." Though I couldn't help wondering what sort of karma Weible would suggest for someone like Snow.

How did a man so in love with historical accuracy feel about an outsider planning to turn his building into a bunch of modern shops and rentals?

Chapter Sixteen

I swung by the Historical Society on my way home.

A tall, lean man in a tweed vest and bow tie met me on the front steps. "We're closing early today," he said. "We'll reopen in the morning." His dark hair fluttered in the wind as he fastened leather buttons on his tan wool coat.

I turned to follow him back to the lot. "I'm Holly Gray," I said.

He squinted against another blast of frosty air. "Orrville Lincoln."

"I was actually looking for you," I said. "Jerry Weible and I just had coffee and—"

Lincoln stiffened and groaned. "Save your efforts if you're here to plead his case. I've been over this with him a dozen times. There's nothing I can do about the sale of that building. I'm not a lawyer. I'm a historian. Hamis Hunter went through all the proper channels to get those approvals, and he's putting nearly two million dollars into the effort. I can't be mad at that. As long as the property meets Mistletoe's aesthetic standards, it's none of my business what else goes on in there. If something illegal happens, notify your husband. Now, if you'll excuse me."

With that, Orrville Lincoln skated past me to a sedan at least twice my age, dropped behind the wheel, and cruised away.

I climbed back into my truck, on autopilot, and took the long way home, lost in thought. Mr. Weible had been pestering the Historical Society over the sale of his building, but why? He'd told me Mr. Hunter had given him cash for the buyout and the right to stay in his apartment for the rest of his life. Did he know Mr. Hunter planned to make two million dollars' worth of changes? Could Mr. Weible have pushed for more money, knowing now how much Hunter planned to spend on property improvements? Did that matter to him?

Perhaps the improvements would positively impact Mr. Weible's apartment as well. And he got to stay in a place he loved.

Every question that popped into mind led to two more I couldn't answer.

With a little luck I'd hear from Mr. Hunter soon, and he'd have details. For now, I needed to check on my folks and inn guests.

A small crowd had gathered near the entrance to Reindeer Games. Cars and trucks lined the road as I drew near. Some people carried candles, their flames flickering in the waning afternoon light. Others carried signs. A few held neatly stenciled well wishes for Mrs. Snow's peace and her son's memory. The remainder possessed harsh sentiments like "How many more will die at this location?"

I glowered at a couple in matching coats, who'd apparently tried to be clever. The message on the woman's sign read: "The Whites Will Be Home for the Homicides."

I had to slow down and squint excessively to read all the words on her friend's sign. "Reindeer Games Family Tree Farm: Go Walking in a Winter Murder Land."

My grip tightened on the wheel, and I fought the urge to flash my high beams or honk until the crowd scattered.

The group turned to gawk as my big truck crept past, stuffed antlers, red nose, logo, and all.

Mom waved from her position among the masses, doling out hot drinks and bagged snacks.

I rubbed my forehead and traveled an extra mile out of the way to access a back road onto the farm. I parked in the main lot and walked toward the gate, but found Mom on her way back and stopped.

"Your turn," she said, toting an empty box in one hand, presumably the transport for her goodies. "Come with me to the Hearth and warm up."

I pivoted and joined her without question. I opened the door and held it for her a few steps later.

"How are you doing?" she asked, shucking off her puffy coat and unwinding the scarf from her neck. "It's been a long day, and I've barely seen you."

"I met with Mr. Weible in town today then stopped by the historical society. I stopped to check on Mr. Moore yesterday, but I missed him."

Mom made a pouty face. "I love that you did that. I spoke to him by phone after lunch. He seemed alert and well. I offered to bring him dinner later, but he said it wasn't necessary."

"There was a blue SUV outside his place when I stopped. No one answered."

Mom shrugged. "He probably took his guests into town." She filled two bright red mugs with steamy apple cider and tucked a cinnamon stick into each as a stirrer. "I met those podcasters you were telling me about. Tate and Harvey. They seem nice," she said.

I rolled my eyes so hard it hurt.

"I love their little nickname for you."

I lifted a finger to stop her. "Don't say it."

"Why? I think it's cute."

"It's not meant to be cute. When did you see them? Where are they now?" I asked, twisting to look toward the closed café door as if I might find them lurking there.

"It's hard to say. Time's a blur without our usual schedules. From what they told me, they've been all over town, so I suppose they could be anywhere."

I frowned. They might've even been downtown to leave the little red cell phone for me. "Great."

Mom set her box on the counter and opened the bakery display. "I ran out of whoopie pies and snickerdoodles, but I want to take some more sweets to the group at the gate. I hate to see them working so hard in the cold like that."

"They're protesting our farm," I said, fixing her with my most deadpan stare. "Didn't you read the signs?"

"Some of them are there to support Violet. I'm sure the others mean well. They just don't understand. Besides, if we shower them in kindness, it'll make it harder to paint us as the enemy."

"You're a nicer person than I am," I said, recalling my urge to flash my lights and scare them away. "If you have to feed them, why not pass out those commemorative cookies? You had more than a thousand left this morning."

"I would, but I can't find them," she said, averting her eyes and sipping her cider.

"What?"

She inhaled long and slow, then used her most polite, customer service voice to repeat that more than a thousand gingerbread men had simply up and vanished.

"Mom," I started, feeling emotion well in my chest. Panic? Fear? I wasn't sure.

"Never mind all that," she said. "My friends and I have been trying to figure out what to do with them, so maybe it's a blessing. Anyway, I've buried the lead. Evan says we can reopen the farm tomorrow. Your dad and his crew are finishing the fencing as we speak. Do you want to see it?"

I wanted to discuss the missing cookies, but clearly I was alone in that. "Sure."

We finished our drinks and headed back into the snow.

As promised, the fence was finished, and we found Dad working alone beneath a new motion sensor light. He and the farm crew had done an incredible job of securing the area and visually blending the white boards with the snowy landscape.

"Hey," Dad said, his contagious smile igniting when he noticed us. "There are my girls." He drew Mom and me into a group hug, then released me without letting Mom get away. A black band circled his left coat sleeve at the bicep.

Mom seemed to notice the fabric at the same time I did. She tugged it gently. "Is this for poor Elijah?"

Dad nodded. "Didn't seem right to put the fence up and pretend nothing happened. A man lost his life. A woman lost her son."

I returned to his embrace and pulled Mom in with me. I held both my parents tightly until I could convince myself to let go.

"Aw," Mom said. "We love you too."

Dad nodded. "We're both unspeakably glad you've decided to sit this one out."

I bit my lip. "Yes, but wouldn't it be nice to get closure for Mrs. Snow before Christmas?" I asked.

My parents' faces moved through a similar series of expressions, from confusion to shock, to horror.

I took a step back and tried to look like their baby.

"Holly!" Mom gasped. "Is that why you've been looking after Henry? Not because you're genuinely worried."

"I am worried," I promised. "I know he didn't do this, but he's the main suspect, and I want to be sure he isn't arrested for lack of options."

Dad made a dismissive, snorting sound. "You think your husband would accuse an old man of murder just because there wasn't someone better to charge?"

"That's not what I said." I raised my hands into the air.

"It sounded like it to me," Mom said. "It also sounds as if you want us to spend another Christmas scared silly while you run headlong into danger."

"I haven't been in any danger this year," I promised. "Mini Mooseketeer's honor."

Dad crossed his arms. "No one has threatened you about this?" he asked, tipping his head slightly in the direction of his new fence.

I wrinkled my nose as memories of the busted cookie on my doorstep and ringing red phone blew into mind.

Something flashed in the distance, distracting me from his question. A vehicle had arrived at the inn. Sunlight glinted off the windshield.

That was my ticket out of the conversation. "I should go arrange the evening tea and snack tray," I said. "I'll send the guests your way around seven."

"We're not finished with this conversation," Dad said.

"Tell them I have pot pies," Mom called. "They can come by anytime!"

I waved, then doubled my pace through the field between the inn and my folks. The car passed me on its way out. Had Gertie and Jackie opted for an Uber over their sleigh? Or were Marcy and Caesar back from exploring?

When I reached the porch, two dark figures sat on the steps, fully cloaked in shadows.

I nearly wet my pants.

A moment later I recognized the loiterers as Tate and Harvey.

"Ugh. What do you want?" I asked, climbing onto the porch with regret. I hadn't seen a guest return. I'd seen these clowns camping out to wait for someone to harass. Lucky me for being next.

Tate hopped onto his feet and extended a hand. "Just hoping to get a word with you."

I glared at his outstretched fingers but eventually caved, accepting the shake. "Fine. Let's get this over with." They were unlikely to leave me alone until I talked, so I'd might as well rip off the bandage.

"Why do you hate us so much?" he asked, a teasing smile on his lips. "You don't even know us. You've probably never even listened to our show."

"Correct," I said. "And I don't hate anyone, but I severely dislike your behavior."

His chin tipped up. "How is what we're doing any different from what you're doing?" he asked.

My jaw dropped. Was he serious? "First of all, how dare you! Second of all, I'm truly concerned by what's happened here, and I want to help. You are capitalizing on a man's death. Those are very different things."

Tate did his best to appear aghast. "We're just making a living. People love this stuff. We'd be the most terrible entrepreneurs in history if we didn't take advantage of an opportunity like this."

I pressed my lips into a tight line, wondering again how far Tate and Harvey would go to increase their number of listeners.

"It's not as if we're that rich investor guy Elijah Snow planned to meet with before, you know—" He drew a thumb across his neck.

"Stop that."

Tate grinned but put his thumb down. "Have you talked to that guy yet?"

"How do you know about him?" I asked, inching closer for a better look at his expression as he spoke.

Harvey rose to stand beside his partner, making it easier to keep an eye on both their faces at once. He dusted his gloved hands against his backside, knocking away bits of snow. "Same way you do," he said. "We asked around, but the secretary at Hunter's company is gatekeeping his access and whereabouts."

"I had a similar experience," I admitted. "I heard he's out of town a lot. Maybe he isn't even in Mistletoe right now."

Harvey shook his head. "Nope. He's here."

"We saw him leaving a fancy restaurant last night," Tate said. "He had some guy with him. We didn't see the passenger's face, but Mr. Hunter was definitely driving."

My intuition spiked. "Does he drive a blue SUV? Subcompact. Maybe three or four years old?"

Tate screwed his features into a comical knot. "He drove a black Mercedes. Luxury class. Next year's model. You realize he's, like, the wealthiest man in the state, right? Maybe the wealthiest on the East Coast."

I made a face I hoped conveyed how much I didn't care.

"I think he was angry when we saw him," Harvey said. "He was glowering and waving his free hand around as he drove away."

The wheels of my mind began to spin. *Why was Mr. Hunter angry that night?* And who'd been his passenger? Did it have anything to do with Elijah Snow's death? Or was this just a series of unrelated details?

Tate rocked on his heels. "What's your next move, Gumshoe?"

"Don't call me that," I said. "And stop harassing people around town. You're asking everyone you see about a man they never met. He wasn't in town twelve hours before he died. You won't get answers like this. You're just stirring up trouble, and Mistletoe doesn't need any more trouble right now. It's Christmas."

Tate stuffed his hands in his pockets, feigning innocence once more. "Like I said before, we're just trying to get the story."

"Well, stop!" I opened the door but paused at the sight of the empty donation receptacle. I reached inside the foyer and flipped on the porch light, illuminating the space. The massive faux gift box was always overflowing with toys, but all I saw inside now was a little snow. "Goodnight," I said absently, dismissing the podcasters before stepping inside.

I waited at the window while Tate and Harvey walked away, making sure they didn't double back to stake out the place or peek through my windows.

Satisfied, I toed off my boots and hung my wrap on the hooks in the hallway.

Cindy Lou Who snoozed in my office, and I went to see her. She'd curled tightly on my desk chair, snuggled into a perfect kitty knot.

I flipped on the light, causing her to blink and yawn.

"Hello, sweet little dumpling," I said. "Did you miss me?"

She leaped onto the floor and stretched into a tall arch, like a Halloween cat. Then she moved into the hall and blinked green eyes at me over her shoulder, presumably leading me to her food bowl.

"Give me a min—" I froze midsentence as the whole of my office came into view. I turned in a small circle, certain my eyes were deceiving me. The room was immaculate and spacious. Utterly devoid of donated toys. Every pile. Every bag, box, and roll of wrapping paper was gone.

Along with all the donations usually found in the porch bin.

And at least a thousand of Mom's cookies.

What was happening?

A soft thud rattled the overhead light fixture and sent adrenaline through my veins. I grabbed my phone and found Evan's number, then hovered my thumb above the "Call" button and inched toward the doorway.

Cindy trotted merrily to the kitchen.

"Did you hear that?" I asked her, pausing at the bottom of the stairs.

Another set of muffled bumps and creaks set my heart rate to a sprint. Was the inn being burgled? Or were my guests horsing around?

The low rumble of a man's voice caught my ear, and I crept silently up the carpeted runner to the second floor. My mind concocted a number of reasonable scenarios for the sounds. Maybe Marcy and Caesar were moving their luggage or looking behind the furniture for something one of them had dropped. Maybe Christopher had come to visit Gertie and brought a large present he'd presented with a thud.

It's not a killer on a murderous rampage, I repeated to myself in my head.

I made it to the end of the second-floor hall before the next thump occurred. Directly on the other side of the wall where I stood. A strangled moan and sharp female squeak pushed me into action before I'd thought better of it. If someone was in danger, there wasn't time to do anything other than act.

In the space of my next heartbeat, I'd flung open the door and slapped the light switch on the wall, dousing the room in bright light.

"Stop!" I shouted, temporarily unable to see and waiting for my vision to clear. "I've called the police!" My foot landed on something unseen, and I fell against the wall, phone outstretched in evidence to support my threat.

Mrs. Snow screeched, and a man shouted. "No!"

It took a moment for my feet to stabilize. Another moment for me to make sense of the situation before me. I'd tripped on a pile of cast-off shoes, for starters. And I hadn't heard an intruder, a murderer, or a burglar.

I'd heard Mrs. Snow and Mr. Moore.

And they were absolutely not fighting.

Chapter Seventeen

I bumbled back to my office and flopped onto my chair. Part of me demanded an explanation for what I'd just seen. The rest of me wanted to never think of it again. I was pretty sure catching Mr. Moore and Mrs. Snow in a heated embrace was more shocking than the threatening phone call I'd received earlier. Unlike the phone call, however, I wasn't sure how to report this to Evan, but it seemed highly relevant.

Footfalls overhead pulled my gaze to the ceiling. I wondered what they were doing up there, then cringed as a dozen images came to mind, followed by one hundred questions.

Had Mrs. Snow invited Mr. Moore to visit her? Was it the first time since her arrival?

Or had Elijah caught them together the way I had on the night of his death? If so, was Elijah defending his mother's honor, and Mr. Moore merely defending himself, when things went south?

No, I scolded myself for the thought. Mr. Moore wouldn't hurt anyone.

But maybe Elijah's death had been an accident. Maybe Elijah had slipped and fallen into the batter, hitting his head on the way down. The giant cookie cutter and tray were both made of metal. A hearty whack on either would easily crack a noggin.

I dropped my cell phone on the desk. My fingers ached from the intensity of my grip, and it took several moments of kneading and flexing to regain proper blood flow.

Around me, the inn was suddenly still. I scanned the space, tuned tightly into every small sound. The soft hum of the furnace, the crackling fire in the parlor. The familiar, rhythmic thumps of Cindy Lou Who's paws on her sealed kibble bin.

It seemed like a good opportunity for an emotional breakdown. If only I had time—the thought was hijacked by my impeccably clean office. I'd returned so befuddled and distracted that I'd nearly forgotten.

Where had all the donated toys gone? And the wrapping paper?

How long ago were they pilfered? Were Mrs. Snow and Mr. Moore upstairs when it happened? Had Mrs. Snow even left the inn today? How long must it have taken someone to move so many toys? Maybe there had been a whole team of toy-stealing bandits.

And what about Mom's cookies?

Two major thefts in a single day on the same farm couldn't be a coincidence. Could it?

I rose on a long exhale and shored up my resolve. I needed to check every room, excluding the occupied guest rooms, for anything that seemed amiss. Maybe the toys and cookies were here somewhere but had simply been moved. I couldn't think of any reason for that to be true, but I couldn't explain a lot of things today.

Everything else in my office appeared to be in order. I gazed through my open door to the foyer. The only things missing there were the usual sets of coats, hats, and scarves. Marcy and Caesar, Gertie and Jackie, must still be out enjoying the town. That was probably for the best. At least for now.

I pocketed my phone and went for a closer look around the inn. I made a loop through the formal dining room, the parlor, and the sunroom, then checked the door to my private quarters. Locked. As it should be. No signs of the missing cookies, toys, or gift wrap. I gave the stairs a long look, then moved on to the kitchen.

Everything appeared to be untouched and exactly as it should be. Though I'd never felt quite so discombobulated.

Something bit my ankle, and I hopped onto the opposite foot. "Ow!"

Cindy glared up at me, blinking luminous green eyes. "Meow."

I scooped food into her bowl, then went to the refrigerator. I didn't have time to argue with her about the hour or her vet's recommended maximum daily intake of treats and kibble. Her weight would have to be addressed after I found all the things I was looking for, most importantly the killer.

She cleaned her bowl and meowed again. Her fluffy sides bulged as she sat.

Maybe she'd eaten the cookies.

"No more," I said. "I have to feed the humans now." I pulled containers of cheese and fruits from the shelves, then lined the island with gold and silver trays. I arranged the foods into small, festive bowls and added a display of hot teas and garnishes. Lastly, I stacked small plates and paper napkins beside the trays and added a collection of mugs with the Reindeer Games logo. Anyone searching for a snack before dinner could help themselves. I put the containers away and added nuts and mints to the arrangement before calling it finished. From there, I set a vanilla and cranberry tart on the candle warmer and pressed play on a compact CD player I'd had since middle school. The festive melody of a holiday tune lifted from the device, and I turned to Cindy.

"I cannot in good conscience feed you more," I said.

She licked her chops and fixed me with a look.

"Okay, let's go." I picked her up with a little effort and, much to her dismay, carried her squirming limbs to the locked door at the back of the home. I fished a key from my pocket with one hand, pressing her fluffy body to my ribs like a football. I dropped her inside when the door swung open.

She made a run for the window, nonplussed, and landed on the sill overlooking our landscaping. These days the view included a set of leafless trees, a smattering of stout shrubs, and a plethora of hungry birds.

I moved to stand behind her and took a long look over her shoulder, checking for signs of a bandit toting a hundred toys and a thousand cookies. When no one appeared, I rose onto my tiptoes to search the ground, hoping I wouldn't find footprints in the snow or other evidence a creeper had lurked outside my window. "Thank goodness," I whispered when the blanket of untouched snow came into view.

I scratched Cindy behind her pivoting ears, then eased away from the glass while she chattered at the birds.

My phone buzzed as I turned my back on the view, and I jumped.

An unknown number graced the screen.

I pressed the device to my ear with suddenly trembling hands. "Hello?"

"Holly White?" a pert female voice asked.

My shoulders relaxed by a fraction. It wasn't the killer or whoever had threatened me on the red phone downtown. "This is Holly," I said, instantly hoping I hadn't negligently announced myself to a reporter or, worse, another podcaster. I had two too many of those in my life already.

"This is Reese Finn," the woman continued. "I'm a resident care manager at Holiday Glenn. Are you familiar with us?"

I ran her name through my mind and came up empty. I wasn't sure I'd ever heard of Holiday Glenn either. "I don't think so," I admitted. "How can I help you?"

"I'm actually calling for Delores Cutter," she said. "You know Delores?"

"Cookie?" My heart rate doubled at the mention of my friend, and I swept out of my private quarters, locking up as I went. "What's happened? Is she okay?" I mentally tallied the amount of time it would take me to get into town at this time of day, then added another fifteen minutes to get to wherever Reese Finn was calling from. "Where did you say you are?"

"Holiday Glenn," she repeated. "I'm sure Ms. Cutter is fine. I'm calling because she listed you as a personal reference."

I stilled, one hand on my coat hanging in the foyer. "A reference." I let the words settle, but they still made little sense. "For what reason?" Cookie was old enough to do as she pleased and rich enough that few people could stop her.

"She's looking to buy a condo here, but there's a careful selection committee and rigid criteria."

"Oh," I said, returning from somewhere in the atmosphere. "What sort of criteria?"

"For starters, everyone in Holiday Glenn must be over the age of fifty-five."

I smiled, then went to take a seat in my office once more. "I'm confident Cookie meets that requirement."

"Of course," Reese continued. "I'm more concerned about the ages of her companions."

"Who?"

The sounds of shuffling papers carried through the phone. "Theodore and his wife, Clementine."

My eyelids fell shut, and I gave my forehead a rub. Who else could she have meant? I smiled as I answered. "I'm not sure about the ages of Theodore or Clementine." But I was certain Reese had no idea they were both goats.

Reese hummed a long, singular note. "It's so odd," she said eventually. "I'd assumed there was a typo here, but she completed the application by hand. Theodore and his wife's ages are listed as five and six. Each number is obviously missing the second digit."

"Perhaps she got distracted," I suggested. "Then she forgot to finish the numbers."

Reese made another noncommittal but contemplative sound. "She's requesting one of our larger units with extended outdoor space and made several specific notes about yard equipment for her grandchildren."

"Cookie doesn't have any grandchildren," I said before I'd thought better of it.

"This definitely says grandkids. Maybe Theodore and Clementine have some," Reese said, her voice a little frustrated. "Residents at Holiday Glen love seeing younger folks visiting their neighbors, and there's extensive outdoor space to be enjoyed, but it is an age-exclusive environment. I suppose I'll need to confirm these details with Ms. Cutter before I can properly conduct this interview. My apologies for not getting things sorted before reaching out."

"No problem."

We ended the call, and I deflated a little at Cookie's unfortunate situation. She needed a place for her growing, if unconventional, family, and I had a feeling Holiday Glenn wasn't the answer.

I swiveled on my chair in slow circles for a few minutes, then dialed Cookie to see how she was doing.

A few tinny rings later, my call connected. The sounds of jingling bells danced across the line. Then a recording of Cookie's voice began to sing, changing all the lyrics to "Joy to the World."

"We're not around to take your call, we're busy with something else. So leave your name and number. Please leave your name and number," she echoed, lowering her voice an octave. "We'll see it when we get home, and we'll know you phoned. And we'll call you back and say hello. Merry Christmas!"

"It's just me," I said, giggling a bit at her perfectly Cookie message. "Just checking in. Let's talk when you have time. Merry Christmas!"

I disconnected and set the phone on my desk before opening my laptop to check my digital storefront. The jewelry orders were piling up again, so I printed several packing lists and gathered the finished products from my inventory.

I loved how much people enjoyed my jewelry. Melting glass bottles into new things had been a fascination of mine for a long while before I'd realized I could make anything I wanted with the help of a microwave kiln. Soon, I'd created custom molds to replicate the holiday sweets and treats I'd grown up with at the Hearth. Gumdrops and sugar plums, gingerbread men and hot chocolates. I'd added the tiny glass versions to posts for earrings and onto loops for charms. Now, the colorful little delights were a reliable income stream all year round.

When all the new orders were filled and the packages were labeled for shipping, I grabbed my coat and pocketed my phone. Neither Mrs. Snow nor Mr. Moore had come downstairs since I'd obnoxiously barged in on them, and I realized I didn't want to be around when he left. I imagined watching them say goodbye would be incredibly awkward for all of us.

I'd see if I could help Mom with anything at the Hearth since I wasn't needed at the inn. Maybe I could distribute more hot drinks to the protesters or get Mom's feedback on Cookie's housing situation.

My phone rang again as I closed the front door behind me, and I recognized the number at once. Liesel, the gallery manager, was returning my call. I answered with a smile I hoped she'd hear across the line.

"It was great to get your message," she said. "We're low on all your pieces. Please bring anything you want. Your jewelry never stays on our shelves for long."

"I love to hear that." I performed a mental inventory of all the things I still had on hand, then listed the options for Liesel.

"Like I said, whatever you have, I can sell it."

"Then I guess I'll see you tomorrow," I said, feeling my smile grow. "What time is best for you?"

"The earlier the better," she said. "With only a few days until Christmas, and this being a Friday, I'm expecting the crowds to double over the next two days."

"Not a problem," I said. "I'll be there."

Chapter Eighteen

I woke early the next morning, mind swimming with unanswered questions, not the least of which was what to get my husband for our first anniversary. Shopping was the only answer, so I bundled up for a trip into town. With a little luck I'd beat the crowd and have a colossal epiphany or two along the way.

My parents and the Reindeer Games crew were already hard at work as I hurried to my truck. Sidewalks had been cleared and salted outside the inn. Smoke drifted from the chimney at the Hearth, signaling that Mom was preparing for her day, baking for the staff and inn guests. Sounds of machinery in the distance suggested Dad was responsible for my cleared sidewalks and still busily pushing snow from farm roads and pathways, making travel easier for cars and foot traffic when the farm reopened.

The air was crisp and clean outside, the world tucked neatly beneath a blanket of snow. Inside the big red pickup, my breath puffed in little white clouds.

While my heaters warmed the cab, I ran through a mental list of things to accomplish. I only had a couple of hours to spend downtown. Mom needed me back at the farm before lunch to help execute a few reindeer games and announce winners. With the farm reopened, and only six days until Christmas, we were expecting massive crowds, and I needed to take jewelry to Liesel.

I shifted into drive and motored toward the gates, then onto the sparsely occupied main roads. My thoughts wandered to the red cell phone and whoever had planted it so they could threaten me. I wondered if Evan had learned anything from the tech team he'd left the device with, and if he had, would he tell me?

A flicker of lights drew my attention to the rearview mirror and the fast-approaching cruiser. I immediately checked my speed, but I wasn't breaking any law. My muscles tensed and my grip tightened on the wheel. Could the killer somehow acquire a cruiser?

I shook away the silly notion and slowed my pace, then drifted to the edge of the road, allowing the other vehicle to pass. *Not everything is about you, Holly.* I snorted a soft laugh for assuming every emergency had something to do with me.

The cruiser followed me onto the shoulder, slowing as I slowed, then parking behind me when I stopped.

I grabbed my phone and dialed Evan, fully prepared to stomp the gas if he gave the word.

The door on the other vehicle opened, and a tall, broad man in uniform emerged.

My call connected.

"Hey, love," Evan said, now visible in my side-view mirror and striding toward my window.

"Oh, thank my stars." I disconnected and set the phone back onto the seat beside me. "Evan!" I opened the door and climbed out, tossing my arms around him and clinging as if my life depended on it. Clearly, I was more shaken by the week's events than I'd realized. On closer inspection, the cruiser was obviously Evan's. I'd let the fear I so determinedly ignored get the best of me. More than a few memories from the last four holiday seasons had become my ghosts of Christmas past.

"Well, good morning to you too," Evan said, chuckling as he arched his back, lifting me briefly off my feet. "I was on my way to the farm to catch you. I waved when we passed, but you didn't notice, so I pulled a U-turn and tried the flashers." He kissed my head and set my boots back on the ground. He gave me a careful look. "Are you okay? Has something else happened?"

"I'm great," I said. "Just surprised to be pulled over before breakfast."

His brows furrowed. "Why didn't you have breakfast?"

I sighed and deflated against him. "I have a lot on my mind."

"Uh-huh." Evan gripped my shoulders and pushed me back for another long examination. "Like?"

"Our anniversary," I said. *And other things,* I added silently.

His concern turned to care as he held me against him once more. "I promise that no matter what is going on with this murder investigation, on Christmas Eve I'll be with you. Arrangements are already in place. I've made it abundantly clear to everyone at the station that my wife and our anniversary take precedence."

Emotion pricked my eyes. I really had the best possible husband.

And I couldn't even find him a gift.

"Did you just groan?" he asked. "I thought you'd like knowing I won't let this interfere with our anniversary."

"I do," I said quickly. "I love it, and I love you. You're completely wonderful, and I still don't know what to get you."

He grinned, and I lifted a mitten, pointer finger extended inside the knitted wool.

An unexpected laugh broke on my lips, and I lowered my hand. "I've missed you."

"So catch me up," he said. "What have I missed?"

I considered the question a moment, then gasped. My cheeks heated despite the biting wind.

Evan tented his brows. "Is that a blush? You've got my attention for sure now. Do share."

I let my eyelids fall shut a moment as I steeled myself for the story. "I thought I heard an intruder at the inn, so I went upstairs to check it out—" I opened my eyes, lips parted in an embarrassed smile.

Evan scowled. "Why would you do that? Why didn't you call me?"

"Because I wasn't sure which of my guests were there, and I didn't want to alert the authorities if nothing was actually wrong. Anyway—"

"You said you thought there was an intruder," Evan interrupted. He crossed his arms over his chest and put a few inches of space between us. "This is the kind of behavior we talked about."

I bristled and matched his stance. Maybe I wouldn't tell him my story after all.

"You could've asked your dad to check it out," he continued. "What if the killer was up there waiting, drawing you to him?"

"I could've called 911," I said. "Why didn't I do that? I could've brought the calvary to save me from an inn guest who dropped their shampoo bottle in the shower. Instead, I climbed the steps to see what was going on and found zero need for emergency services."

Evan looked at me but said nothing.

I waited.

"Go on," he said begrudgingly.

"You're ruining a good story," I told him. "I was excited to tell it, and now I'm not."

Evan's expression went flat. "Is this related to my investigation in any way?"

"No."

"Holly," he warned.

"I caught Mrs. Snow and Mr. Moore together," I said. I rolled my eyes so he'd know I was still annoyed, even if I was talking.

"What does that mean?"

"It means I broke into her room, prepared to defend her after hearing some soft thuds and a muffled squeal, but I tripped on a pile of their shoes and nearly gave the three of us simultaneous heart attacks."

Evan's brows furrowed. "Their shoes?"

I nodded slowly, and recognition slowly registered in his eyes.

Then he burst into laughter.

"Evan," I scolded. "It's not f—" Before I could finish the sentence, I joined him in raucous giggles. "Stop." I pushed his chest. "It was awful."

"I have no doubt," he agreed, finally straightening himself.

"I was feeling bad for Mr. Moore before that. I'd planned to ask Cookie to help him find friends, but clearly he has at least one."

Evan dragged a heavy hand over his face. "Jeez. Now I have to ask him about this. How on earth am I supposed to do that?" He looked at the bright morning sky. "I'll have to address it with Mrs. Snow too."

I doubled over in fresh laughter.

"Hey," he said. "This is your fault."

I gasped for air as tears rolled from my eyes.

"Go on, keep laughing," Evan said. His green eyes danced with delight. "What made you think Moore was lonely? He's been a part of this town his whole life. Everyone knows him and vice versa."

I sobered, recalling my reasoning. "I stopped by his place to check on him. He didn't answer the door, but there was a blue SUV parked outside." I wasn't sure why I'd mentioned the SUV, but once I'd said it, the image stuck in my head. Who had been there? Why was Moore in the bath while he had company? Did I want to know?

More importantly, why hadn't I taken a picture of the vehicle or plate. I nearly groaned again at the thought.

"You assumed Moore was lonely because he had company when you stopped by his place," Evan said. "Am I missing something?"

I nodded, my mind still wandering over that day. "His living room was covered in old photo albums and letters. They were open on his desk and spread across the floor. I thought it meant he was missing the people who weren't in his life anymore." A sudden, belatedly obvious realization hit like an iceberg. "He was missing her," I said. *Ugh. Of course, he was.* "Seeing her had to be hard after all these years. Then to see her with her son, then to see her grieving her son, and he couldn't do anything to comfort her. He must've felt so miserable and helpless."

"Are you talking about Violet Snow?"

"Yes. He said he loved her while he was doped up after the hospital, and then I found them together at the inn. It would make sense that at least some of the photos and letters I'd seen were from her."

Evan looked in the direction of the tree farm. "Right."

"What did he say when you talked to him?" I asked.

"Nothing." Evan returned his eyes to mine. "He leaned into his bumbling old man facade and told me about all the stuffed squirrels and chipmunks dressed as locals and law enforcement in his living room."

I pressed my lips into a line to squelch another fit of laughter. "The taxidermy was another reason I thought he might need friends."

Evan grunted. "I've got no argument with that logic. And I keep saying this, but you need to leave my murder investigation alone. I've got a solid lead and plenty of help. I want you to enjoy your holiday and clear your evening plans for our anniversary."

I smiled despite myself. "A lead, huh? Do you have a suspect who isn't Mr. Moore?"

"Maybe."

"And you're building a case right now?"

"Yes, so stop poking the bear," he said. "If I can limit the threats made against you to a broken cookie and one angry phone call, I'll call this a holiday miracle," he said. "Frankly, it's all I want for Christmas. Please let this be my gift." He reached around me and opened my truck's door. "For now, you should get out of the cold and run your errands before the crowds converge."

"One more question." I smiled, and Evan frowned. "Have you learned anything about the phone I found?"

He shook his head. "No. Tech services says it's a pay-as-you-go device purchased online with a prepaid Visa. If the buyer used a personal credit card to load up the Visa, we'll have a name, but—"

"If they went to that much trouble, they probably also paid cash for the card," I said, picking up his thought.

"Yes, but all those cards have serial numbers, so tech will figure out which store sold the card. From there, they can contact the store and get a time the receipt was printed." He grinned.

And I took over again. "Then the store can use cameras to see who made the purchase." I rose onto my tiptoes and kissed him, then climbed behind the wheel. "Law enforcement is so interesting."

He whistled and tipped his head in the direction of a box on my passenger seat. I'd used the safety harness to keep it from sliding around as I drove. "Looks like you've been busy."

"I have." I'd completed and packaged all my outstanding jewelry orders over coffee at daybreak. I'd been lucky to have a box large enough to carry them all.

Evan motioned for me to buckle up before he closed my door.

I powered down the window. "I love you."

He planted another kiss on my lips. "Be safe, Gray. I love you too."

I drove away, seeing him in my rearview mirror, hands on hips, shaking his head as he watched me go.

* * *

My usual spot in the alley behind a dumpster was available again, so I angled my truck into the hidey hole and counted my blessings. I looked both ways before climbing out and shouldering the quilted tote bag I'd filled with a curated collection of my jewelry. I beetled to the closest end of the alley, where shoppers had begun to appear, and beeped the doors locked with my fob as I rounded the corner.

Making my way to the gallery was easy with the sidewalks so clear. The square was mostly empty this early in the day, and the gallery was on the next block. The same route would be nearly impassable when I went home, filled with last-minute shoppers and tourists enjoying our adorable town.

I paused to take in the five-story structure lined in twinkle lights and pine greenery. Electric candles flickered in every window, and a series of crimson flags billowed on brass poles near the roof. It truly was a gorgeous building. I couldn't imagine it as it had been originally, filled with kilns and workers. A national paint and wallpaper company had thrived here for decades, transporting goods around the country via the local railroad.

I adjusted the tote bag on my shoulder, then slipped inside.

The lights were bright, gleaming reflectively against the high-polished floor. Creative displays were scattered throughout the space, showcasing the town's many artistic talents and beautiful creations, including a few of my own.

"Good morning," I called, tugging off my mittens and putting them into my pockets.

"Holly?" Liesel popped into view from behind the register. Her brown eyes were wide, her thin brows arched high. "I was just counting bags." She stood with a bewildered grin. "Every November I'm sure I've ordered far too many for the season, then the week before Christmas I'm sure I'll run out! I imagine sending shoppers home with items in their pockets, because I can't get more holiday bags here fast enough."

I laughed. "Well, here are a few more things to put in those bags—or pockets," I teased. I slid the tote from my shoulder and set it on the counter, then unpacked the boxes of earrings, necklaces, rings, and charms. "What do you think?"

Liesel cupped both hands over her ruby-red lips and leaned in for a closer look. "I love these!"

"Thank you."

"You're so incredibly talented. I'm not sure why you still let me sell these here. I know exactly how popular your online shop has become. I might've bought a thing or two for myself in the offseason. Regardless, I'm grateful for the chance to showcase your work." She gathered a stack of boxes and headed for the far wall of shelves. Long dark hair swung against her back as she moved.

I followed close on her heels.

"Liesel," I asked carefully. "I'm sure you heard about what happened at the farm. Did you know the man who died? Ever hear his name or see him around?"

She stilled, then turned back to me, boxes still in hand. "No, but—"

I waited, sensing there was something of interest to me still on her tongue. When I thought she'd changed her mind about whatever she'd planned to say, she performed a long sigh.

"I shouldn't be saying anything," she said. "I don't want to get involved in this thing. And you shouldn't be asking about him. You know what happens when you start down these paths."

I bristled. "I'm only asking," I said as breezily as possible, "because it was a shock to my family and me, and I'm trying to process. How could a man who'd only spent one night in this town be killed before dawn? It doesn't make sense. Someone had to know him and be upset about something. It makes me wonder if he'd been here before, maybe meeting with other businessmen or checking out the town." He might've even had online meetings, video conferences, or any other sort of interactions, I realized as I spoke. Whoever killed Mr. Snow didn't necessarily have to meet him in person before that awful night. And that was devastating to my investigation, because anyone with the internet and an interest in Snow's plans to turn our historic downtown into a cash cow of micro rentals could join my suspect list. And anyone who was staunchly against it as well.

"Oof." The sound left my lips in a rush of air.

Liesel looked at the front door, her gaze wandering across the shop window and the increasing number of passersby. "Okay." She rubbed her hand against one eyebrow, then tipped her head toward the register. "Let's talk."

I trailed her back to the countertop and folded my hands in an attempt to look less frantic than I felt.

She put my jewelry back on the counter. "Snow stopped by once or twice last summer."

I gasped, and Liesel's eyes widened.

"Sorry." I cleared my throat. "Please, go on."

"The first time he came to the gallery, he was with Orrville Lincoln and Mr. Weible," Liesel said. "Weible and Lincoln have been friends for years. They were telling Mr. Snow all about the building's structure and history. Mr. Lincoln loves those details. He works for the Historical Society, and Weible has worked on half the historical structures in town, plus he lives here, so they really geek out about this stuff, you know?"

I nodded. The vast majority of folks in Mistletoe lived here because they loved the historical aspects and town-wide fervor to protect the past. The older I got, the more I connected with those feelings and goals.

The new information caused another set of questions, however.

Had Elijah lied to his mother about never being in Mistletoe before their arrival this week? Or had they both lied to me for some reason I couldn't yet understand?

A bout of laughter pulled my gaze to the shop window, where a group in Victorian attire bustled past. I couldn't imagine living anywhere else, but I'd met plenty of people over the years who felt differently.

Liesel watched me expectantly. "Anything else?"

So much else, I thought. "Did Mr. Snow seem interested in the information about the building's historical significance?" I asked.

Liesel barked an ugly laugh. "Not even a little. He was focused on how many individual shops, condos, or tourist rentals this building could support and how much it'd cost him to create the new spaces. He even tried pitching the concept of a family pizza and games center like Chuck E. Cheese or Dave & Buster's, except Christmas themed. I could practically see the other men's eyes gloss over. He had a clipboard with a list of all the shops in town and was trying to think of what was missing and how to capitalize. Everything was about the money to him," she said. "And time, but then he pointed out that time is also money, so—"

I wrinkled my nose. "Wow."

"Yeah." She nodded. "And that guy was a liar. He probably didn't deserve what happened to him, but I wasn't exactly shocked when news of his demise made it to the gallery."

I clenched my teeth to stop myself from gasping again.

"Sorry." Liesel appeared remorseful when her eyes met mine. "That was really mean," she said. "I get carried away. I love this town, and I think life is about more than money. The way he walked around, nose in the air, scowling at everything because it wasn't shiny and new . . . well . . . it peeved me off."

I forced a small smile at the self-deprecation in her tone and the softening of her features. "I get it," I said. "Trust me, when it comes to defending this place, I'm the queen of carried away."

"It's strange that he's dead," she said. "He was the kind of guy you'd expect to grow old yelling at kids to get away from his sports car. A modern-day Ebenezer Scrooge."

He'd seemed uptight when we met, but I hadn't known him long enough to agree or disagree with her conclusion, and something she'd said earlier circled back to mind. "Did you say Elijah was a liar?" I asked. I was sure she'd said it, but she hadn't explained the reasoning behind the accusation.

Liesel's expression pinched and her lips flattened. "Maybe it doesn't matter in the big scheme of things, but he said he was buying us out, and that wasn't true. It turned out to be Hamish Hunter, that billionaire on the hill, who was actually buying. That guy probably spends less than a week in Mistletoe all year long. I did some research on him, and I think he only keeps his offices here because of a big tax break he negotiated before I was born, when the town wasn't as well known and heavily visited. The mayor gave folks like him major financial incentives to set up their companies in town. The initiative was supposed to bring commerce to the area, and most of the new businesses did, but not Hunter's. He went remote from the start. Even before the internet, he hired workers around the country and used teleconferences for communication. He's never set up a proper, populated office as the deal intended. Nothing in the paperwork specified otherwise, probably because remote work wasn't common then. The joke was on the old mayor, I guess."

"And the town," I said. I could only imagine the amount of tax breaks a company making billions might receive. What did a billion dollars even look like? The concept was too foreign to be real. Somewhere beyond a million, my mind equated everything to Monopoly money, or something equally abstract.

Liesel's cheeks appeared redder than they had a moment before. Her jaw tightened as she peered through the window, apparently lost in thought. "I just wish an art gallery fit their new vision for the space."

My eyes widened in shock. "The gallery is closing?"

"It was," she said. "I don't know about now. Mr. Snow seemed to be the idea man, and Mr. Hunter was the money. I'm thinking of contacting all the artists who show their work here. Maybe if I can prove the gallery is an asset and major attraction to the community, it can stay. It doesn't make as much money as other stores, but art is important. It's part of who we are in this town. Without the gallery, I'll be heartbroken and out of a job."

The little bells over her shop door jingled, and a group of women moved inside, dusting snow from their hats and shoulders.

Liesel leaned in my direction and gave me another apologetic look. "I am sorry about what I said earlier," she whispered. "It wasn't kind, and I didn't mean it. I just get all riled up over what went on, and honestly, Snow had the personality of a rock. An incredibly pretentious rock," she amended. "Anyway, I'd better go." She shot the women a welcoming smile, then her eyes locked back on mine. "For what it's worth, you should know I'm well aware of what you're up to. The whole town knows what happens when someone dies the way Snow did. I think you'd be wise to let this one go before you get hurt."

I leaned back, the flash of heat in her eyes raising my internal temperature several degrees.

"I'll see you later," she said, then glided toward the shoppers without a backward glance.

Chapter Nineteen

Traffic outside the farm was backed up for a mile. I took a detour to our private entrance at my first opportunity, bypassing a half-dozen tour buses and countless family vehicles in the process. From there, I parked outside my parents' farmhouse and walked across the property to the Hearth, where I was officially late to start the Reindeer Games.

I made it within a few dozen yards of my destination when a low wall of snow came into view. I stopped short to ponder the purpose of this new creation. A familiar figure straightened from a crouch as I approached. "Dad?"

My father wiped the back of one glove across his forehead, nudging his hat up by an inch. "Hey, Holly. What do you think?" he asked, readjusting his knit cap.

"I like it," I said. "What is it?" I vaguely recalled hearing the sounds of machinery when I'd left this morning, but I'd assumed he was plowing.

"It's a snow maze for the kiddos." He opened his arms like a six-foot gameshow host. "We moved all the excess snow from the roads and paths into one place, then the guys and I sculpted this. We're etching lines in the walls now to make it appear to be made of big ice blocks. What do you think?"

I walked closer to the chest-high attraction. "Holy holly berries. This isn't a kiddie maze. This is a whole pint-sized labyrinth." Dozens of dead ends and sharp turns filled the space that was nearly a quarter football field in size. The paths were neatly arranged with two entrances at opposite corners, but any savvy kid could easily climb out if they couldn't find their way. "How long was I gone?"

He chuckled. "It wasn't as hard as you'd think. Your mom helped me draw up the plans and mark the ground where the walls would go. The crew and I moved the bulk of the snow yesterday, and we stacked and shaped the snow this morning after feeding the horses."

"Oh, is that all?" I asked, nudging him with my elbow. "You're kind of amazing. You know that?"

"I'm just out here keeping your mother happy." He grinned.

I hugged him. "Kids are going to love this."

"Fingers crossed. I overestimated the amount we'd need, so the excess is over there."

I followed his gaze to an eight-foot mound of snow, then looked back to Dad. "I'll have to give the maze a try later. I'm behind schedule at the moment. I promised Mom I'd lead the outdoor games today."

Dad patted my beanie. "You'd better get going. No need to make her wait or worry."

"Absolutely right." I paused, attention returning to the big hill of snow. "Dad, I might have an idea for a new reindeer game."

His brows rose, and I filled him in on the concept. "I love it," he said. "The crew and I can have things set up inside an hour."

"Perfect! Thank you!"

I turned back in the direction I'd been headed, waving to the farmhands when they came into view, determinedly etching lines into the snow as Dad had been. A walk through an adult-sized snow maze would be a lot of fun, and Evan would be the first to try to beat me through it. Unfortunately, we'd need a lot more snow for construction of something that big.

A row of rectangular folding tables stood outside the café. Each wore a thick red and white checked cloth stacked with cooking supplies. A faceless bust wearing a red chef's hat was piled high with aprons. My childhood karaoke machine was plugged into an exterior outlet by a fifty-foot orange extension cord. The giant foam core board leaning against the tables had four large words stenciled on it: "Great Blizzard Bake-Off."

Waving to the cluster of guests milling around the area, I lifted the microphone on my old karaoke machine and powered the device on. "Merry Christmas!" I called.

The gathering crowd returned my greeting.

A moment later, Mom's face appeared in the nearest Hearth window. She smiled brightly, then mouthed the words *thank you.* I formed half a heart with my free hand, and she raised curved fingers into view, forming the other half of my heart.

Several guests took notice and giggled and murmured a round of *aws*.

"My name is Holly," I said, "and I'm so glad you're here. There's nothing my family and this place love more than some reindeer games, and today we're packing in a bunch. If you have time, I hope you'll stick around and play a few. For now . . ." I paused briefly for dramatic effect. "Welcome to the Great Blizzard Bake-Off!" I dragged the final words out like a sportscaster, then raised my mic in the air and cheered.

I waited for the crowd to settle before I began my overview. "The first thing you want to do is break up into teams of two and grab one of everything from the tables," I instructed. "The supplies are stacked together, but they don't have to match or coordinate. Everyone gets an apron, one cookie sheet, a tray with spray bottles, and a snowball maker—that's the one that looks like a giant melon baller," I explained. "Also, one set of cookie cutters, a spatula, and a bowl of berries and greenery per team. Then line up in pairs when you have all your baking supplies."

I pressed "Play" on my ancient CD player while a swarm of family members, friends, and farm guests gathered their supplies. Holiday tunes lifted into the air, and my head began to rock along.

Shoppers from Santa's Village noticed the commotion and made their way in our direction. Rosy-cheeked newcomers snacked on candied nuts and kettle corn as the players settled into a row.

"Okay," I called into the mic, lowering the music volume by a smidge. "Decide who will be team member one and team member two. Rock, paper, scissors works well for this if you aren't good at making decisions."

The players chuckled, consulted, then put their eyes back on me.

"Great! Team member ones, line up here." I motioned to the general area in front of me. "Team member twos, stand in front of your partner, about ten feet away." I took three giant strides, then stopped. "Over here."

I waited for the partners to line up. "Perfect! Now, each team needs to make one dozen holiday snow cookies. The first team finished wins, but every cookie has to go through the following steps. First, team member ones"—I spun to face the other line of contestants—"use the snowball roller to gather snow into balls and deposit those onto the tray. Flatten the balls, then use one of the cookie cutters to shape the snow. When the tray is full, slide it across the snow to your partner. Don't worry, the snow between you will get smoother and slicker with each pass of the trays, and I'm guessing you'll need to repeat the process three or four times to make a dozen completed and unbroken cookies. Any questions?"

I scanned the players and the onlooking crowd. No one voiced any concerns, so I moved on.

"Team member twos," I said, spinning back to look at the other group, "when you receive the tray, you need to decorate the cookies with the spray bottles you were given. Each is filled with environmentally friendly, animal-safe, colored water. Spray the cookies with one or more of the colors, then add the sprinkles. Those are the leaves, nuts, and berries in the bowls. Finally, you need to remove the cookies from the tray, using the spatula. Don't let them break, or they won't count," I warned. "Then slide the tray back to your teammate so they can make more cookies. In the event more than one team finishes at the same time, the crowd will judge both teams' cookies by attractiveness, so speed isn't the only goal here. Any questions?"

The teams chattered and laughed. The crowd whistled and called out words of encouragement.

"Everyone playing will receive a coupon for a complimentary hot drink from the Hearth when we finish. There are several kinds of hot chocolates, ciders, teas, and coffees, so be sure to check them out. The winning team will receive two baskets of fresh baked goodies and two gift certificates for the café. Now," I said, dragging my gaze over the players, one by one, "are you ready to play the Great Blizzard Bake-Off?"

Everyone cheered, and I yelled, "Begin!"

The row of adults before me dropped onto their knees and began gathering snowballs.

I scanned the crowd for signs of familiar faces, giving each a friendly wave. I didn't notice any of my inn guests or Mr. Moore.

The sounds of sliding cookie trays on snow pulled my eyes back to the Bake-Off. Players on the opposite side of the game board crawled rapidly to where their tray had stopped, then dragged it back to begin decorating. A squirt of red, a spray of green, a dash of nuts and berries.

Cookies were levered off the trays, often crumbling and breaking midair. Sounds of disappointment rolled over the players and crowd.

Then—*whoosh!*—the empty trays skated back to where they'd begun.

Each team had two surviving cookies at the end of round one and a lot of advice being shouted from the crowd.

I pumped up the music when the opening notes to "Jingle Bell Rock" began, and I made a show of shimmying my shoulders as I mouthed the words. I'd leave the actual karaoke to Cookie, but pretending to dance and sing was a whole lot of fun.

When team four proved victorious several minutes later, I delivered coupons to the other players and certificates for goodie baskets to the winners.

"Thank you all so much for playing and for watching the Great Blizzard Bake-Off! I'll see you all near the stables in about thirty minutes for the annual Blindfolded Sledding Challenge!"

I powered off the karaoke machine and set the mic back on the cradle. In the following silence, my favorite voice drifted to my ears. I smiled as I turned in his direction.

Evan's words were muffled when he spoke again, and I followed the sound to the newly erected fence outside the recent murder scene.

"Evan?" I asked, shuffling through thick, untraveled snow.

He stepped into view before I reached the fence. "Hey," he said, pulling me into a short embrace. "I heard the commotion over there. Sounded like I missed a good game."

"You did," I agreed. "But have you seen the kiddie snow maze Dad built?" I made an obnoxiously excited face. "Am I ten years old, or is that the coolest thing ever?"

"It's pretty cool," he said, nodding. "Care to see if we can find our way out later?"

I beamed. "You are my favorite person ever. I absolutely want to try to the maze with you."

He pressed a kiss against my forehead and squeezed me once more.

"I'm glad you're in a good mood," I said, "because I'm about to ask what you're doing behind the fence, who you were talking to, and where they went."

He rolled his eyes. "Your dad called me. One of his crew members noticed a lot of footprints around the pole barn where the cookie had been stored the night Mr. Snow was killed. I came to check it out, and I've been here ever since. I was probably on another call when you heard me."

"Do you think the killer was looking for evidence accidentally left behind?" I guessed. "Or maybe it was a podcaster in search of a story? Assuming the two aren't one and the same," I grumbled.

Evan made a sour face. "Did you have any luck in town?"

I opened my mouth to complain about his graceless change of subject, then froze, recalling exactly what I'd done in town versus what I'd said I was going to do. Maybe he already knew I hadn't actually shopped for his gift, as I'd planned. I'd spoken at length to Liesel about Elijah instead. And in the end, I might've added her to my suspect list. She'd be at the bottom, but she had admitted to meeting him before his death, and she wasn't shy about the fact she didn't like him. Was it reason enough to kill?

I'd purchased a large hot chocolate and a slice of pie after that to help me mull things over. All I got from the effort was a sugar buzz.

"Holly?" Evan prompted. "Shopping?"

"Oh." I refreshed my smile. "No luck. I dropped some of my jewelry off at the gallery then stopped at the post office and pie shop before heading home."

He hooked an arm around my shoulders and drew me back to him, then set his chin atop my head. "You really don't have to buy me anything. I know this time of year is madness for you and your family, and basically everyone in town, maybe in the world."

I wrapped my arms around his middle and squeezed him with my appreciation.

Liesel's frustrated face returned to my mind's eye. Was there a possibility that she'd lashed out at Elijah Snow? Could she have sought him out to give him a piece of her mind, and things got out of control?

"Um, hon," I said, mentally cursing my voice when it cracked, "what did you say the coroner determined to be Elijah Snow's time of death?"

My cheek bounced against Evan's chest as he performed a low, unnatural chuckle.

"I didn't say."

I pulled back and tipped my chin, daring a look into his steely green eyes. "Would you like to?"

"No."

I sighed and dropped my hands to my sides. "No fun." I checked the time on my watch and smiled. "I've got to go lead the Blindfolded Sledding Challenge. Do you want to play?"

"Yes, but I'm on the clock," he said. "I'll walk with you, though. I got a call from Libby right before you showed up. She said someone stole over a thousand cookies from your mother."

"That's right," I said, baffled. Somehow, I'd completely forgotten to tell Evan.

"You knew." He stopped moving. "When did this happen? And why didn't you tell me?"

I shrugged. "Mom didn't seem to care, so I just put it in the back of my mind until—"

"Until?" he asked, nearly growling the word.

"Until I got back to the inn last night and realized someone took all the donated toys and gift wrap from my office too."

A little swirl of smoke seemed to lift from my husband's head. It might've been from my breath on the cold air as I spoke, but I was pretty sure it was smoke.

He schooled his darkened features, and a vein began to throb on his forehead.

I wrinkled my nose. "I planned to tell you last night, but then I heard the noise upstairs, and you know how that went. Afterward, my brain was useless. I worked on orders and went to visit Mom. Then you didn't sleep at the inn." I bit my lip, realizing I'd treaded on yet another sore subject.

"This is one more reason we need to sell the house," he said. "We should be living together." He shoved his hands into his pockets the way he did when trying to rein in his temper or regain composure.

"I'm sorry." I meant it to my core.

"I know." He met my gaze with quiet resolve. "I'm not mad at you. I'm frustrated with our situation, but then I feel guilty for being upset about having too many places to live when so many people don't have anywhere to live." He huffed a sharp breath and removed his hat to run his fingers through his hair. "I don't want to live in two places like some set of estranged billionaire spouses. I want to live together like the regular, perfectly average, run-of-the-mill married people we are."

"Me too." In truth, nothing about my husband was average, but I knew what he was trying to say, so I kept the thought to myself. "I promise we'll figure things out after Christmas, which is only six days away. We're almost there." His mention of the word *billionaire* brought Hamish Hunter to mind, but it wasn't a good time to mention that. For now, I wrapped one arm around Evan's back and let him walk me to the next reindeer game.

Chapter Twenty

Two hours later, my nose was frozen, my fingers were numb inside my mittens, and I was finally starting the last of the outdoor reindeer games. The sun was low in the sky, casting gorgeous golden and apricot light over the glistening snow, and the farm had come alive with endless strings of twinkle lights. Chasing bulbs outlined the café and other buildings on our property. Icicle lights hung from the wooden perimeter fence and on the branches of trees. Massive colored bulbs danced to music in the sixty-foot spruce near our gate. Our farm was beautiful by day, but this time of year, when twilight arrived, the property became a winter wonderland.

I increased my pace as I carried the last of our black rubber inner tubes to the pile of snow Dad and his farmhands had left over after building the maze. They'd spent the previous two hours packing and smoothing the mountain into a wide, flat slide with steps carved out on the backside for climbing.

The final outdoor game of the night would be a fast one. Literally.

"Okay," I yelled, projecting my voice above the din of chatter. I was too far from an outlet to use my mic, but everyone quieted to wait for instructions. "I've got a pocket full of coupons for free hot apple cider and warm, old-fashioned donuts at the Hearth. All you have to do is carry a tube to the top of Mt. St. Christmas over there, have a seat, then coast down. The catch is you have to grab one of these inflatable gingerbread men on your way." I pointed to the minefield of toys I'd arranged on the snow moments before. One strong wind would send them all into town, so we needed to move quickly and hope the breeze stayed away. "If you catch a gingerbread man, bring him to me, and we'll trade for a coupon. One per player, until all the gingerbread men have been captured, but you can try as many times as you're willing. Ready?"

A mass of adults and children headed around the backside of the mountain, inner tubes in hand.

I waited until the first face became visible at the top. "On your marks!"

One woman struggled to still her ride, then fell on top while trying to mount the tube.

Swoosh!

"I guess, Go!" I called, laughing as a woman in her forties spun wildly down the mountain and into the snow, a casualty to gravity. Her arms pinwheeled, trying to regain control, her boots in the air, body only partially on the tube.

She screamed as the speed increased with her struggle.

"Use your feet to stop!" A man called seconds before she collided with a mound of loosely packed snow fifty yards away. A smart safety addition by my troubleshooting dad.

She rolled off the tube with snow caked to her hat and cheeks. It took several steps before she got her land legs back, but she laughed all the way back, to try again.

"Next year we should add cameras like the ones at amusement parks," I said.

One by one, the sledders shot down the mountain, some with arms and smiles wide, leaning in the direction of my plastic cookie men. Others covered their eyes and screamed, intimidated by the wild, out-of-control experience.

I jumped to safety repeatedly as child sledders hit the smallest bumps and catapulted from their tube, rolling to stops in fits of giggles.

Snow flew and joy-filled screams cracked the air until all the inflatable gingerbread men were captured and all my coupons were gone. I stacked the tubes on a pole to stop them from sliding or blowing away, then tucked the last of the inflatable cookies into a mesh bag and headed for the Hearth.

Mr. Weible raised a toddler in a pink snowsuit onto his shoulders and held her legs against his chest for safety. A woman several years younger than me walked along at his side.

"Mr. Weible!" I called, unable to help myself. He was clearly having a nice family outing, but I'd never been one to let opportunity pass me by.

"Oh, hello, Holly," he said, looking a bit fatigued.

I hoped the expression was a result of chasing the kid and not due to my sudden presence.

"Hello," I said, making brief eye contact with each of the three people before me. "It's good to see you. Are you just getting started, or have you been here long enough to take a sleigh ride and play a game or two?" I asked. "The Hearth has some indoor games going on later, and the cookies are pure magic." I grinned at the little girl on his shoulders, then the woman I presumed to be her mother.

"I'm Natalia," the woman said. "This is my daughter, Anna, and you know Dad."

"Apologies," Mr. Weible said. "I assumed you'd met before."

"Nope," I said. "But it's nice to meet you, Natalia and Anna." The family looked alike, each with a pleasant round face, small features, and matching brown eyes.

Mr. Weible wore a black wool coat and jeans. Mother and daughter wore puffy white ski coats and yoga pants. They looked like the kind of family featured in ads for local shops and outdoor experiences.

"We've been here for hours," Natalia said. She pushed a lock of thick raven hair away from her cheek, and I felt a pang of envy because of my own mousy-brown hair. "I think we've done everything twice. It's a wonderful place. My parents brought me here every year when I was small. Sadly, this is the first we've brought Anna, but it won't be the last."

I smiled, but a little voice in my head wondered how many hours, precisely, they'd been at the farm. Had they been there long enough for Mr. Weible to make footprints in the snow around the crime scene?

Anna wiggled on Mr. Weible's shoulders, attempting to get back into the snow.

He set her down and took her hand. "I think we'd better keep moving. Someone's getting tired."

Natalia offered an apologetic smile. "We bow to the demands of the princess. Do you want to meet me at the car?" she asked her dad. "I'm going to stop at the café for a box of holiday cookies." She looked to me. "I don't have the time, patience, or skill to come close to the things made in there, and we're hosting a holiday event tomorrow night."

"Wonderful!" I said a bit too enthusiastically. "I was just headed that way. I'll walk with you."

Mr. Weible lifted a hand, then let his granddaughter lead him away.

Natalia and I headed for the Hearth.

"It's nice that you were able to spend all day here with your daughter and your dad," I said. "That must feel incredibly nostalgic."

"It does," she agreed. "Anna wasn't old enough to really participate in the activities before this year, but she had an incredible time. I knew she would. And we ran into a lot of friends we don't usually have time to visit with, like other teachers from my school, with their families; old neighbors I haven't seen since I moved; and lots of exhausted mom friends." She laughed. "We even saw Liesel and Orrville. It was fun."

"Orrville Lincoln?" I asked, recalling how deftly the man had blown me off outside the Historical Society.

"Mm-hmm." She paced herself beside me, eyes on the prize as we neared the café. "Do you know him?"

"Kind of," I said, weighing my words. I knew Orrville Lincoln because he was on my suspect list, just like her father.

"So you grew up here? That must've been amazing."

I laughed. "It really was. I run the inn now, and my folks have a home on the property, so I still see them every day. Do you and Anna get to see your dad often?"

"As often as we can," she said. "I teach full time at the elementary school, and Dad—well, he's retired, but he never stops moving. I think he's as involved in town events and projects as he was while I was growing up. Maybe more since he doesn't have to punch a time clock these days."

"I can imagine," I said, chuckling lightly at her mystified expression. "I had coffee with him this week. He turned me on to Cup of Cheer. It's fabulous if you haven't been there. Anna would love it. He mentioned being with you guys last Friday night."

Her steps faltered, and she released a long, low, humorless laugh before suddenly picking up her pace. "So that's what this is about," she mused. "I guess it's true. When Holly White takes an interest in you, it's probably because she thinks you're a murderer."

"What?"

She stopped so suddenly that I nearly walked past. "You know exactly what I mean. The whole town knows exactly what I mean. Thanks to that obnoxious podcast, the whole country knows what I mean."

I frowned. "I don't think you killed anyone. If you're referencing *Dead and Berried*, I am not a fan of that show, and I'm just making small talk."

"About me and my dad," she said. "The kind where you want to know if we have alibis for the night of a murder. Just because we hated Elijah Snow doesn't mean we killed him."

"You hated Mr. Snow?" I asked. The words broke from my lips the moment they reached my mind. "Why?"

"Oh, I don't know," she said. "Maybe because he wanted to turn my childhood home into a bunch of cheap rental units and destroy the history and beauty in everything for the sake of making a few dollars. He and his partner, Hamish Hunter, undercut the value of the place and offered my dad a tiny portion of its true worth without telling him the whole story." She crossed her arms and shook her head at me, disappointed. "Dad tries not to complain about the deal he was cut, but he's a retired electrician, not a Rockefeller, and after losing Mom this year, I wanted a big win for him, not a deal that was merely adequate."

I bit my lip, not realizing Mr. Weible's wife had died so recently or that poor Natalia had said goodbye to her mother. "I'm so sorry for your loss."

She raised a palm to stop me, eyes misting with emotion. "Don't. Just know my mom's medical bills are astronomical because my parents did everything they could for as long as they could to beat her disease. He'll die still paying that debt, which is why he even considered selling the building, and he was thankful to be given the right to stay there as long as he wanted, regardless of what they did to the rest of the space. But no one told him they were considering adding bars, family game locations, and a half dozen other things that will cause continuous traffic in the hallways and noise until two in the morning most nights. My dad isn't a twenty-something frat boy. He's in his pajamas before I typically eat dinner. The money Dad agreed on seemed fair based on the limited and skewed information he was given and the awful financial position he's been in for years. Those investors did him dirty, but he's not a killer."

I hated everything she said. Losing a spouse and parent. Being so strapped for money that as a result he was forced to sell a property that meant so much to him. Then learning he'd been somewhat hoodwinked. All terrible. Then a sliver of hope rose into mind. "If the deal isn't final," I said, "maybe it's not too late to negotiate for more."

A look of exhaustion crossed Natalia's pretty face. "Guys like Snow and Hunter think money is all that matters, and they get away with everything because they can buy people's silence."

My mouth opened, then closed. Nothing she'd said was expected, and this was the second perfectly nice woman to turn on me for no reason. She and Liesel would have plenty to talk about if they ever got together. Apparently, neither were fans of Snow, Hunter—*or me.*

"And to answer your question," she continued, "yes, Dad was with me on the night of the murder. He read a book and sang his granddaughter to sleep, then stayed for a glass of wine with my husband and me. It was a lovely moment and memory until you tainted it." She rolled her eyes and turned away, heading for her dad and daughter in the distance instead of to the Hearth as planned.

Mr. Weible loaded Anna into a white minivan parked in our lot.

I wasn't sure when preschoolers went to bed, or the exact time of Mr. Snow's death, but I guessed they were hours apart. The farm had been open until nine, and Dad made his rounds at ten. The killer had had the rest of the night to drive over and confront the victim.

My conversation with Natalia didn't remove her dad as a suspect, as I'd hoped, but after hearing her rant, I considered adding her to the growing list.

Chapter Twenty-One

The next night, I scootched into my favorite booth at the Hearth, already occupied by Ray and Libby. Most of the other seats were full, and Mom's friends were waiting tables.

On the small makeshift stage in one corner, Cookie pranced, mic in hand. She wore a headband with stuffed reindeer antlers, a red clown's nose, and a crimson velvet dress trimmed in white faux fur. The introductory notes to "Winter Wonderland" began, and she sang along in her most British of accents.

Ray hummed along to the tune, tapping thin fingers against a mostly empty mug of hot chocolate before him.

Libby watched Cookie in pure delight. "This will never get old. I don't care if I live here until I'm eighty. What was I even doing with my life in Boston when I could've watched a white-haired lady, tipsy on forty-proof tea, dress like a cross between Rudolph and Mrs. Claus while singing Christmas karaoke?"

I snorted a laugh, remembering how hard Libby had tried to dislike our arguably quirky little hamlet. She'd thought her brother was bonkers for wanting to live here, and now look at her. Delighted by Cookie doing Cookie things. "How'd you get the night off?" I asked. Typically, it was all hands on deck so close to Christmas.

She looked at Ray and grinned before returning her attention to me with a smirk. "I asked nicely." Her Boston accent seemed to cling to the words, something that always happened when she was being smug. Or mischievous. Which was often.

Cookie's suggestion that Libby and Ray had been acting hinky returned to me, and I narrowed my eyes, attempting to pluck the full version of Libby's answer from her mind. Why had she asked for the night off? Did she just feel like a date night? Or was there more she didn't want to say? If so, what was it? And why couldn't I know?

Her smile grew. She locked her arm with Ray's and scooted closer to him. "What do you think of our sweatshirts? They were a gift from his mother."

It took a moment for my brain to switch gears. Then I noticed the coordinating hoodies. Hers was cream with a small female elf embroidered over the left pocket. The figure wore red and white striped tights beneath a flared miniskirt with scarlet crinoline peeking out at the bottom. She held a candy cane to her open-lipped smile and flirtatiously peered over one shoulder. Ray's shirt was maroon with a male elf embroidered over his right pocket. The way the two were seated, their elves were mere inches apart, and Ray's elf had wide, appreciative eyes turned her way, clearly enjoying the view.

"Those are completely adorable," I said on a laugh. "Incredible, really. Where can I get one?"

"Ray's mom made them," Libby said, lifting her mug to her lips for a sip. Scents of peppermint floated on the air to my nose, and my mouth watered. "She got a cool new sewing machine that does any kind of stitching and embroidery you want. All she needs is an image to download."

"Impressive." I still struggled to reattach fallen buttons, but who was I to hate? "She could make a fortune selling those online, or in town."

"Probably," Ray agreed. "She'd hoped to be here tonight, but she's packing for her trip."

Ray's mom had remarried two years ago at Christmastime, and she and her husband took an annual vacation every December to commemorate the event. Usually someplace warm.

I thought of the lovely seaside town where Evan and I had spent a week drinking iced teas and learning about the long, enchanting history of another charming place. Which reminded me I still needed to choose an anniversary gift for him, and time was running out.

"What happened?" Ray asked. "You were smiling. Now you look like someone stole your puppy."

"Kicked her puppy," Libby corrected.

He turned to her, an expression of horror on his handsome face. "Who would kick a puppy?"

"That's the expression."

He continued to appear aghast. "Why would you even think of that?"

She flattened her shiny red lips. "Watch it, Griggs."

The room exploded into applause, and Cookie took a bow. "Thank you," she said into the mic. "That's very nice of you. I hope you'll all stick around for a pint of hot cocoa or cider. And a cookie or two. Don't rush off before Holiday Bingo begins. Cards and markers are coming around now," she added, drifting into Oliver Twist territory with the accent. "I'll call a number and you mark it with a peppermint, then Bob's your uncle, ay?"

Libby cracked up.

Ray and I followed suit.

"One more song for the road!" Cookie changed the music, and my skin pebbled in goose bumps as "Santa Claus Is Coming to Town" began. I saw the red cell phone on the bench in my mind's eye, heard the familiar lyrics warning children that Santa saw them when they were sleeping and awake. Then I heard the raspy whisper telling me I was going to get hurt if I didn't leave this murder investigation alone.

Mom arrived at our booth with a tray of bingo supplies and a bright "Merry Christmas" welcome.

I nearly jumped out of my skin.

Mom and my tablemates looked at me while she doled out bingo cards and set a bowl of red-and-white-striped peppermints at the table's center. "Can I get you all something to eat or drink? Everything okay, Holly?"

I nodded.

"I'd love more tea," Libby said.

Ray downed the dregs of his cocoa and smiled. "Yes, please."

"One tea and another hot chocolate," Mom said. She swung her gaze to mine. "How about you, sweetie? What'll it be?"

"Cider sounds amazing," I said. "And snickerdoodles."

"Easy-peasy, anything else?" She scrutinized me, but I looked at Ray.

"Maybe a cookie assortment for the table," he said. "Cutouts, whoopie pies, wedding cookies, thumbprints . . ." His pupils widened, and his voice grew a little breathy. "Peanut butter blossoms."

"Okay, that's enough," Libby said. She snapped her fingers in front of his face. "Come back to earth, you little sugar fiend."

Mom giggled, patted the table, and moved away.

"She's going to bring the cookies, though?" Ray asked.

"Yes," Libby assured. "Have a mint while you wait."

I smiled as she passed him a piece of candy. "I heard a little rumor that you two are up to something," I said, hoping to trick them into spilling whatever beans they had canned.

The couple's eyes met, then snapped to mine.

"What do you mean?" Ray asked.

Libby pressed her elbow against his ribs.

"Ow."

I raised my brows. "Anything you want to share with your dearest friend? Or do I have to hear it on the street like a commoner?"

"We aren't up to anything," Libby said. "We're just happy."

"Speaking of happy couples," Ray said, popping the mint into his mouth, "have you decided what to get Evan for your anniversary?"

I eased back in my seat. "No, but I'm wide open to ideas. Maybe your mom could make him a sweatshirt."

Ray looked unimpressed.

"It's better than showing up empty-handed," Libby said. "Especially considering what he's doing for you."

My jaw dropped. "What's he giving me?"

Her smirk returned. "You've got a few more days to wait and see."

"Mean," I said.

"Yeah," she agreed. "Feels good. Feels right."

Ray laughed.

Feedback from the microphone quieted the room. Then the sound of bouncing bingo balls inside the spinning cage started the excitement again.

"All righty," Cookie called, "we're playing a traditional round first. One straight row. Up and down, side to side, or corner to corner. Don't forget to cover your free space. Here we go!"

Ray, Libby, and I placed peppermints onto the center space marked "Free."

"B-11," Cookie said.

Libby and I covered the spots on our cards. Ray crunched his mint and reached for another.

"Have you heard anything more about Cookie's quest to find new housing?" I asked, recalling the woman who'd phoned from Holiday Glenn, the fifty-five-and-over community. "Someone called me for a reference, but I don't think she knows Theodore is a goat."

"He's not a goat," Ray said. "He's family."

"Right," I agreed, "but even if Cookie gets approved for that place, they'll take the offer back as soon as she pulls up with a livestock trailer."

Libby watched Cookie as she called another number. "It's too bad Theodore's wife has to live with them. Not all couples do that, I hear."

"Hey," I said. "Let's keep this friendly."

She grinned.

"I've been thinking about what Gertie said the other day when Cookie mentioned needing a new place. Gertie said Cookie belonged here. I think she was right." Though I wasn't sure how Gertie knew. "There's plenty of room on the farm for Theodore, his wife, and as many kids as they want. I'm just not sure where Cookie would live."

Ray unwrapped another mint. His attention fixed on Cookie. "She's pretty attached. I think she'd be sad without him."

Mom returned with our drinks and cookies.

We thanked her and dug in.

A few minutes and several bingo calls later, Libby dusted crumbs from her lips and sighed. "So good."

Ray's eyelids fluttered as he bit into a whoopie pie. "Yes."

Libby's lips quirked up one side in response to her being entertained by her goofy man. "All right," she said, swinging her gaze in my direction. "We've been here more than thirty minutes, and you haven't told us anything about your investigation. Is it going that poorly?"

Ray stopped chewing. "I thought we agreed ot-nay o-tay ask-kay."

"Well that plan is foiled," I said, "because she already asked, and I'm afraid I've broken your secret code."

He turned offended eyes on me. "That message wasn't meant for you."

I laughed, and he grinned.

"Seriously," Libby pressed, "what's going on, and how can we help?"

I placed a peppermint on my bingo card, covering I-26, then set my mug aside. I filled them in on everything I knew so far and ticked my suspects off on my fingers.

Libby folded her hands on the tabletop and leaned forward. "Okay, let's dig in. We've got a daughter upset on her father's behalf, a retired electrician who got a raw deal, a gallery manager who's potentially out of work, and a rich investor."

"And the podcasters," Ray said.

Libby didn't look interested in Tate and Harvey as suspects.

"Never underestimate a person's determination to succeed at something," I said. "Remember the Olympic figure skater who hired a thug to disable her opponent?"

Libby drummed her crimson nails against her mug. "We need to cut that list down."

"I'm trying," I said. "I'd hoped I could mark Mr. Weible off the list by speaking to his daughter, but I wound up adding her instead. I can't reach the investor, but I've left a message, and I'm going to stop by the Historical Society tomorrow to talk to Mr. Lincoln again."

"Maybe we should do that," Libby said. She hooked a thumb in Ray's direction. "You've got a ton on your plate already, and keeping you out of harm's way will be our gift to my brother and your mother."

Ray huffed a little laugh.

"I don't know," I said. I didn't want to put either of them in harm's way. Or get them involved in a mess I'd created.

"Come on. You're always rushing around at this point in the season, trying to care for your inn guests, fill last-minute jewelry orders, wrap toy donations, and hand-deliver Christmas cards because you missed the deadline to get them to the post office," Libby said. "We'll talk to the guy at the Historical Society and see what we can learn."

I frowned, offended, and feeling like a child whose candy had just been stolen. "I am not rushing around this year. I'm caught up on my jewelry orders and the holiday cards. One of my guests barely leaves her room, and the others are rarely on site." Gertie and Jackie had been out exploring more often than resting, and as far as I could tell, Caesar and Marcy only came back from town long enough to sleep each night. Everyone seemed happy, but none of the guests needed me at all.

"And the toy donations?" Ray asked. "Do we have a day and time for the annual wrapping party?"

I shook my head, lips pursed. "That's canceled."

Libby's eyes narrowed. "Don't tell me you wrapped hundreds of gifts by yourself. I'm still struggling to believe you're caught up on all the other things."

I looked from her to Ray then back. "Remember how all those gingerbread men cookies disappeared?"

"Yeah? And?" she asked.

"Mom told me about that, and then I walked back to the inn, and all the toys were gone."

Libby's mouth opened, then snapped shut.

"On the same day?" Ray asked.

I shrugged. "I guess so." Mom hadn't been one hundred percent clear on the timing of the cookie disappearance, but it was safe to assume the day was one and the same.

"What did Evan say?" Libby asked.

"That he'd look into it." I didn't bother adding how unhappy he'd been to know I'd forgotten to mention it right away.

I took a long drink from my cider, savoring the warm apple and cinnamon on my tongue. All around me, the energy in the room lifted my spirit, and I smiled.

"Bingo!" someone called, and the crowd cheered for the winner, likely a perfect stranger to most.

Ray stretched long legs beneath the table, knocking into my boots before pulling back. "I guess it's a good thing you're caught up on your jewelry orders," he said. "Otherwise, all that could've been taken too."

The possibility made my stomach sink. There would've been so many unsatisfied consumers. So many unfulfilled orders. A potentially fatal number of lost customers.

"A definite silver lining," I said. Then the flaw in the argument hitched in my mind. "Wait. I filled all those orders after the toys went missing."

Libby cringed. "I guess the thief wasn't impressed with your work."

"Or they didn't want dozens of the same few pieces," I said. Not to mention, most locals would be able to identify my items if someone tried selling them around town.

Cookie set down the mic, and a deep thump echoed through the speakers. She stepped off stage and moved in the direction of the door. She posed for a selfie with the bingo winner, then handed him a gift certificate.

Another round of applause went up. This time I joined in.

A moment later, the Hearth's front door opened, and a leggy blonde walked in.

I waved an arm overhead. "Caroline's here."

She spotted me easily, seated in our usual booth, and led her boyfriend, Zane, through the dining area to join us. They looked like an ad for holiday couture in coordinating ensembles. Her black dress coat was tied at the waist; her heeled boots and bag were matching and designer. His dark wool coat was unbuttoned to reveal a black sweater and dark jeans. Her thick blond hair fell over her shoulders in perfect waves. His neatly trimmed beard was enough to be masculine and attractive without crossing the line into rugged or woodsy.

I scooted to the far side of the bench and let the happy couple sit beside me. We exchanged greetings while she and Zane removed their coats, gloves, and scarves. He hung them on the post attached to our booth.

"What have we missed?" Caroline asked. Her gold necklace and earrings sparkled in the café lighting. She set her hands on the table, fingers laced and nails painted a shimmering white.

"Karaoke and the first round of bingo," Ray said, helping himself to another cookie. "But we have plenty of sweets to share." He nudged the plate in their direction.

Caroline waved him off, but Zane chose a reindeer cutout.

"Do you want to play?" Libby asked. "I can grab two more cards."

"No," Caroline shook her head. "We're not staying long. I've been on my feet at work all day and would probably be asleep by now if Zane hadn't insisted we come. He said I'd regret missing our annual game night, or at least the gossip, and he was totally right."

Libby smiled. "One more reason I've always liked you. Prioritizing small-town gossip over sleep is a must. Especially when there's been a recent murder, and your BFF is the Gumdrop Gumshoe."

"Do not," I warned, pointing a finger at her. "Never say that again."

"So," Caroline said, fighting a smile, "fill us in."

I finished my cider and two snickerdoodles while Libby and Ray gave the newcomers a rundown of everything we'd talked about.

Caroline turned to me with pink lips pulled into a frown. "You still haven't chosen an anniversary gift?" she asked, focusing on the most Caroline part of the story. "Cutting it a little close, aren't you?"

I dropped my forehead onto the table and covered my head with my hands.

Someone patted my shoulder. "Look at the bright side," Zane said, shifting away when I sat upright. He settled his long arm around Caroline's shoulders, and I realized he'd been the one to pat me. "You were great on the podcast today. I laughed more than once, and I don't even like podcasts."

I turned slowly to face him, eyes narrowing, and temper boiling. "I wasn't on a podcast today." Or any day. But I had a pretty good idea of the show he was talking about. "Explain."

"Maybe you taped it earlier," he offered. "I just heard it today. The one with the murders and recipes." He looked at the ceiling. "What's it called?"

"*Dead and Berried*," the rest of the table answered in jumble of voices.

"Right. Wait. What am I missing?" he asked.

"I do not like those guys," I said. "They're becoming my nemesis. My nemeses?" What was the plural of nemesis? Could I have more than one? *Probably,* I reasoned. Especially since these dingbats were a set. "Those two only came to Mistletoe to get more listeners. Now they turn up everywhere I go, and they gave me that ridiculous nickname. I'm not completely convinced they didn't hurt Elijah Snow for the ratings."

A distant, tinny sound that reminded me of my voice stopped me mid-rant.

Across the table, Ray and Libby huddled over Ray's phone, listening as Tate and Harvey thanked me for taking time from my busy day to speak with them.

I gasped. "I did not participate in that!"

"Shh," my tablemates said.

We listened as Tate introduced me to his audience as the adorable Gumdrop Gumshoe, then played an obviously recorded round of applause. Next, he explained my role at the inn and talked about my family's legacy in town. "It's an impressive lineage you have here," he said.

"Did you know my husband is the sheriff?" my voice responded.

I guffawed. "I asked him that when he was poking around the farm!" I looked at each of my friends. "He must've been recording our interaction!"

Harvey's voice interrupted the fake conversation to say I looked lovely in my red dress.

Caroline barked a laugh. "She'd never wear a dress to a podcast interview. I'm lucky to coax her out of jeans twice a year."

"It's Christmas," my prerecorded voice explained.

The temperature in the room seemed to double as I imagined all the ways I wanted to throttle both podcasters. Surely, I could sue for this—or at least press charges.

Tate was back at the mic, providing details related to Mr. Snow's death. "We've run into the Gumshoe a number of times while executing our own investigation. I hope we didn't get in your way."

"No, you weren't," the recorded me said.

I pointed at the phone, beyond the point of outrage. "They absolutely are in the way!" And apparently they'd recorded more than one of our conversations.

"What can you tell us about the case?" Tate asked. "Better yet, what do you find most compelling?"

"He wasn't in town twelve hours before he died," my voice said.

"You've been hot on the trail of whoever was so eager to see this man dead," Tate said. "We're seriously impressed. You've befriended the main suspect, been seen with him at the hospital and visiting his home. You're checking in with all the key players and had lunch with another suspect, someone with good reason to hate Elijah Snow. And I hear you've already received a threat or two. Do you want to tell the audience about that?"

"No."

He chuckled. "Understandable. Any advice to our listeners thinking of putting on a detective hat the next time someone bites it in their town?"

"It's not a game," the recorded me said.

"That's so true, and there you have it," Tate agreed. "I'd ask what we're pairing with this murder, but something tells me it's gingerbread."

Ray tapped his phone screen and set the device on the table. "*Dead and Berried* gained a ton of new followers since that aired today."

"I'm going to kill them," I said.

Libby pressed a finger to her lips. "No. You aren't. And you should probably never say that again about anyone or anything. At least not while these two are in town recording you."

Something potentially worse occurred to me then. "They've broadcasted my meddling."

I wouldn't have a chance to kill them because Evan was going to murder me first.

"Hopefully the killer wasn't one of the people who listened to the podcast," Caroline said. "Can you tell how many people have played it?"

Ray wrinkled his nose. "Less than one hundred . . . and twenty . . . thousand."

I felt the air leave my lungs. I was in very deep trouble.

Even if Evan accepted me for the curious woman I was, having my escapades announced from a platform that size would give him a dozen ulcers and six consecutive strokes. Maybe I wouldn't need to come up with an anniversary gift after all. He'd just divorce me.

Caroline set her hand gently on mine. "Don't worry. This will work out. Everything always does. Maybe you can ask a certain someone for a little help." She worked her neatly shaped brows. "Put in for a Christmas miracle."

"Christopher isn't Santa Claus," I said. "And Gertie isn't Mrs. Claus. And even if they were, they'd deliver toys to children, not murderers to law enforcement."

"I don't know," she said. "Christmas magic is Christmas magic, and it can't hurt to ask."

The way things were going, I wasn't so sure.

Chapter Twenty-Two

Nearly an hour later, Cookie left the stage with a gift certificate for the final bingo winner of the night. I'd completely forgotten the game was happening. My bingo card was empty, and Ray had eaten all the peppermint markers. I was still stewing over the podcasters' audacity.

Cookie approached the booth, a bottle of water in hand. "This is for you," she said, sending it down the table in my direction like the bartender at an Old West saloon.

My hand opened and caught the bottle on instinct.

"Good reflexes," she said. "And you look like you can use that. You're pale as a ghost." She turned to face Caroline and Zane, then nudged her way onto the seat across from them. "Scootch," she told Libby, bumping her against Ray.

"Aren't we cozy," Libby said, looking a little like a redheaded sardine.

Ray looped his arm around her, perpetually unbothered. I suspected he'd cheerfully sit on the floor if we asked, and I wished for a bit of his easygoing nature. At the moment I was imagining all the things I wanted to say to Tate and Harvey.

"Well," Cookie said, folding her hands on the table and calling the court to order, "what's the word on this year's murder?"

Libby laughed, and I sank in my seat a little.

"The gals in my Swingers group are taking bets the killer is Henry Moore," Cookie said, clearly eager to get started. "I can't see it. Someone said he's been sweet on Violet all his life. Hurting her son wouldn't make any sense."

"Who said that?" Caroline asked, voicing the immediate question in my head.

Cookie raised her brows. "What?"

"Details," Libby said, poking a finger against Cookie's arm. "Context."

"The Swingers are the dancers—"

"Not that," Libby interjected. "We've all met. Tell us what they said about Moore and Violet."

"Oh." She turned one palm to face the ceiling. "I guess they were lovers in high school. Probably because their families were at war. That Romeo and Juliet stuff can be a real aphrodisiac, plus kids love to break rules."

"How do your friends know that?" I asked. I could only guess Cookie's age, but she was definitely older than Henry and Violet, and so were all the Swingers.

"Gossip." She selected a cutout cookie and bit the head off a snowman. "My friend, Henrietta, was an office aide when they were kids. You'd be surprised how much the teachers and administration talk about the students. They have their favorite couples, the ones they hope will finally get together, others they wish would break up. Sometimes they choose partners for assignments just so they can place kids together who they think will hit it off."

Zane laughed. "Lucky kids."

Caroline knitted her brows. "I was always paired with meatheads."

Ray leaned forward, peering down the table, past Libby, to Cookie. "Do they really do that?"

"Sure. People have to make fun where they can, and most teachers want students to be happy. That's what the Swingers say, anyhow."

"They worked at the school?" I asked, digging for the crux.

"Not all of them, but a few. When we were your age, women were a little more limited on career opportunities. Homemaking was popular, but those ladies only got to meddle in their own kids' lives," she said looking a bit sad for the homemakers.

I circled a finger in the air, rolling it toward me. "Let's back up. Millie and Jean went to school with Violet and Henry, and they didn't say anything about them being a couple."

"They weren't a couple," Cookie said. "It was forbidden, remember? Their families had already been feuding for decades."

Libby gave her a disbelieving look. "How did your friends know if other students didn't even know?"

I nodded. Being interested in the kids at the school, and even intentionally partnering students for assignments, was one thing. Knowing their secrets was another entirely.

Cookie's blue eyes widened, and her pink lips pinched in delight. I leaned in, sensing an excellent story on the way. She glanced around the busy café, then lowered her voice. "Henry was a helper in the art department, and sometimes he stayed after school to clean up for the next day. The janitor let him in and out. It wasn't a big deal until the art teacher forgot something and went back after dinner to pick it up. Henry was still there—with Violet—in the supply closet."

Caroline gasped.

I tensed, waiting for more.

Cookie grinned. "Henry was supposed to be cleaning up, but according to my source, he was getting dirty that night."

"Cookie!" Caroline exclaimed.

Zane erupted in laughter and Ray followed.

"Really," Cookie said. "Paint everywhere."

Libby leaned back, ignoring the cackling men and the goofy turn Cookie's story had taken. "How did they keep something that scandalous from getting out in a town this size, way back then?"

Cookie frowned. "Wasn't that long ago. And the art teacher was discreet. She had a private conversation with Violet's parents, and that was that. A couple weeks later there was a 'For Sale' sign in their yard. Her dad got a job in another town, and the rest is history."

"What about Henry's family?" Libby asked. "Who talked to them?"

"I don't know," Cookie said. "Men are heroes for that kind of stuff. Ladies were chastised or forced to get married. I supposed the course of action was up to her dad, and he chose to leave."

Caroline crossed her arms. "That's so sad. I can't imagine being torn away from my first love so dramatically, especially over a feud between family members who were probably dead before I was born."

"I don't know," Ray said. "Couldn't be all bad. She met and married the love of her life almost immediately. They were together forty-five years. Maybe the move was a blessing."

Zane watched as I worked through the new possibilities. I could feel his curious gaze on my cheek. When I made eye contact, he said, "That helps your case, right? Moore wouldn't have killed her son if they had a history like that."

"I don't know," I said. "It could be argued that he confronted her for breaking his heart. He never married because he never stopped loving her, but she married immediately."

"A heartbreak carried for more than forty years could fester," Libby said.

I hated the possibility that might be true.

* * *

I stayed with my friends until the Hearth closed, talking about everything from our extracurriculars in high school and our first loves to what we wanted most for Christmas. I wanted to know the truth about what had happened to Elijah Snow. I wanted justice and some measure of peace for his mom. Everything else in my life was relatively great.

My thoughts drifted repeatedly to Violet as I walked back to the inn. Snow blew in swirls around me, rustled up by the wind and dispersed in glittery wisps. I was nearly home when I realized I needed to tell Evan what I'd learned. He wasn't a fan of gossip, and the reason Violet's family had left town forty-five years ago was basically a cold case, but confirmation of a teenage relationship between Violet and Henry seemed like need-to-know information.

"Hey," he answered on the first ring. "I'm on my way to you. Everything okay?"

My steps stuttered at the announcement, then picked up the pace. "Really? You're staying here tonight?"

"Every night—at least that's the plan until Christmas," he said. "You need to be there while the inn is full, and I need to be with you, so I'll keep you company."

My heart swelled. "Thank you."

"I'll only be a few more minutes. How were the games tonight?"

"Fun," I said, thankful for the segue I needed. "Cookie was having the time of her life singing karaoke and calling bingo. The guests were eating it up. She sat with us when she finished."

"Why do I sense there's a story behind those words?"

"Because there's always a story when Cookie's involved?" I asked.

"Or because I know you, and I recognize that tone," he said. "Let's hear it, Gray."

I reached the inn and kicked the toes of my boots against the steps on my way up to the porch. "Cookie had an interesting bit of gossip." I let myself inside and shivered. "I'll tell you all about it when you get here."

A fire roared and crackled in the parlor to my left. I suspected the chill had followed me in from outside.

"Deal," he said. "I wish I'd had luck finding all those missing toys. It's really bugging me that so many kids will go without a gift under the tree this week because some creep stole their surprise."

"You're so kind," I said. "You've got a full plate this time of year, and you're in the middle of another murder investigation, yet you're still thinking about the kids and their toys."

"Guess what else," he said.

"What?"

"I spoke to a few of your mom's friends about the missing cookies, and one of the ladies gave most of them to Gertie for Christopher's men. She'd forgotten to mention it to your mom. So, there's at least one mystery solved,"

The word *most* clung in my mind. "What happened to the rest?" I asked. I hung my coat on the hook in the foyer and did a double take as the parlor caught my eye. "Oh my stars!" The room was stuffed to the rafters with so many beautifully wrapped Christmas gifts I could barely see the tree.

"Holly?" Evan asked, a note of tension in his voice. "I'm almost there. What's wrong?"

"I think someone wrapped all those toy donations and returned them to the inn!"

He barked a startled laugh. "Are you sure? All of them?"

I flipped the overhead light on and inched into the room. "I think so," I said. "There might actually be more than before. I can't be sure, but it's a lot."

I couldn't be positive the gifts were toys, but the wrapping paper matched what had been stolen. It would be a nightmare to try to peek inside each gift to confirm, but it would be worse to deliver something inappropriate for a child on Christmas morning. I imagined a small boy unwrapping a large woman's robe and slippers, or a toddler receiving a hammer and nails. "I think we have to make sure these are all toys before we let the collection team distribute them."

Headlights flashed over the window, and Evan's cruiser came into view outside. "No problem. We can get started tonight over cookies and hot chocolate."

I turned and crossed the hall toward my office, smiling as I watched him arrive. "That sounds per—"

Crunch.

I froze as my foot connected with something on the floor. I dropped my gaze to assess the situation and discovered what appeared to be the rest of those missing cookies. "Oh no."

Piles of broken gingerbread men spilled from my office chair. Tiny, iced arms and legs were mounded on the seat, topped with heads and torsos. Additional cookie parts covered the roller pad beneath my chair and surrounding floorboards.

I eased my foot off a crushed cookie, heart rate climbing with each short, shallow breath.

Outside the window, Evan jogged toward the inn. "Don't worry," he said. "We've got all night to peek inside the packages. I can't believe someone took them and did all the wrapping for us." He laughed. "But I'm not surprised by anything in this town anymore, and I'm starting to believe in Christmas miracles."

"Evan," I said, swallowing a fist-sized lump in my throat. "I think I also found the missing cookies."

The front door opened, and Evan came in on a gust of icy air. He scanned the room quickly before his gaze stuck briefly on mine. I wasn't sure what he saw there—horror, I presumed—but he was at my side in a heartbeat, pulling me into his arms.

"Hey, you okay?" he asked.

I set my cheek against the cold material of his coat and nodded. "Better now."

We were quiet for several seconds, surveying the strange combination of threats and treasures.

He raised a finger when I stepped away. "Wait here," he said. "I need to take a look around the inn, then grab some evidence bags and a couple of boxes from the car. We'll collect the cookies and then search the space for evidence of who else has been in this room."

Passing me a pair of protective gloves from his pocket, he headed into the foyer to look for hidden bad guys.

I stretched the blue latex over my fingers and crouched to give the cookie pile a closer inspection.

Something caught my eye beneath the mess, along the edge of the mat for my roller chair. I brushed the cookies aside carefully, and my chest tightened with each breath.

"Holly?" Evan called, returning to the space outside my office.

"Down here," I said, mouth dry and words sticking in my throat. "You should see this before you get those evidence bags."

He darted into the office and crouched at my side. Cuss words poured from his lips the moment he saw what I did.

Deep scratches in the floorboards formed two angry words.

Final Warning!

Chapter Twenty-Three

I woke early the next morning to have breakfast with Evan before he started his shift. The sun was yet to rise, and the inn was magically aglow from the lights of a dozen Christmas trees tucked into every nook and corner.

I made coffee. Evan made pancakes. Then we curled onto the padded red gingham bench rested against the far wall of the large kitchen, our meal plated before us. For a lengthy, silent while, we ate in companionable contemplation, both exhausted from an excruciatingly long night.

Evan's deputies had stayed late, examining every inch and fiber of the inn, determined to find some indication of who had carved the threat into my floorboards. Their efforts were tedious and thorough.

Also, fruitless.

Mrs. Snow had been horribly shaken when I let her know what had happened. I wasn't specific about the threat, but I felt obligated to explain the sudden and ongoing presence of lawmen onsite. She hadn't come down for dinner after that. Caesar and Marcy had been out until the deputies were preparing to leave. The duo had seemed surprised but were otherwise undeterred by my news. I'd fed them cookies and cocoa while they'd regaled Evan and me with stories of local attempts at holiday records. Neither seemed to notice the strain in our smiles or fatigue in our eyes. Gertie and Jackie had only returned long enough to see the commotion and leave again. Shockingly, none of my guests wanted to check out. I was thankful for everyone involved. It would be nearly impossible to find another place in town for them to stay, so close to Christmas, and it would be nice for me to know I'd rarely be home alone.

I moved another pancake from the platter to my plate and smothered it in butter and syrup. Today was sure to be an all-sugar, double-the-caffeine kind of day. And I needed to prepare.

"What's on your agenda?" Evan asked, fighting a yawn on the final word.

"I want to check in with my folks, hang out at the Hearth, and keep an eye on the inn," I said. "The usual."

He turned to look at me for a long, silent beat. "Maybe we should sell the house in town and try to find something closer to the farm. Then we aren't choosing that house or the inn, but something literally in between."

"What?" My sleep-deprived mind replayed his words, struggling to comprehend. We'd never even discussed the possibility of a new home. "Where's this coming from?"

"I think part of the problem is how far away our other place is from your family. You want to be here when the inn is full, which is most of the year, and especially during the holidays. Commuting is inconvenient in the best of weather, and it can be dangerous in the winter. The private quarters here are cramped for two adults and not conducive to long-term living. Plus, we either have to buy two of everything or make continuous trips between houses to fetch the things we need."

I was well aware of the complications our housing situation caused, but I was not in the right headspace to think about adding a third option to the conundrum. Available properties in Mistletoe were few and far between, as well as overpriced because demand consistently exceeded supply. “I do enjoy seeing my folks every day, but I still think this is a conversation for after Christmas. Meanwhile, we should stay put and figure out who’s leaving threats.”

“We should get a camera for the doorbell,” Evan said. He sipped his coffee, eyes fixed in the direction of the foyer. “And a number pad with a key code for the lock. Every guest should have their own code. Then there will be a digital log of everyone entering the premises, complete with time stamp.”

I pushed a bite of breakfast between my lips to stop myself from saying anything cranky. I didn’t disagree that his way would be safer, and I understood where he was coming from, but we’d had this talk at length, and more than once. A change like the one he described would drastically alter the inn and the inn experience. The thought saddened me for my parents’ sake and for all the future guests. It seemed unjust to give a criminal that kind of power.

My parents had dreamed of this place all my life, and the inn had been carefully crafted to replicate a historic home. Every detail was strategically chosen to accurately reflect other homes built the year the town was founded. From the octagon tiles on the bathroom floors, to the old-fashioned faucets and knobs, to the carpets and the paint palette; to the curation of custom trim work, handrails, and spindles on the stairs. My parents’ dreams were visible in every aspect of this place. So, how could I willingly add cameras, keypads, and alarms? A modern-day, technology-driven eyesore attached right to the front door? That felt like the real crime.

I let my head fall back in exasperation.

“Don’t forget, your office is a crime scene,” Evan said, still talking to the air.

I set my fork aside and turned to stare at him until he met my eye. “In what universe could I possibly forget?”

“I wasn’t suggesting you would. It’s just a gentle reminder,” he said. “People run on autopilot and habit all the time. You wouldn’t let me put the yellow tape across the threshold, so now there's no visual reminder."

My eyes narrowed. "I didn't want to upset the guests."

"Or ruin the aesthetic," he added under his breath.

I twisted on the bench to look at him more directly. "What was that?"

"It would be easy to walk in there without thinking, that's all."

I turned back to my breakfast, my irritation growing. Logically, I knew none of this was Evan's fault, and he was only doing his job, both as the sheriff and as my husband, but I wanted to scream.

He finished eating before me, then carried his things to the sink. "I'm going to head out. I want to stop by our house before work."

I forced myself upright and met him at the counter with my mug, plate, and fork.

Evan took everything from my hands and set the items aside. His arms were around my waist in a second, towing me close before I could protest. "I love you," he said. The sincerity and concern in his tone melted the steel from my mood, and I leaned into the embrace.

"I love you too," I said. "I can't believe this is happening again. I hate that I've brought madness and chaos to the inn. That my behavior has inadvertently ruined my parents' beautiful floor and possibly their vision for how the inn will look in days and years to come." I imagined the keypad on the door again and gagged silently.

Evan stroked messy hair away from my face and kissed my forehead. He kissed my cheeks and nose, then looked into my eyes. "You didn't do this. A criminal did this. If you played any part, it was only that you let that big, justice-seeking heart of yours drag you around once in a while. And on occasion, sure, you might follow it willingly," he amended.

I laughed softly and tightened my arms around his middle.

"Even then, this isn't your fault," he said. "I know it, and your adoring parents also know it. No one blames you, and I'm confident

Christopher can replace the scarred boards without any trouble. Things happen. It's fine. Also, I plan to remove the damaged boards and take them in as evidence so the lab can get an idea of what was used to make the cuts. They don't match any of the knives in the house."

I suppressed a dramatic sigh and walked Evan to the door. I flipped the dead bolt for good measure after saying goodbye.

All my guests were safely in their beds. Anyone else wanting inside would have to ring the bell.

"Meow." Cindy Lou Who rubbed against my ankles, purring and vocalizing as I returned to the kitchen and loaded the dishwasher.

"You've already had breakfast," I told her. Evan had fed her before making pancakes, so she'd be less interested in harassing us while we ate. Apparently, my time was up.

"Meow," she retorted. "Meow. Meow. Meow."

The complaints were distorted by the volume of her purrs, causing each to shake and rattle in her furry chest and throat.

"Aww." I bent to scratch behind her ears, enchanted by the happy sound.

She bit me.

"Hey." I straightened with a frown. "Mean."

Realizing I wasn't getting her treats, Cindy turned and marched away.

"Merry Christmas," I told her backside as she bounded up the steps.

Alone again, I scanned the room, then hit the nearest light switch, thankful for the instant illumination and absence of shadows. A ne'er-do-well had been inside the inn yesterday. Had been inside my office. And they'd carved a threat deep into my floor. There'd been nothing tentative about those marks, each drag of the weapon had splintered the polished wood, creating a mass of angry, jagged gashes. I could only assume Elijah Snow's killer was the culprit, and

I tried not to wonder if that person had imagined me in place of my floorboards as they'd worked.

A shiver rocked down my spine, and I pushed the thought away.

The crowds on the farm had been thick last night while I'd sat inside the warm Hearth, having a lovely time with friends. Anyone could've let themselves in and out of the inn during that time, and they could do it again if I wasn't more vigilant. I'd have to start locking all the doors and asking guests to do so as well.

I hated the necessary change. Our town had never been like this before. Never in my childhood. Never in my teen years. People had been trustworthy. Not homicidal. But I wouldn't be a victim for nostalgia's sake or put anyone unnecessarily in danger on my watch. So, the doors would stay locked, and guests would need to take their keys when they went out.

I checked the back door and turned that lock as well.

Footfalls on the staircase spun me in that direction.

Caesar froze. "I'm so sorry. I didn't mean to scare you. I thought I was the only one up."

"Wrong," Marcy said, her legs appearing on the steps behind him. A moment later, the rest of her came into view. "I've been up for an hour, reviewing the photographs and videos we took yesterday. I even drafted an article to go with the images. I love this town."

Caesar chuckled and finished his descent, with her close behind.

I zipped back to the kitchen island, turning on the remaining overhead lights as I moved. "Let me get you something to drink and snack on."

"Just coffee," Caesar said. "We have plans for breakfast at the pie shop. Since Marcy's up and ready to go, we probably shouldn't wait long."

She climbed onto a barstool. "That pie is the reason I woke before dawn," she said. "It smells like heaven every time we walk past, but there's always a line around the block."

I smiled. "It's a very popular place." Evan loved the pie shop. It was where he spent much of his time on duty. The little bakery and café was Mistletoe's gossip central. People went in for pie and coffee, then got all jazzed up on caffeine and sugar and said way too much. As a new sheriff in town, Evan had gotten a lot of his information via this channel. As a local teen, I'd gotten in a lot of trouble via that channel.

Caesar took a seat on the stool beside Marcy. "Folks in Mistletoe are incredibly creative. We could spend every day for a month listening to their pitches for world records. It's been a lot of fun."

"Oh yeah?" I asked, knowing the part about our citizens' exceptional creativity, but curious if anyone else had won. I was torn between hating that Mom didn't reach her goal with the cookie, and excitement for others to reach theirs. Not to mention, Mistletoe could use the extra positive vibes.

I passed each of my guests a mug of coffee.

Caesar shook his head solemnly. "Most world records involving groups require a greater headcount than Mistletoe's entire population, but y'all have heart. There's no doubt about that."

"And spirit," Marcy said. "My favorite efforts so far were the not-quite-largest collection of Mrs. Claus memorabilia, and the goat lady's mass of straw ornaments."

"Cookie?" I asked.

"No, thank you," Marcy said. "I'm holding out for pie."

I blinked, taken aback by the strange response. I laughed when the misunderstanding registered. "No, the goat lady," I said. "Was her name Cookie? Her goat is Theodore. She's a good friend of mine."

Marcy shook her head. "No, this lady's name is Alice. She's from Sweden and had about three hundred straw ornaments at her café. Unfortunately, there's a man in Sweden with four thousand."

"Yeesh," I said. Where did anyone store that many of anything? I barely had enough room in my closet for all my puffy coats and winter boots. Then I recalled Alice's kind smile when we'd met, and my mouth watered a little as I recalled her delicious sweets. "I just met her at the Cup of Cheer. She's lovely."

"Cookie must be the one with the calendars," Caesar said.

I grinned. "A Goat for All Seasons."

Marcy returned my smile. "That's the one. I liked her too. Everyone is so nice here." Her body stiffened slightly. "I mean other than the murderer and whoever did that to your floor."

"The floor issue was unfortunate," I said. I took a beat, considering how best to redirect the conversation. "But someone also wrapped hundreds of donated toys for local children and didn't even take credit for it."

She nodded, and the tension in the room dissipated by a fraction.

Evan and his deputies had tediously examined gift after gift, making sure no unsuspecting child would get a dangerous surprise on Christmas morning. They'd taken the packages they hadn't had time to check to the station. Evan would bring them back if they were all safe as well, but we still had no idea who'd taken them and wrapped them in the first place. The same person who had carved my floor? Surely not.

And if there were two people in my office last night, had the gift wrapper seen the killer?

"I enjoyed the hand-crafted mitten collection," Caesar said, gamely changing the subject. "And the mass of Christmas-themed jigsaw puzzles."

Marcy's focus was steady on me. "Should we feel guilty for enjoying ourselves so much when a man died here this week?"

Caesar and I exchanged awkward looks. "I don't think so," he said, running a palm across the smooth granite expanse between them. "Making the most of our trip while remembering a fellow houseguest is grieving, it's a fine line, but we're doing okay. Sadly, lives end every day. Perhaps that's the best reason for the rest of us to keep appreciating every day we can."

Marcy listened intently, then added, "I hear her crying at night."

My heart ached, but I wasn't sure what to do. "I can move you to a new room," I offered. "We have one more—" I stopped, recalling why we had an open room.

Elijah Snow no longer needed it.

"No, thank you," Marcy said. "That would definitely be worse."

"Right." I poured myself a cup of coffee and willed my brain to work faster before I stuck my foot in my mouth again.

"Good morning." A thin voice turned us in the direction of the stairs.

Mrs. Snow stood silent as a kitten on the bottom step.

I nearly dropped my mug.

Her slippered feet on the thick carpet runner had masked her approach.

"Good morning," I said. "Come on in. Let me pour you some coffee."

Caesar tipped his mug back, finishing the last of his drink. Marcy pushed hers aside. "We're on our way to the pie shop," he said. "Can we bring you back anything?"

Mrs. Snow looked blankly at him and then Marcy for a moment. "Pie," she said.

Marcy frowned. "What kind—"

Caesar set his hands on her shoulders and steered her away. "Will do."

Mrs. Snow took a seat at the island, accepting the coffee when I set it before her. "I didn't mean to scare them off."

"Not at all," I fibbed. "They're just really excited about the pie."

Her lips twitched in a failed smile. "Well, I suppose this is best. I owe you an apology and an explanation for what you saw the other day when you barged into my room unannounced and uninvited."

I pressed my lips into a flat line as heat rose up my neck to my cheeks, scalding the tips of my ears. "I am profoundly sorry," I said. "I heard a commotion. I thought there was an intruder and you needed help."

"I did not."

I dropped my gaze to the floor as a gamut of unwanted images returned to my mind. "I got that."

"I don't make a habit of behaving in that manner," she said. "Just so you know."

"Please don't explain. I was in the wrong. I know that now."

Violet cupped pale hands around the steaming mug and stared into the dark liquid. "I've loved Henry all my life. I'm struggling right now, and he was a comforting place to land."

I darted my gaze around the room, wishing there was some kind of work to busy my hands and train my focus. Anything but looking into her eyes while recalling her in Mr. Moore's embrace.

"Henry is Elijah's father."

My eyes jerked to hers, all previous thoughts abandoned. "Pardon?"

Violet's cheeks grew redder than the mug in her hands, but she sat tall, shoulders back and chin high. "My husband knew," she said, apparently deciding not to repeat herself. "Matthew and I married quickly, before he was deployed, then pretended Elijah was a honeymoon baby and a preemie. Matthew never cared about Elijah's paternity. He loved us with every ounce of himself. It didn't matter whose DNA the boy carried; he was our son, and that was the only thing anyone needed to know. We even gave him Henry's name as his middle name."

I thought of the day I'd met Elijah, and the embroidered square of silk in his pocket. EHS. Elijah Henry Snow.

She relaxed a little, shoulders lowering, as if the weight had been lifted. "Henry always suspected. The timing of my pregnancy was a dead giveaway, but my marriage made him question himself. I pretended it wasn't true when he asked, but I think he knew. We exchanged letters while Matthew was stationed overseas, but I kept my distance to make things easier for him. When Matthew returned, I stopped writing and responding to Henry. It seemed the only right thing to do. I could've come back to visit any time after my parents passed. I wanted to. Every day I wanted to. But I didn't, out of respect for all the men I loved."

My heart broke as I imagined the triangle she described: a soul mate, a husband, and a son. She was grieving Elijah now, but she'd been grieving the loss of Henry for forty-five years. From the look on her face, she'd grieved the life she'd been denied as well. A life where she wouldn't have loved anyone other than her husband, but that was never meant to be.

"Henry sent condolence cards and flowers to the funeral home when I lost Matthew. That was when I knew it was time for me to come back to Mistletoe. Elijah was on board as soon as I mentioned the mayor's invitation. He did his research and found a project to get involved in." She smiled a little at that. "He was just like his father." The smile faded abruptly, and I wondered if she was thinking of Matthew or Mr. Moore.

"I told myself I'd confess everything to Elijah and Henry when we arrived. Perhaps take them both to dinner, make proper introductions." Her eyes misted, and her gaze went distant. "But we'd barely checked in before Henry confronted us outside. He didn't give me a chance to explain. It was as if he knew the truth the moment he set eyes on Elijah. I could see it on his face and hear it in his tone. He asked if Elijah was his son. I didn't know what to say. I was stunned. That wasn't how I'd planned to tell them. Elijah was horrified. He didn't understand why anyone would say something like that to me. I'm a well-respected woman. A pillar in our community. And I'd been with his father for a lifetime. With Matthew," she clarified. "You saw what happened then. Elijah lost his temper, and Henry just stood there, stunned while Elijah said the meanest things. Your father had to tell him to settle down. It was awful. I can't imagine what he must've thought."

"For whatever it's worth, I don't think my dad knew what Elijah was upset about, and he's not one to pass judgment," I said. "And I don't believe Mr. Moore hurt Elijah," I said. "He wouldn't hurt anyone."

She wiped a renegade tear from her cheek. "I agree."

Henry Moore had waited more than forty years to meet Elijah, suspecting all the while that he was his father. No wonder he'd been so shocked when he'd seen Elijah in the cookie batter. He'd waited too long to confirm the truth, and now he'd never get to know the boy he'd fathered or the man he'd become.

"Mrs. Snow," I said, drawing her eyes to mine. I hoped my tone conveyed the utmost respect as I carefully crafted my next question. "Did you know any of the men Elijah planned to meet in Mistletoe? Mr. Hunter, Mr. Lincoln, or Mr. Weible?"

"Not personally," she said.

"Did you know this wasn't Elijah's first trip to Mistletoe?"

Her brows knitted. "No. Why do you say that?"

"I've been asking around, and the local gallery manager recalls meeting Elijah several months ago. He'd visited her building with two of those men."

Violet's surprise turned to disappointment. "I didn't know. I suppose I shouldn't be surprised that he kept it from me. He knew how much I wanted to introduce him to my hometown. But he was a planner, and he really wanted things to work out here. I guess it makes sense that he prepared as much as possible. I just wish he hadn't involved Hamish Hunter. I've never heard a single good thing about that man."

Chapter Twenty-Four

I spent the morning at the Hearth, chatting with Mom and assuring her I was safe and happy despite the recent threats. She didn't care about the damaged floorboards. I knew she wouldn't, but I cared very much. And she wholeheartedly agreed with Evan about the digital keypad and cameras. I was officially outnumbered on that front because Dad always sided with Mom, and I knew the safety of humans came before the aesthetic of the inn. But I still hated how one or two criminals could force everyone and everything else to change. As if my world should adapt to their poor behaviors.

When I told her Evan wanted to buy a house closer to the farm, she buzzed with enthusiasm I didn't share. I took a seat in an empty booth, with a notepad and pen, then started a pros and cons list for both living at the inn and living at the house in town. We already had two homes. I couldn't get my mind around looking for a third.

My phone rang as the café began to fill with farm guests in search of caffeine to fuel their morning of holiday fun.

"Hello?" I answered, hoping for good news and not another threat call.

"Ms. Gray?"

I didn't recognize the number, but I knew the voice immediately. It was Hamish Hunter's admin.

"Yes!" I stood quickly, drawing Mom's attention as she passed pastries to a couple at the counter. "This is Holly."

"You are receiving a return call from Mr. Hunter." She placed me on hold without further comment, and the soft notes of instrumental holiday music began.

A zing of anticipation jerked me onto my feet. Memories of Mrs. Snow's earlier comment about the investor raced circles in my mind. She didn't know him, but she hadn't liked whatever she'd heard, and that was enough to move him up my suspect list by at least one small notch. I paced out a small loop in front of my booth, pinching my bottom lip between thumb and forefinger as I waited.

Mom approached with narrowed eyes. Her pretty red sweater had a list of all Santa's reindeer down the center and sparkly snowflakes on both arms. Matching snowflake earrings dangled from her earlobes, their sleek silver design flashing beneath the lights. The tiny red bow on each post had tested my patience to its very end. But whenever I saw her smile, the work became utterly worthwhile. "What are you up to?" she asked, her perpetual cheer on a sudden back burner.

"Nothing," I promised, a knee-jerk reaction from my adolescence.

"Why are you pacing like that?"

I bit the insides of my cheeks. "I've been waiting for this call."

At my ear, a male voice spoke my name.

"Yes," I said, "this is Holly. Thank you so much for getting back with me."

Mom glanced at the line forming at her register and reluctantly walked away.

Mr. Hunter cleared his throat. "My notes indicate you're interested in purchasing property in Mistletoe, Maine," he said. "Is that still the case?"

"Absolutely," I lied, having too many places to live already.

"What is your budget?"

My budget. If I were in the market to buy a home, I couldn't afford to browse a catalog of homes Hunter was selling. His clients would want to spend big money, and I needed to play the role, so I lied again. "A million dollars." The words arrived so smoothly that a small piece of my mind worried I might have a problem.

Mom stopped mid-step across the room and fixed me with a look.

I forced a goofy smile and waved a hand, hoping to convey the number was spoken in jest. Some bit of a conversation she'd missed the rest of and couldn't possibly understand.

She moved on, ringing up customers while gifting me with significant side-eye.

"I have a few properties coming available in January," he said. "I should be back in the states by then. Should we set a time to meet?"

I returned to my seat. "You're not in town?" I asked. Heck, he wasn't even in the country. "How long have you been gone?"

"I like to spend the holidays in France. It's rather marvelous here, especially compared to the congestion and chaos in Mistletoe this time of year. I fly out before the seasonal hoopla takes hold, then do my best to stay away."

Apparently, he really had only set up his office here for the tax breaks. And he didn't know a good time when he had an office overlooking one.

I couldn't bring myself to agree with his nonsensical statement or lie about my beloved town, so I forced a tight laugh instead. If Hamish Hunter hadn't been in Mistletoe, he couldn't possibly be Mr. Snow's killer. I supposed Hunter could be lying about his whereabouts, and I wasn't sure how I could confirm it if needed, but my gut said he was speaking the truth. His tone and demeanor made it clear he'd never intentionally deal with a Christmas town at Christmastime. As if the notion was absurd, or at the very least, too commercial and pedestrian.

Yet the podcasters had claimed to see Mr. Hunter in a fancy black car very recently, allegedly arguing with a gray-haired man. He couldn't be in Mistletoe and in France. Did that mean Tate and Harvey were mistaken? Or were they lying? And if the answer was the latter, then why?

"When will be a good time for you, Ms. Gray?" Mr. Hunter asked. "Generally, I find afternoons better than mornings until March. It gives the road crews time to salt and plow and allows temperatures to work themselves up to zero."

"That's true," I agreed. "But I think you're cutting out." I had no need to continue this conversation or the farce of finding a million-dollar home. What I needed was a way to determine if Hunter had been in Mistletoe the night Elijah died. "Oh, dear. Seems like a bad connection on my end," I said. "I'll have to call you back when I get away from the mountains."

Mom turned to face me again, one hand on her hip, a tray with cookies and a kettle of tea balanced on the opposite palm. Her narrowing eyes asked, *What kind of nonsense are you up to now?*

I turned my back to her, disconnected the call, and tucked the phone into my pocket. I needed to cross someone off my suspect list. Mr. Weible and his daughter had each other as an alibi. I needed more information to eliminate Hunter and the podcasters. I hadn't asked Liesel where she'd been on the night of the murder, but at least I had an idea about how I could find out.

Liesel was my least likely suspect and my lowest hanging fruit, so I started there. She'd said she'd be heartbroken and out of a job if the investor didn't include the art gallery in his new vision for the building, as Mr. Snow had intended. She'd been angry when she explained the situation, but I wasn't convinced it was a solid motive.

Evan would probably say people had killed for less.

I opened an internet browser on my phone and navigated to the gallery's website, then searched the calendar for events. It only took a moment to see there had been a book launch party that night. The author of a popular Christmas mystery series had been in town to meet readers and sign books. I hated that I'd missed the event. I'd collected a few real-life experiences the author could probably use in her next book. Assuming there was a market for stories set in charming Christmas towns like mine and tenacious but loveable amateur sleuths.

Next, I searched the most popular social media platforms for the author's and Liesel's accounts. From there I scrolled, searching the images for Liesel and possibly a clock to tell me how long the event had lasted.

A post titled *Show Time* was time-stamped 7:11 PM and included photos of the crowded gallery, stacks of books, and long buffets of finger foods, desserts, and a hot chocolate bar. The author looked marvelous, her hair twisted up from her neck and joy all over her face.

A parallel post titled *That's a Wrap* included photos from the same angles, minus the people, books, and refreshments. The author's hair was down, and she smiled into the camera, one arm slung over Liesel's shoulders. The time stamp was after midnight, and the gallery was a mess. The included message thanked everyone who'd come out to support the book and the launch.

I tapped my cursor into the search bar again and looked for the gallery's account but found pictures from the start of the party. Finally, I scrolled through Liesel's posts.

"Got it," I whispered, pausing on a photo of Liesel seated on the gallery floor. The place was clean again, buffet tables gone. All evidence of the party erased. She looked as if she'd run a marathon in her little black dress. Hair stuck to her sweaty neck and cheeks. Her heels lay beside her on the tile. She held up one thumb. The timestamp was nearly three AM.

Could the exhausted woman in the photo have made a trip to Reindeer Games, confronted, then killed Elijah Snow before dawn? I didn't know the exact time of death, but it seemed unlikely my friend was a killer.

I relaxed against the seat back, thankful Liesel wasn't the one who'd been threatening me. I wished I'd thought of researching the suspects online earlier, and that I knew more by now than I did. But I was an innkeeper and jewelry maker. The humble servant of a fabulous, if demanding, calico cat. I wasn't a detective or the sheriff. And clearly being the sheriff's wife didn't provide any more investigative prowess than being his friend or girlfriend had.

I stared into the blue light of my phone screen, wondering who to research next.

Caesar and Marcy appeared before I could decide.

"There she is," he said.

I waved them over, hoping I hadn't dropped the ball on something they needed.

The duo took seats across from me, strange expressions on their faces.

Mom trailed them with a coffeepot and a smile. "Can I get you anything?"

"Yes!" Caesar said. "A few minutes of your time would be incredible. You seem to know everyone in this town, and we have an idea."

Mom and I exchanged a look.

"For?" Mom asked.

Marcy beamed, her small frame vibrating at Caesar's side.

I wasn't sure if she was cold or excited, but I felt my knee begin to bob in anticipation.

"A world record for this town," Caesar said. "We've loved and appreciated all the attempts we've seen this week. Mistletoe clearly loves Christmas, and we want you to take home a win. Especially after what's happened. We've been brainstorming, and we think we can help."

Marcy shifted forward, hands in prayer pose, smile wide. "If we can get everyone to dress in Victorian garb and go to the town square at the same time, we think you can break the record for largest Victorian Christmas Village. There are already enough historically correct buildings, and there aren't any motor vehicles on the central roads right now, thanks to your husband." She looked to me with a conspiratorial grin. "We'd just need to make a few tweaks and collect enough participants. What do you think?"

"I love it," I said.

Mom took a seat beside me, eyes misting with emotion. "I wanted a world record for Mistletoe this year so badly. This town deserves something nice for everyone to think about. Something to help us focus on the magic and not the . . . other things that sometimes go wrong."

Caesar smiled. "I think we can make that happen if you can help us get as many people as possible to the square at the same time. All dressed appropriately, of course. I'm guessing not everyone in your town has Victorian era clothing or a costume on hand. That could be a problem."

"You'd think," I said. "But there are a lot of exceptional seamstresses here, and a few small theater groups with substantial wardrobes, who might be willing to lend a hand as well."

Marcy made an eager squeaking sound.

"Why am I unsurprised?" Caesar asked. The gleam in his eyes said he was also quite pleased. "To be as authentic as possible, we'll also need at least a couple of animals and several more horses. Acquiring and transporting livestock will need to be arranged."

Mom nodded. "Bud and the crew can do all that."

Another happy idea popped into mind. "What about the tents and booths from Santa's Village?" I pointed through the window for clarification. They'd been created to reflect and support the town's Victorian theme, and each sold unique, handcrafted holiday items.

Marcy clapped silently. "That would be perfect. The booths look amazing, and they're right on track with the overall theme. Plus, we can use them strategically to block roads and modern things like stop signs. We've really got to sell this if we want to win. There's a village in Germany that's held the record for nearly a decade."

Hope fluttered in my chest, and I looked at my mom. "We just have to spread the word. I'm sure anyone available will want to help."

She pointed to my cell phone. "This is going to take a Christmas miracle, and a whole lot of coordination. Better call Caroline."

"Who's Caroline?" Marcy asked.

"She owns Caroline's Cupcakes," I said. "She's my best friend and possibly the world's most organized human."

"Ohh," Marcy whispered, pupils dilating. "I love the cupcake lady."

"She'll love knowing you called her that," I assured her.

Caesar patted the breast of his coat. He removed glasses and a phone from hidden pockets. "I'll pull up all the stats from the record holder. We'll have to go above that number as much as possible, just in case they've increased their scope or participation this year. The gathering is an annual town-wide event for them." He perched the glasses on the bridge of his nose, then glanced at Marcy. "Is anyone covering that this year?"

"I can find out," she said.

"Good. If so, let's keep tabs on their progress. We can use them as a baseline."

My eyes stung with a burst of unexpected emotion. We could really break a world record this year. Not just a giant cookie win for our farm and family, but a win earned *by* our town, *for* our town. My heart rate rose, and the previously fluttering hope began to soar. "I can ask Ray to create a digital flyer, and then I can send it to everyone on the Chamber of Commerce email chain, which includes most of the businesses in town." Reindeer Games had been part of the local chamber all my life, and I'd recently joined when my jewelry business gained traction. "I'll attach it to a message with details and ask every business owner to consider sending it to their family, clients, and staff email lists as well. Recipients can print and post the flyers on their windows in case anyone visiting town wants to join us."

Mom shimmied. "I've got goose bumps."

"Me too," Marcy said. "Who's Ray?"

"A local photographer," I explained. "He works for the newspaper and helps make the Goat for All Seasons calendar every year."

I felt my eyebrows draw into a frown. I hadn't thought of it before now, but no one had mentioned the calendar this year. Was that because Cookie had spent all her time looking for a new home? I wished again that I could help her. There had to be a way.

Caesar stuck out his hand, palm down, near the center of the table. "Mistletoe rocks on three," he said.

The rest of us placed our hands on top of his.

"One, two, three," we chanted. "Mistletoe rocks!"

The smattering of guests throughout the café clapped and cheered, though they had no idea what we were talking about. Yet.

Mom quickly rose and filled them in. "So stay tuned," she finished a few moments later. "I'll post details on the window when we have them!" She turned to me, rubbing excited palms down the front of her jeans. "I've got to call your father. He'll be thrilled!"

He definitely would. He'd been more heartsick than Mom when her dream of baking the world's largest gingerbread man had fallen through. And he'd do anything to make her smile.

"I'll call Caroline," I said. "And Ray."

Marcy pumped a fist into the air. "I love when a plan comes together."

Chapter Twenty-Five

My annual wrapping party had been canceled when the toys went missing, but every person I called showed up for an all-hands-on-deck brainstorming event. The shindig was serious business, and no one hesitated when I told them what we were up to or that they needed to clear their entire evening schedule for the next two days. As it turned out, with only four days left until Christmas, and after evaluating the availability of costumes, livestock, and people, then coordinating those things with Caesar and Marcy's flights home, tomorrow was determined to be the only possible day left to break a world record this year. Aside from timing, the local meteorologist was predicting a major strike against us. Tomorrow would be a cold and blustery day with high winds, falling temperatures, and drifting snow. On the bright side, we weren't expecting any additional accumulation. So, we counted our wins where we could.

And tonight we planned.

Mom and her friends had made enough food for an army, and I set up an excessive coffee station with multiple pots to keep the caffeine flowing. Samantha brought an assortment of wines, and Cookie provided peppermint tea. I made a little sign to advise the tea also contained alcohol, and wondered belatedly if the warning should've stated, "Peppermint schnapps—also contains tea."

Caesar and Marcy welcomed the group at promptly seven sharp and explained the gist of the evening itinerary. Libby and Ray helped Mom and Dad prep and deliver plates of roast, carrots, mashed potatoes, and rolls to everyone in attendance. Evan and I kept their glasses and mugs topped off.

When stomachs were full and hopes were high, thanks to the unbridled enthusiasm of Caesar and Marcy, Zane distributed a stack of fully prepped and bound handouts. Caroline powered up her pink portable projector and used a nearby wall as her screen. Then we settled into baked apple desserts and followed along as she presented. I had no doubt that by the time I went to bed tonight, Mistletoe would have an airtight plan for breaking that world record tomorrow.

Mrs. Snow sat on the staircase, looking as dejected and forlorn as ever. She wouldn't leave town until the coroner released Elijah's body, and not a single soul had come to stay with her. I hoped the sound of hope and merriment raised her spirits, even a little. Eventually Mom joined her, offering a cup of hot cider and silent companionship.

In addition to my usual crew, mom's friends had come with their husbands; several members of the farm staff had brought their spouses; Cookie's entire book club and the swingers showed up early and volunteered to help clean up afterward; Samantha and a number of Winers made an appearance; and several shop owners came by as well. I was especially stunned to see Mr. Weible and his daughter, Natalia, but I welcomed both with a warm hug and smile. After my last conversation with Natalia, I'd expected her to look away if we ever crossed paths again.

Caroline announced a break around ten PM and directed us to put all the things we'd learned to use, reaching out to our contacts by text and emails immediately, sharing the flyers Ray made for shop windows and doors, and spreading the word in any way possible. The sooner the better. Ray promised to get the call to action into the morning paper, and Caesar couldn't have been happier.

Natalia approached during the break, her coat and hat back on. "Holly?"

"Hi," I said, unsure what to expect. "Are you leaving?"

"Yeah. My husband is with Anna, but I'm exhausted. This is my bedtime." She laughed. "I wanted to be here tonight to show you how sorry I am for my bad behavior the other day. I get defensive when it comes to my dad. He's a good guy, you know?"

I looked for Mr. Weible but found my dad near the tree, speaking with friends. My heart swelled at the sight of him. I knew how I'd felt when Evan accused him of hurting someone once. "I get it," I promised. "I'm sorry for even suggesting—"

She shook her head. "Friends?"

We shook hands, then shared a short hug.

"Natalia?" Mr. Weible called from the door.

"I should go," she said, stepping away.

I waved to her dad, then to her. "Merry Christmas."

The pair took their leave, and I leaned against the kitchen counter, lost in thought while I piled the dishwasher full.

The gentle ting of silverware against crystal drew my attention back to Caroline, calling the group to order once again. "Now we need to secure enough costumes for anyone who shows up and figure out transportation for livestock and the Santa's Village booths."

The chatter died down as guests took turns making suggestions and offers.

I watched Evan as he approached. "Hey," I said softly, my heart incredibly full.

"Hey." His voice was low and gravelly as he pulled me against him. "You want to see something?"

"Always," I said.

He gave me his phone. "Look."

The website for the *Dead and Berried* podcast centered the screen, along with a candy cane graphic and the words "Help Mistletoe have a merry Christmas." A rolling number beside it kept track of the dollar amount collected and the first names of everyone donating, along with their city and state.

"I don't understand," I said.

Evan scrolled, revealing a paragraph with details about our desire to break a world record, and quotes from all the people who'd heard the plea and wanted to help. "They're encouraging their listeners to help however they can. Some will drive here to be a part of the Victorian town tomorrow. Some are donating Victorian costumery, others are giving money to support the cause. The goal was a thousand dollars for props and costumes."

I touched his phone screen, pulling the candy cane back into view. "That says fifty-two hundred, and it's growing."

"Yep."

I turned wide eyes on him. "How did you find out about this?"

He smirked. "I became a faithful listener the minute I realized these guys were talking to everyone in town about my case. Tate didn't know, so he called to tell me about the donations. They've set up an account in town and added me to it."

"Not the mayor?" I asked. "Or someone from the Historical Society?"

He shook his head. "Tate said they've spoken to hundreds of people this week, and there is a small group of individuals everyone trusts. Neither the mayor nor anyone from the Historical Society made the list."

"You did," I said, a wealth of pride growing in my chest.

He nodded. "As did you and your parents." He nodded in their direction. "Cookie, Caroline, Ray, and Libby."

I pressed a palm to my heart. "All my people."

"*Our* people," he corrected.

I hugged him. "Our people," I agreed.

* * *

Evan and I met the podcasters for pie the next day so we could thank them properly for the shoutout on their show. I grumbled as they approached, and my husband pinched me under the table. "Be nice," he whispered. "This was your idea, remember?"

I refreshed my smile but narrowed my eyes a moment at him for the assault.

"Hey," Tate said, smoothly sliding onto the bench across from us.

"Morning," Harvey added, falling into the space beside his cohost. "I'm incredibly glad to see you both."

"Thanks," Evan said, cordially. His mouth opened again, but the words stalled as Tate passed Harvey a ten-dollar bill.

"Sorry," Tate chuckled. "We place bets on all kinds of things to keep the job interesting. Keeps things light, you know?"

I sucked my teeth and hiked my brows. Then I pinched Evan, because I'd told him these two were the worst. "You showcase murders paired with recipes," I said.

"The food keeps things light," he said.

I forced myself to remember the time I'd spent exploring their podcast's website with Evan, and the fact they'd been live from eleven PM until dawn on the night of Elijah's death. Apparently, the duo who irked me to no end wasn't all bad. They'd hosted an event they called Money at Midnight as part of a charity fundraiser where they regaled listeners with unsolved mysteries all night in exchange for donations. "Thank you for coming," I said. "We wanted to thank you in person for helping us spread the word about today's event."

Tate folded his hands on the table and fixed his attention on me. "Yeah?"

I nodded, lips tight. "Yep."

"Really?"

I nodded again.

"How thankful are you on a scale of 'not really' to 'I will finally agree to that interview'?" he pressed.

I looked at Evan. Would he arrest me if I hurt Tate the Great? Or look the other way?

"Holly?" Evan nudged, clearly enjoying my frustration. "Feel like an interview? A chance to speak for your town?"

I dragged my attention back to the waiting podcasters. "Call me after Christmas?"

"Awesome." Tate elbowed his partner, and Harvey returned the ten-dollar bill. "Told you she'd cave," Tate gloated. "We should go before she changes her mind."

The men quickly exited the booth.

"Talk to you soon," Tate called.

The waitress appeared in their absence, and my eye began to twitch. "Merry Christmas! Can I take your order?" she asked.

Evan and I stayed for nearly an hour, enjoying the pie and the time together. The wind was cold when we finally headed outside. As promised, there hadn't been any additional precipitation, but the falling temps were freezing every drop of melted snow from yesterday's warm sun.

Dad and a large group of men worked on the corner, backlit in rays of crimson and gold. The last of the booths from Santa's Village had been moved from Reindeer Games to the square. Mom would bring him dinner and something Victorian to change into soon, before it was time to count heads.

"It's looking good," Evan said. "It's really starting to feel as if we're back in time. At least on this one block anyway."

I heartily agreed.

Traffic had been blocked from most of downtown all month, but the Victorian Christmas village we were creating for the World Record Book was tightly focused on the square. Caesar felt the scope should remain small and densely packed with all things fitting our theme. We were aiming for authenticity and number of participants over square footage.

The results so far were outstanding.

My phone rang, and I checked the screen. "It's Mom," I told him before raising the phone to my ear. "Merry Christmas," I said.

"Holly, are you with Evan?"

I tensed at the urgency in her tone, then pressed "Speaker" before answering. "Yes. He's right here. What's going on?"

"I'm with Violet Snow," she said. "She's concerned about Henry Moore. She hasn't seen him since he left the inn a couple of days ago."

"He hasn't called," Violet added, her voice smaller and distant. "And he hasn't returned my messages."

Evan caught my eye. Concern drew lines across his brow. "Mrs. Snow? This is Sheriff Evan Gray. I'm going to check on Mr. Moore now. I'll come to see you at the farm when I finish. Sit tight, and I'll have news for you soon. Carol? Stay with her, okay?"

"Of course," Mom agreed.

"Thank you," Violet said.

I disconnected the call, and Evan kissed my cheek.

"Meet me at the farm in an hour," he said. "Drive safely—the roads are slick."

"Back at you," I said, and he broke into a jog away from the square.

I bought some candied pecans on the way back to my truck and forced worried thoughts from my mind. Evan would find Mr. Moore and handle anything that was wrong. My job was to enjoy the day. I'd promised Evan that much over coffee and pie.

All around me, the Victorian town square took new, more authentic shape by the moment. I couldn't wait to see it after sunset, filled with hundreds, maybe thousands, of participants.

Cookie and a group I recognized as her choir friends arranged themselves on the corner across the street, hooded cloaks on their heads and fur muffs over their hands. Their voices rose over the chatter and bustle of shoppers. The chorus was angelic, and I fought the urge to stay until the end. The sights and sounds, and the scent of rich hot chocolate on the wind were enticing, but the bite in the air kept me moving.

I smiled at babies bundled inside strollers and parents with pink cheeks and noses. I waved to friends and locals. And I counted my many, many blessings with each careful step. I turned onto the empty side street at the next corner, thankful for the no-motor-vehicle rule on this block, then made the first available turn into the alley where I'd left my truck.

I started the engine remotely as soon as the pickup's tailgate came into view. I pulled the receipt off my windshield, then used my phone's flashlight to peek under the vehicle and into the space behind my seat before climbing aboard and promptly locking my doors. I'd had enough bad experiences during perfectly lovely holiday moments to understand that even the most blissful times could quickly turn dangerous.

Seat belt buckled, and truck heater pumping, I eased away from my spot beside the dumpster and headed for the steady stream of cross traffic at the alley's opposite end.

Vehicles plugged along in the distance, routed toward the high school and away from the square, occasionally slipping on patches of newly frozen ice in the ever-increasing wind. I pointed the heater vents at my frozen fingers and wiggled the digits to keep my blood flowing.

Up ahead, a set of headlights turned into the alley.

The alley was narrow, barely accommodating my truck and the dumpster between buildings. Another vehicle would never fit.

When the incoming vehicle crept forward, I shifted into reverse, backing up to make room.

The headlights moved confidently forward, matching my speed and angle instead of passing as I'd intended.

"What are you doing?" I asked, confusion becoming mild panic in my chest.

I bounced my gaze from the rearview mirror to the encroaching set of lights, making sure not to hit anything as I reversed, and keeping an eye on the vehicle before me as well. I imagined this was what being herded felt like.

Eventually, I reached the cross street I'd used to access the alley on foot, and I turned my wheel, reversing out of the alley completely. The strict no-motor-vehicle policy meant the road was clear, and now the intersection was as well. The other vehicle could carry on, and I could go home to keep Mom and Mrs. Snow company until Evan arrived.

I shifted into drive and waited for the other vehicle to pass. From my new vantage I could see more than the headlights.

A blue SUV crept to the alley's edge, then idled a dozen yards away. The vehicle looked a lot like the one that had drawn a frown on Mr. Moore's face at the farm, and the one parked outside his home.

Shadows cast from buildings streaked the windshield, making it difficult to get a clear view of the driver. A dark knit cap covered the person's head to their eyebrows. A thick scarf wrapped their neck and chin.

I motioned the other driver to leave the alley. Turn out in front of me or cross the empty street where I now waited. I didn't care as long as they stopped forcing me to back up.

The SUV flashed its headlights, signaling that I should go instead of them.

This felt a lot like the sort of trouble I'd worried about while walking to the truck. At least, I was safely inside and out of danger. I raised a tentative palm to the other driver in thanks, then set my foot on the gas pedal and opted to leave while I could.

The SUV jolted forward, colliding with my door when I tried to roll past the alley. My body jerked and swayed against the seat belt.

My head yanked one way, then the other. Pain raced up my spine to my neck.

The other driver backed up.

I blinked at the little blue SUV, confusion setting in. Was this a supremely strange accident? A misunderstanding? Or did the driver really think his SUV could hurt my farm truck?

I jammed my foot against the gas pedal when the other vehicle started toward me once more. My tires spun on black ice for a long moment before finding purchase. Then my truck shot forward.

"Call Evan!" I ordered, praying my phone would hear me and do as I asked.

The little device skidded along the bench at my side, then crashed onto the floor. I wheeled onto the next available street, searching for traffic, or at least a few witnesses on foot.

Crunch!

My truck jolted forward as the SUV pushed against my rear bumper, setting me on an icy collision course with a slow-moving tour bus.

"Ahh!" I screamed and pulled the wheel, maneuvering away from the giant vehicle. "Call Evan!" I ordered. "Please, please, please!" I couldn't reach my phone or take my hands off the wheel to access my dashboard features.

The SUV hit my rear bumper once more, and I skirted onto a side road heading away from town. "Shoot!"

I couldn't believe I was under attack again.

Exactly what my parents, friends, and husband had warned me would happen.

And I'd promised would not.

The sound of a ringing phone echoed through my truck's speakers, and I nearly sobbed at the realization my call had connected.

"Hey," Evan said. "I can't talk. The roads are awful, and we've got fender benders everywhere. We might have to call off the—"

"Evan!" I blurted. Tears of relief clogged my throat, but I forced out one more word. "Help!"

"Whoa. Where are you?" His voice changed in the space of a heartbeat. The easygoing sheriff had become my protector. There were few men more formidable when he was in that mode. Thank my lucky stars.

"I'm on County Route Seven," I said, wiping a trembling hand across my brow. My fingers encountered a smear of fresh blood. Had I hit my head on the initial impact? I glanced at my window and saw a scarlet stain there too.

"Holly, I'm on my way, but I need more information."

A car door slammed in the distance and soft engine sounds rose through the speakers.

"Holly," he repeated. "Details."

Heavy winds whooped and howled, jostling light posts and street signs, causing the boughs of ancient trees to whip and bend. My big, non-aerodynamic truck headed toward the double yellow lines. I strained against the gust, forcing my ride back into its lane. A mass of drifting snow rose suddenly from the ground, then covered my windshield with a slap. I fumbled for the wipers, my jostled mind working overtime to manage the most important things. "I'm in my truck," I said, projecting my voice above the wind. "Someone is chasing me—"

The SUV rammed my bumper once again, and my wheels lost traction on the frozen road. I screamed and my eyes blurred, probably with tears, maybe with blood from my head wound. "I'm on Route Seven," I said, my voice quieter than expected.

"You already said that." Evan growled. "Are you hurt?"

My teeth chattered, and my grip tightened painfully on the steering wheel as another gust of wind pushed my truck toward the center lines. "I'm scared."

"Can you pull over?" Evan asked. "Are you still driving?"

"No."

"You aren't driving?"

"I can't pull over." I needed to keep moving until Evan or one of his deputies found us. More importantly, I needed to stay on the road. "Come get me!"

A colossal thud shoved me against the steering wheel, and my arms flew out to my sides.

The tailspin was so sharp and sudden, my pickup and I left the road. My head flopped uncontrollably with the force of the turn, and for one excruciating moment, the pickup tipped partially off the ground. I prayed it wouldn't begin to roll.

The truck smacked hard onto its tires a moment later.

My head connected with the steering wheel. And things went dark.

Chapter Twenty-Six

I blinked open my eyes, no longer in the truck or outside.

Exposed brick covered the walls of a room I'd never seen, and high-polished wooden floors stretched beneath my cheek. I pried my face away from the cool surface and squinted against the light, then moaned in pain.

Across the way, Mr. Weible moved a suitcase and pile of framed photos into an ancient, gated elevator. He wore tan khakis and a navy-blue sweater with moccasins. He looked like any other mild-mannered man I'd ever seen, working contentedly, utterly unbothered. Then he caught me staring. "Darn," he said, adjusting glasses on the bridge of his nose. "You're awake."

I frowned, then winced. Every muscle in my body ached. I wondered what had happened, and the thought registered with an avalanche of graphic memories. Adrenaline coursed through my veins anew. I'd been chased over the icy roads in my truck and hit repeatedly by a blue SUV.

Mr. Weible's SUV?

I'd seen him climb into a white minivan at the farm, but he'd been with Natalia and Anna. My stomach sank. His daughter must've driven that day.

I rolled onto my back and turned my head to keep him in my sight. Irrational sadness overcame me as all the missing pieces flowed together. I also felt a little betrayed. I'd liked this guy! We'd had coffee, and I'd met his family. He'd even been at my house last night. *Probably to collect information,* I realized. Like where he could next find me alone. My eyelids slowly closed as I recalled telling a few of Mom's friends about my favorite place to park, in case they needed it.

"I was hoping you'd sleep longer," Weible said. His steady footfalls drew my eyes open once more. "I can give you something to help." He pulled a prescription bottle from his pocket. "My wife took them for pain near the end."

I shook my head and flattened my lips. *Hard pass,* I thought, taking a physical inventory. Aching head and nearby killer aside, I seemed to be okay.

"Suit yourself," he said and placed the pills on the floor near my head.

I willed my limbs to cooperate and levered into a seated position, using core strength, and realized my wrists and ankles were bound.

Evan was going to be livid.

"Why are you doing this?" I asked, already knowing the answer. "Is it because you killed Elijah Snow?"

"That wasn't what happened," Weible said. He shook a scolding finger at me before returning to the elevator. He returned with an old metal container and unscrewed the cap. "I only wanted to talk to him. I thought he could help, so I drove to the inn. He was out wandering in the snow when I arrived. He'd been drinking and blathered on about finding his mom with a man and meeting his real dad. He wouldn't focus or listen. He climbed onto that big metal thing to ask the sky if his whole life was a lie." Weible sighed and rolled his eyes. "Everyone is so dramatic these days. In my time, people shook things off, we kept our chins up, and we did better."

So, I'd been right that day, when I'd suggested someone had gotten drunk and fallen into the batter. I made a mental note to tell Evan.

Weible swung the unlidded can gently, tossing streams of liquid onto the floor.

I coughed as the scent reached my nose; then I winced from the resulting pain. "What is that?"

He looked at the can, then carried on, dousing curtains, sparse furniture, and boxes in it as well. "Turpentine. It's highly flammable. I found dozens of these cans in the basement where the factory used to be. Turpentine was used for thinning paints back in the day. It's not good to breathe."

"Yeah?" I coughed. "Why don't you untie me and we can get out of here?"

He chuckled darkly but made no move to help.

The comment about the factory and paint thinner helped me confirm our location. We were inside his building, maybe even his apartment. "You're not going to burn down your own home, are you?" I asked, though that certainly seemed to be his plan.

Then again, Weible didn't own the building anymore. And he'd killed Snow over the subpar deal.

I wiggled my wrists and strained for a better look at the knots. I nearly smiled when I recognized them. My years as a Mini Mooseketeer were paying off tonight. I knew how Weible had tied the ropes, which meant I could also untie them, assuming I could reach them.

"Anyway, he fell," Weible said. "He slipped on the icy metal tray, hit his head, and sank into the batter."

"Did you even try to save him?" I asked, hoping to buy time before Weible put down the turpentine and picked up a match.

According to the coroner Elijah had frozen to death. He'd had a head injury, but it wasn't fatal.

Regardless, I thought, *Weible was there, and Elijah didn't have to die.* "Why didn't you call for help?" I asked. "Or dial emergency services. You could've done anything, but you just left him there."

"He was dead!" Weible yelled. "He hit his head!"

"He died of hypothermia," I said. "The fall didn't kill him."

I looked desperately toward the dark world beyond the apartment windows, and I willed Evan to find me. The most I could do from my position was keep Mr. Weible talking long enough to free my wrists and ankles. Then I was sure I could outrun him, even with an aching head, because adrenaline was my friend.

Weible stared into my eyes for several long beats. "I saw the blood. I used my pocket light for a good look at the wound. The gash was deep and wide from the sharp edge on that big cookie cutter." His gaze slid away, then fixed back on me. "I covered him with one of those thermal tarps in the barn and ran. I thought I lost the light, but I must've put it back in my pocket. I was sure my footprints in the snow would give me away, but I had a plan for that too. I was merely curious, heartbroken, and visiting the site as a memorial."

That explained the tracks Dad found near the murder site. And how the dough got covered.

"Why'd you go there to harass him anyway?" I asked. "Hamish Hunter gave you the bad deal, not Snow."

"Because this was all Snow's idea!" He threw the emptied can onto the floor. "He wanted to turn this building into a bunch of modern chain businesses, a brewery, and an arcade. People would be coming and going late into the night. There'd be loud bells and whistles from all the electronic games and machines. Every morning instructors at the fitness place would blast music and yell into headsets at their classes. I'd be the only real tenant left. All the other apartments would become short-term rentals decked out in technological advances and gadgetry. Snow planned to erase the history of this building by gutting and redesigning until it was nothing more than an outward facade to maintain required aesthetics. I tried to tell Orrville and the Historical Society members, but no one listened. It was as if no one cared about the complete demolition of the interior craftsmanship. Orrville told me to stop calling him, and we've been friends for decades!"

Weible paced, apparently lost to a new flood of anger. "Snow planned to turn my home into a mockery, and he sold the idea to Hunter, who undercut me and stole my legacy. I've spent a lifetime preserving the heritage and historic authenticity of this town. It's been my life's work, my calling, and my passion." He raised a trembling hand to his head. "I wanted to leave this building to Natalia and Anna, but I needed money to help with my wife's medical bills. I thought making a deal with Hunter and Snow was the answer, but I had no idea what they planned to do. To make it all worse, neither of them needed the money the way I do, yet they intentionally gave me the short end of their stick."

When his gaze turned to the window, I curved into a ball, stretching my fingers to reach the ropes around my ankles.

"Maybe it's not too late to change your mind," I said. "When we had coffee, you told me the contract hadn't been signed by Mr. Hunter." If that was still true, couldn't either party back out?

Weible turned dark, exasperated eyes on me. "Don't you think I tried that? I called every day until he flew back here to meet with me and talk it out. We had dinner, and I explained my need to renegotiate based on the new information. I was calm and professional. He told me to be happy with what I'd agreed to because it was incredibly generous."

Another lightbulb snapped on in my head. Mr. Weible had been the man the podcasters had seen in Mr. Hunter's car.

"Hunter said he can back out, because he hasn't signed. I, on the other hand, am stuck in a bad deal, dodging local law enforcement and a bevy of nosy locals while he's off enjoying Christmas in Bali."

"France," I corrected. I worked my fingertips into the loosened binds at my ankles, making slow, careful moves, hoping not to draw attention. "And I think he lied. I'm sure the deal isn't final until both parties sign."

Turpentine fumes scorched my lungs. My eyes, nose, and throat burned with each new breath. But my ankles were inching apart with every tug and pull.

"Well, the last joke's on him," Weible said. "I'm burning the place down. At least then I can collect the insurance money before the property transfers to his name."

"What about your family?" I asked.

"They're fine. They're meeting me on the square in a few minutes, along with the rest of this town," he said. "By the time the interior of this place fills with enough smoke and flames for anyone to notice, it will be a total loss."

"And what about me?" I asked. "You're going to leave me here to die? You're not a killer. You're a nice man." He should've told someone Elijah fell into the cookie, but it didn't seem the time to split hairs. "You can't just leave me here to burn alive."

He turned for the elevator.

"Wait!"

Weible paused. "What?"

"Um . . ." I scraped my rattled mind for something more to say. "What about the nosy locals?" I asked, his words returning to mind. "Do you just mean me?" I was the only one tied up at the moment after all.

"I wish. There were those obnoxious podcasters, for starters," he said. "I know they're not local, but they were here. They were everywhere. They made me nuts!"

"So annoying," I agreed, feeling the binds loosen further as I wiggled my ankles.

"And you," he added. "And Moore. The sheriff. His deputies. It started to feel as if I was being watched every minute."

"Mr. Moore," I said, as much to myself as Weible.

Mrs. Snow said he was missing, and Evan had gone to check on him. Would he tell Evan about his suspicions? Would he share enough of what he knew to direct Evan to me? Would there be enough time?

Weible's expression crumpled a little. "Do yourself a favor. Take the pills. He did." Weible's gaze darted to a pile of blankets near the far wall. On closer inspection, the blankets might've been covering a man.

"Henry's got a bad ticker," Weible said, patting his heart. "He hasn't been well since Snow turned up in that batter. He confronted me when he learned about the building deal. He suspected I knew something about what happened to Snow. I don't know why he cared. He'd never even met Elijah Snow. But he kept coming back with more questions. Badgering me. I tried to convince him he had it all wrong, but eventually, I had to do something. So I invited him over for coffee."

Tears welled in my eyes as I stared at the lifeless form across the room. "You drugged him? How long ago? How much did you give him?" What if the pills interacted poorly with whatever Henry took for his medical condition?

"Enough," Weible said. "I didn't want to, but I'm also not trying to spend my golden years behind bars because some guy got drunk and hit his head on a giant cookie cutter."

He stepped into the elevator and closed the gate. He sighed and shook his head, features cloaked in disappointment. "This elevator is more than one hundred years old, with the original cast iron gate. The interior is copper-washed steel, and until it was updated in the 1950's, this crank was used to move the car manually. I hate when people ruin historic treasures with technology. Don't you?" He glanced briefly in my direction, then back to the elevator door. "It's never an upgrade, and it's always a tragedy." The apparatus shimmied slightly, then Mr. Weible began to descend. "I'm truly sorry to do this, but it's the two of you or me, and Natalia has already lost a mother. Do yourself a favor," he said again, gently. "Take the pills or some deep breaths. Smoke inhalation is a less painful way to go."

I straightened and kicked the rope off my ankles the moment he was out of sight. Then I worked frantically on the ties on my wrists. "Mr. Moore!" I called. "Wake up!"

The old elevator gate rattled from deep within the shaft, and I suspected Weible had reached the ground floor.

I flipped onto all fours, wrists still bound, and crawled at high speed in Henry's direction.

The scent of turpentine was powerful and nauseating. I wondered where else Weible had spread the chemical liquid. Based on the air's potency, we'd be lucky if friction from the elevator wasn't enough to send us up in smoke, or through the roof, if the stuff was combustible.

"Mr. Moore," I tried again when I reached his side. "It's me, Holly!" I bumped my joined hands against his head, then shoved his cold cheeks with my knuckles and leaned my mouth close to his ear. "Wake up!"

He spluttered, and I coughed for the better half of a minute while he slowly roused.

"Holly?"

"Yes," I croaked, choking on the residual itch of smoke in my throat. *Oh no,* I thought. The smoke was new. "Help!" I screamed, unsure who could hear me. The bank of mailboxes downstairs, all devoid of names save Weible's, suddenly suggested something different than they had before. His neighbors weren't more cautious, as I'd originally thought. They probably weren't here! If the place would soon be shops and rentals, Weible might already be the only remaining tenant.

Outside, wind whistled around the windowpanes, violently shaking the glass.

"Fire!" I called. "Help!"

Mr. Moore creaked into a sitting position. He worked his bushy eyebrows like bug antennas, trying to make sense of the scene. "I came for coffee."

"And he drugged you," I said. "Then he tied me up and set the building on fire."

"Dear." Moore removed glasses from his pocket and put them on. "I don't think I can stand."

"Can you help me with these ropes?" I pushed my joined hands forward, and he pulled them in for a closer look.

Dark gray smoke rose through the elevator shaft and spilled into the room like an apparition. I fought another round of coughs.

Henry made easy work of my bindings. "Those were tight."

"Yes," I agreed, rubbing my tender wrists as I searched for the door. "Thank you."

"Mistletoe can wind tightly enough around a tree limb to break it," he said.

"Okay." I patted his arm.

I sat back on my haunches, staying low as heat and smoke filled the room.

Mr. Weible's apartment was on the fifth floor. We couldn't jump through a window from this height, and we couldn't use the elevator, but we could try to beat the fire to the central staircase.

"We've got to go," I said, reaching for Henry's hand. We had to move before the flames reached us, before the floor collapsed or there wasn't any oxygen left.

He rubbed his forehead. "I'm very dizzy, and it's quite warm. My heart's not well."

"I know," I said. "But we can't stay."

His eyelids drifted shut, and his body went slack, listing back to the ground.

I looked to the ceiling in desperation, and a lightning streak of flame licked across the plaster.

"Help!" The word broke as smoke hit my lungs, and I crouched low to cough. The fire had arrived, and my time was up. I needed to move more than I needed a plan.

The wind picked up outside again, lashing snow at the glass until I thought it would break.

I grabbed the corners of the blanket beneath Mr. Moore and began to pull. I scooted across the heated floor on my backside, dragging him toward the nearest doorway. Coughing and wheezing, I made it into the next room and spotted the front door behind a low wall of flames.

"A little help!" I screamed at the universe. The sound was swallowed by a loud boom somewhere below.

I stripped off my coat and pressed it against the little rug fire in front of the door, then wiped sweat from my eyes.

"Violet," Henry muttered, "I'm so sorry."

My throat tightened for new reasons, and my thoughts raced to Evan. I, too, was deeply sorry. We'd only been married a year. It was too soon for me to die. We were supposed to have a family and grow old together. I didn't want to miss any of the things Henry and Violet had. I wanted it all.

I patted my pockets in search of my cell phone, then recalled it on the floorboards of my truck.

I unlocked the dead bolt with shaking hands, thankful the metal was still cool. The knob turned easily, but the door didn't open. "Come on!"

Had the wood swollen from the heat? Or was something else going on?

I released the blanket, and Henry's head thudded against the floor.

I hacked and coughed as crackling flames rose in clusters around me. All else seemed invisible in the smoke.

I pounded my palms and yanked wildly on the door while tears poured over my scorching cheeks.

Next, I turned to Henry. I patted his body from chest to hips, searching for the telltale shape of a cell phone. In the form of a true Christmas miracle, I found what I was looking for.

I pulled the collar of my sweatshirt over my nose and mouth as I pressed one of Mr. Moore's fingers against the sensor, then dialed.

"Sheriff Gray," Evan said, voice hard and sharp. The sounds of carolers echoed in the background.

"Help!"

"Holly?"

I coughed until I thought I'd be sick before regaining enough composure to speak again. I lowered myself to the floor, the carpet uncomfortably warm. "I'm in Mr. Weible's apartment on the fifth floor of the building with the art gallery. It's on fire."

Evan cussed and began barking orders to someone unseen.

"Mr. Moore is with me," I continued, feeling my head lighten with each breath. "He was drugged. We can't get out. The door is stuck."

"The front door?" he asked, breaths coming in quick gasps.

"No, the apartment door. Weible left in the elevator. He's going to the square."

Sweat dripped over my temples, and the cloudy gray room began to spin.

"I'm on my way," Evan said. "EMTs and firefighters are en route. Holly?"

I imagined his handsome face on our wedding day, the most perfect of days.

The sound of breaking glass registered as we danced in the barn, our first moments as husband and wife. We were the dearest of friends.

"Stay with me, Holly!" he demanded.

Cold air raked my skin, cooling and soothing me as I grabbed hold of the memory with my entire heart and held on.

Always, I thought. *I will always stay with you.*

Then I drifted into the abyss.

Chapter Twenty-Seven

The words to "Silent Night" pulled me from the depths of sleep. An angel choir roused me slowly from the darkness, urging open my heavy eyelids.

"Oh, thank heavens!" Mom's voice was crisp and near. "She's awake!"

"She's awake!" A grandiose voice echoed, and the choir paused.

I cringed at the pain in my head and throat as my parents came into view. Behind them, a sea of people in Victorian attire clapped and cheered.

Beside me, the sky glowed orange as Mr. Weible's building burned.

Emergency lights circled, and the sound of an ambulance faded into the distance.

Mom flattened her torso against mine in a cry of complete joy. "Sweet baby girl!"

I raised my arms to hug her, and found an IV plugged into one hand.

"Holly?" Evan's voice was next to register. His face came into view as Mom pulled away.

"Hi," he said, a pained expression twisting his lips.

"It's a miracle," Mom said.

"She's a miracle," he corrected. Then he pressed a kiss to my forehead. "Hey." He shoved hair away from my stinging cheeks. "You gave us all quite a scare."

"I have an IV," I told him. My breath puffed back, trapped inside an oxygen mask, I realized.

"You need that," he said. "Don't take it off, and don't talk more than necessary. The medic says you inhaled a lot of smoke, and you need to save your energy. Firefighters found you just inside the apartment. They said the wooden door was swollen from the heat and stuck tight."

I'd thought the door was somehow blocked.

Evan turned his gaze to a man in an EMT uniform, and I realized belatedly I was strapped to a gurney, outside the open doors of an ambulance near the square. "Mr. Weible!" I gasped. My hand flew up to remove the mask, but Evan stopped me.

"What did I just say?" he asked with a quiet chuckle. "So predictable."

I frowned.

"I had the pleasure of arresting Mr. Weible after seeing you were in good hands."

I sighed in relief, then choked a little on the raspy breath. "My hero."

"Always." Evan's eyes crinkled at the corners, pride and love burning in their depths. "You could make it a little easier for me. I wouldn't complain."

I laughed, and pain clawed deeply in my chest, causing me to cough.

"Easy," he soothed. "Let's talk more after you've been fully evaluated at the hospital."

The gurney began to roll, and I grabbed Evan's hand. "Mr. Moore."

"Already en route to the ER, and I'm guessing he'll be okay thanks to you."

Gratitude pricked my eyes and spilled over my cheeks. "It wasn't too late?"

Evan shook his head. "No. They know he's been drugged and exactly what's in his system. They found a pill bottle on the floor in Weible's apartment. I'd say he's got a really good chance. And no less than four thousand seven hundred and eleven people praying for him."

I blinked through the tears, returning my attention to the Victorian-themed crowd pressing in around us. "Did we win?"

"I think so," Mom said, elation in her tone, tears streaming over her cheeks. "I know I did." She moved into the space beside Evan and stroked my cheek. Dad stood behind her, hands on her shoulders, his eyes on me.

A sudden boom from the burning building sent a ripple of screams through the masses and lifted everyone's eyes to the sky. Scraps of brightly colored, somewhat scorched, paper rained down like mangled confetti.

"What the—" Evan's brow furrowed, confusion blatant.

"Wallpaper," I croaked.

He turned his still bewildered face to me.

A pair of EMTs bookended my gurney. "I think that's our cue," one of the men said before I could explain.

Dad began to speak, and I knew he'd fill in the blanks about the building's history.

Evan rubbed his forehead as he listened, and the partially lit shreds of old wallpaper drifted on the breeze.

My gurney rose into the waiting ambulance, and Caroline's dad came briefly into view. He stood at the square's center with a microphone, apparently acting as master of ceremonies and official announcer for those without a good view. I hoped the mic and speakers had arrived after the head count for the record book, because neither had existed in the Victorian era.

"She's headed to the hospital," our mayor announced. "Wish her well."

Then thousands of costumed people began to wave and shout.

Evan hopped into the ambulance, and I smiled as the doors closed over the town I loved.

Mine really was a wonderful life.

* * *

Christmas Eve was the warmest day in nearly two weeks. My inn guests had all checked out, and I felt better than I had in quite a while. The recent near-death experience had provided a lot of clarity I hadn't realized I needed. It wasn't the first time I'd come face to face with a killer, but it was the first time I'd truly thought I would die. Waking on the gurney, surrounded by people and a community I loved, had brought my world into sharp focus.

Decisions had been made that night.

The doorbell rang, and I wiped my hands on the nearest dish towel. "I'll get it," I told Mom, slipping away from the inn's island, where we'd worked companionably for the last hour. Setting up a Christmas Eve feast was just one of the many traditions I never wanted to miss.

I checked the app on my phone to see who was on the porch, then unlocked the dead bolt with a wide smile. "Merry Christmas!" I called, pulling Caroline into a hug.

"Merry Christmas," she said. She left air kisses beside my cheeks, then stepped aside to make room for Zane on the interior welcome mat.

I no longer cared if the presence of security technology negatively impacted the inn's overall aesthetic. In fact, I'd cheerfully agree to a chain-link fence and armed guards if that meant keeping my family and guests safe. The upgrades had been sufficiently masked to meet the Historical Society's aesthetic standards, and I was happy.

The couple knocked snow from their boots and slipped out of their coats and hats.

Zane passed me the gifts he'd been carrying. "These are for the exchange. You might not want to go far—we weren't the only ones pulling into the lot."

"Thanks. Mom's in the kitchen," I said. "I'll put these under the tree and be right there."

I dropped off the gifts in the parlor, then greeted Cookie, Ray, and Libby when they reached the porch.

Dad was next, arms stacked with casserole dishes from their farmhouse across the property.

Evan was running late, but I didn't fault him. He'd get here as soon as possible, and we had all night to celebrate.

I joined the small group of friends in the kitchen, drinking in the spicy scents of warm wassail and sounds of laughter.

Twinkle lights danced around the windows. Christmas trees glowed proudly in every corner. My heart grew impossibly fuller, as it had every moment since the fire.

Some of my muscles still ached from the accident, but I was healthy, happy, and grateful.

Mr. Moore had made a full recovery, and when he was released from the hospital this morning, Violet Snow had been by his bedside. He accompanied her and their son's body back to their hometown for burial. My family sent flowers.

Zane refilled his mug, then moved to stand beside me. "What's the scoop on Weible?" he asked. "I've been out of the loop the last day or two." His gaze drifted to Libby.

I looked at Caroline to see if she noticed, and her small cat-that-ate-the-canary smile suggested she had. Clearly, I was missing something.

"Well," I began, eager to get this part over with and never mention his name again, "Mr. Weible confessed to everything when he was interrogated at the sheriff's station." He'd cracked within a couple of hours, after his clothes and hands tested positive for turpentine, the accelerant used to start the fire. Then the hospital matched the drugs in Moore's system with the ones found in Weible's apartment, a prescription written to Weible's late wife. Plus, Henry had survived, and so had I. We were both able to make a statement about the whole thing. Additionally, the SUV he'd chased me with had been purchased online this month and registered to a new LLC, which took less than an hour to trace back to him. The SUV was damaged from all the times he'd rammed into my pickup, and some red paint from my truck had transferred in the process. "He was a mess," I added, hating that I felt so badly for him despite everything he'd done. He'd been acting on emotion instead of logic. Angry with Hunter about his intent to destroy the building's history and everything he'd worked so hard to maintain. Grieving the loss of his wife. And deeply in need of a therapist. "I hear he's pleading temporary insanity."

"Wow." Zane nodded. "I'm guessing he'll get some serious jail time regardless. Snow's death and the attempted murder of you and Moore. The threats. Abduction. The car chase."

"He'll have rightfully earned every day of his sentence," Dad said, cheeks going red with the words.

Mom stroked his arm in comfort.

Caroline worked up a bright smile, hopefully intent on changing the subject. "Tell me. What was it like having Mrs. Claus stay here?"

I laughed, relieved and immensely thankful for the turn of topics. "Gertie isn't Mrs. Claus."

"How do you know?" she challenged. "Did you ask?"

"No." I rolled my eyes. "But I bet she signed the guest book." I went to grab the gilded leather tome and opened it to the page marked with the crimson ribbon.

Gertie and Jackie had checked out while I slept, and I regretted not having had the chance to say goodbye. They'd left their keys on the island and their rooms as tidy as the day they'd arrived.

Everyone leaned silently inward as I set the book on the island.

I trailed a fingertip down the page to a line written in glittery red ink. *"A lovely inn and even lovelier innkeeper and family. The perfect place for an exciting holiday getaway,"* I read. "She signed this 'Gertie K,' so we can rest this case. Claus begins with a C."

"Kringle doesn't," Cookie said. "Hey, what's that?"

I followed her gaze to the corner of a cream-colored paper poking out from between the pages of my guest book. I gave the material a tug and discovered it was an envelope. My name was scripted in neat black calligraphy on the front. I raised the high-quality linen stock up for all to see.

Caroline made a long whistling sound. "Fancy."

"Open it!" Cookie said.

I peeled the flap away and slipped a piece of bright white parchment from the sheath.

Holly,

Thank you for a wonderful stay. Christopher was right, Mistletoe is truly an enchanted town, and your family's farm is the highlight. I'm sorry Jack and I weren't around the inn more, but there was just so much to see and do. We're sorry about the weather, but we hope that wrapping all those gifts for the toy drive eased your burden a little.

Merry Christmas,
Gertie & Jackie

"That's nice," Mom said. "I really liked them."

I read the note again, letting each word settle in. "So, Gertie and Jackie wrapped all the gifts?" It made sense, I supposed. They'd had access and time, plus they'd volunteered to do the job early in their visit. I was thankful for the closure. That mystery had been making me bonkers.

I thought of the night the presents had reappeared and how little I'd interacted with Gertie and Jackie since then. The threat carved into my office floorboards had distracted me thoroughly, and I'd barely seen the ladies again before they'd checked out.

"Wait a minute," Cookie said. "What about the reservation? I'll bet we can see her whole last name there."

Caroline perked. "That's a great idea."

"Gertie didn't make the reservation," I said. "I'd remember if someone tried to reserve a room under the last name Kringle so close to Christmas."

"Check," Caroline said. "Please?"

I pulled my phone from the pocket of my oversized cardigan and found the inn's registration app. "Looks like Jackie made the reservation." I turned the phone to face them as proof.

Cookie squinted, then gasped and tapped a finger against the screen. "Look at her last name."

I gave the reservation another look.

"It's Frost," Cookie said. "Gertie apologized for the weather, and her friend's name is Jacqueline Frost."

Dad laughed. "Jack Frost? That certainly would explain a lot."

"No." I shook my head at him. "That explains nothing. Except maybe that Jackie's parents had a sense of humor."

Ray made a low humming sound. "Actually," he said, "have you read the article about the fire in today's paper?"

"I know too much about that already," I said.

Frankly, I'd rather continue speculating over the existence of Santa Claus.

"According to the fire marshal," Ray said, "a preliminary review of the property is complete, and it was determined that the windstorm eventually broke the windows."

I shrugged, uncomfortable as a series of memories returned in a rush.

"That was probably what saved you," Ray said, "and what killed all hope of saving the building."

My insatiable curiosity reared its head. "What do you mean?"

"I mean, you would've died from smoke inhalation, but the oxygen provided by the broken windows probably saved you. Unfortunately, that also fed the fire. It's like a trade was made, and the best part is that no meteorological reports from that day show winds nearly strong enough to do that."

Zane leaned onto the counter, brows knitted, attention rapt. "Interesting."

"It is," Ray said. "I followed the story as far as I could, and also discovered no other town in Maine had the severe low temperatures we had during the few days before and after the fire." He hiked his brows. "I hadn't thought much of that until now. Maybe our unique weather was a result of Jack Frost being in town."

I opened my mouth to tell him Jack Frost was as mythical as the Clauses, but the security app on my phone chimed. I peeked at the notification and smiled instead. "Evan's here."

I rushed to greet my husband and give him a kiss. "You're earlier than I expected."

"I hurried," he said. "It's our anniversary after all."

Soon our group relocated to the parlor, stomachs full and spirits bright. It was officially time for the gift exchange.

Cookie started the fun. "This is from Theodore and his wife," she said, passing a shiny red bag to Evan.

He pressed his lips together, then unwrapped a thermos with a Boston Red Sox logo. He opened the lid and inhaled. "Whoa."

"I filled it with my peppermint tea," she said.

He wrapped her in a hug. "Please tell Theodore and Clementine it's perfect."

"I guess I'm next," Evan said. He passed a piece of paper to Caroline. "I didn't have time to wrap it, so I printed the receipt instead.

She took the paper with a curious smile. A moment later, she rose from the couch to hug him. "Thank you!"

"What is it?" Zane asked, lifting the paper from the seat where she'd left it. "A new security system," he read, nodding in approval as he scanned the sheet.

"It's for your cupcake shop," Evan said.

"I love it," she assured him.

Apparently, everyone was getting a security upgrade this year.

"My turn," Caroline said. She selected a gift from beneath the tree and passed it to Mom.

A moment later, Mom unwrapped a personalized cake stand with a glass cover. The words *Home is where the Hearth is* were etched into the glass.

Mom thanked Caroline, then passed a gift to Cookie. "This goes hand in hand with Libby and Ray's gifts."

The couple rose, and I looked to Evan.

His prideful smile suggested he knew something I didn't.

Ray raised his palms. "This is a multipart announcement. First, and most importantly, I've asked Libby to marry me—"

"Knew it," Cookie said.

"And, she said yes." Ray looked at his fiancée with reverence, then kissed her before moving on. "I knew Libby would want a destination wedding, so I've been saving up all year, and with a little help from Mom and Pierce, we're going to take all of you with us."

"What?" Mom asked, one hand pressed to her heart. "Where?"

Ray rocked onto his heels, eyes and smile bright. "This year, everyone gets plane tickets and a room at the resort in Rio where we will tie the knot." He fanned out an array of envelopes in his hands. One for each person in the parlor.

The room was on its feet in seconds, shouting and laughing in celebration. We passed Libby and Ray around in a massive congratulatory hug.

"All right," Libby complained, when we'd carried on too long. "We aren't done."

The group did our collective best to quiet, but the energy racing around us was palpable. Beside me, Evan looked as if he might explode with delight for his sister's happiness.

He squeezed my hand. "Confession," he said softly. "Ray asked for my blessing since our dad is gone. I've had to keep this from you for the last couple of days. I know how much you hate being left out of the loop."

I leaned against his side. "I think I'll give you a pass on this one."

How could I not understand his reasoning on something so wonderful? It was the perfect Christmas surprise.

"Is this the thing they've been keeping?" I asked him. "You wanted me to look into it, and I never had a chance."

"I sure hope so," he said. "I can't imagine what else it might be."

"I'm moving out of the guesthouse and into Ray's place," Libby said.

"Our place," he corrected, and Libby's smile grew exponentially wider.

Evan leaned closer to my ear. "Maybe it's also that."

"Which means," Libby said, swinging her attention to Cookie, "if you're still looking for somewhere to stay, the guesthouse is going to be available."

Mom passed the small gift in her hands to Cookie. "It's a key to the house," Mom said. "And we know how much Theodore loves the barns and horses here, so we hoped he and Clementine might consider Reindeer Games for their home as well."

Cookie's eyes filled with tears. "We couldn't."

Dad barked a laugh. "You absolutely can."

"We insist," Mom said. "If that's what you want."

"I do!" Cookie exclaimed, reaching out to hug my parents.

"Still more," Libby said, her Boston accent thick with humor and feigned impatience.

Evan frowned. Apparently, his sister hadn't let him in on all her secrets.

I leaned forward, eager for what she might say next.

"I've put in my notice at the Hearth," Libby said. "Carol is looking for an official replacement now, but her friends are helping in the interim."

Mom nodded proudly. "I hate to see you go, but I love watching all your lives unfold." Her gaze moved from Ray and Libby to Evan and me.

"What are you going to do now?" I asked. She'd been a student in Boston. Was she thinking of going back? Maybe commuting to a school closer to Mistletoe?

Libby and Zane exchanged another look. "I've been taking classes to get my private investigator's license," she said. "A friend and I are going into business in the new year."

Evan made a choking sound. "Absolutely not." He turned to me. "You can't."

"I can too," I told him, "but she's not talking about me." I did, however, have an idea about who that friend was.

Ray pointed at Zane, confirming my suspicion.

"What?" Caroline squeaked.

Zane grinned. "I love working security annually here, but the commute back and forth to my town is killing me. So, I'm moving to Mistletoe and partnering with Libby on this. I've had my PI license for years, so I'm good to go."

"Seriously?" Evan asked.

Zane bobbed his head. "I've always had an interest in investigation, but I knew I didn't want to go into law enforcement. Too many rules."

My mom swept her gaze from Libby to Zane and back, then silently signed the cross.

We were all determined to worry her, it seemed.

Cookie was the first in motion to hug Libby. "Whoo-hoo!" she called. "A real life PI! Like Magnum! That Tom Selleck knows how to wear a mustache. Theodore's beard is nice, but I've always liked a good mustache."

"I'm not growing a mustache," Libby said.

Ray stroked the light-colored hairs barely visible on his top lip. "Already on it."

Caroline hugged Zane, and the rest of us joined in another massive round of congratulations.

I suspected someone should gift Evan a gallon of antacid next Christmas.

Dad cleared his throat. "While we're talking about living arrangements," he said, "I'll go next. Holly, Evan, we've had the farm surveyed and parceled this year."

My breath caught. "You aren't selling any of it are you?"

Mom beamed. "No, but we are gifting an acre and a half to our daughter and son-in-law."

"Just in case you ever decide to build a home and want to do that here," Dad said. "No pressure, of course."

"You're kidding," Evan said.

Dad shook his head and moved in our direction, arm extended, a manila envelope in his hand.

Evan ignored the envelope, pulling him into a hug instead. Evan had just suggested we look for a home closer to the farm. Now we had an opportunity to build a life on the land where I'd grown up. On the land where my dad and granddad had grown up.

I cried.

I'd been completely wrong earlier when I'd thought news of Ray and Libby's engagement was the perfect Christmas surprise. This was far greater in every way.

"Thank you," I told them in earnest. "This is amazing."

I stood with Evan, looking at my parents. One generation of strength in union facing another. "I'm moving," I said abruptly, surprising myself with the words. I'd planned to save my news for later, because it was the anniversary gift I'd chosen for Evan.

"There's no rush," Dad said.

I chuckled. "No. I meant I'm not going to live at the inn anymore. I want to live with Evan, and that will be much easier at the house in town." At least until we could afford to build a home on the farm. I could tell by the expression on Evan's face he was already trying to work out the possibilities. "I'll just commute to work like everyone else." I'd given the concept plenty of thought, and I was sure I could manage the inn without calling it my home. "We can turn the private quarters into an elaborate holiday suite."

Cookie stepped forward. "I can help out here as much as you need," she said. "Now that I'm going to be living at the guesthouse, you can work less and be with your husband more."

"I like the sound of that," Evan said. "What do you think?" he asked me.

I pulled him in for a kiss. "I love it."

Next, I found the gift I'd bought Dad under the tree and watched in delight as he opened it. The new axe was top quality and handcrafted. His name had been burnt into the handle above the words My father. My hero. My friend.

His eyes misted, and he nodded in lieu of speech. "Love you, baby girl."

"I love you too." I released Evan in favor of hugging Dad once more, and I watched as Evan made his way to Libby's side.

They didn't have their dad anymore, but they had mine now, and the wrenching mix of heartbreak and joy nearly caused me to sob.

Outside the front window, a sleigh arrived.

Everyone turned to look.

Evan moved in my direction. "Ready for your anniversary gift?" he asked.

"What about the gift exchange?"

Dad stuffed his hands in his pockets. "I got Zane a new barn coat."

"Cool," Zane said, and I chuckled. The gift was still under the tree.

"We'll tell you all about the rest later," Caroline said. "Go enjoy your anniversary."

Mom smiled. "We'll probably all be here when you get back anyway."

Evan helped me into my coat, then led me to the sleigh. We took a ride along a candlelit path to the barn, just as we had the year before, on our wedding day.

The sleigh stopped, and we departed. Our driver, a man who'd been part of the farm crew most of my life, simply said, "Merry Christmas," then drove away.

Evan led me to the giant barn doors and parted them for me to enter.

Faux candles filled the cavernous structure, which had been decorated in much the same way as it had when we'd exchanged our vows. A table for two was set near the center, reminiscent of Evan's ultra-romantic proposal two years ago tonight.

"Evan," I whispered, completely aghast. "This is beautiful." I turned in a slow circle, taking in the views. "It's amazing."

"Did you know," he asked, drawing me close and beginning to dance, though the melody was only in his heart and head, "the night I proposed was the greatest night of my life until the day I married you?"

I smiled. "Oh yeah?"

He smiled, eyes soft and expression immensely peaceful. He set his forehead against mine as we swayed. "Every day since then has been a close second."

"I love you," I said, tightening my arms around him. "You are my favorite gift of all time."

"In that case," he said, pressing a tender kiss on my lips. "Merry Christmas."

Acknowledgments

Thank you, dear readers, for joining Holly and her friends on another Mistletoe adventure. Your love for these characters and the holiday season keeps this series alive. Thank you also to my dedicated editorial team and my critique partners Danielle Haas and Jennifer Andreson for reading every word I write and making them better. And to my brilliant ninja of an agent, Erin Niumata, you are making my dream possible. There simply aren't enough words to thank you.